Dreaming of Love

The Bradens

Love in Bloom Series

Melissa Foster

ISBN-13: 978-1-941480-08-3
ISBN-10: 194148008X

This is a work of fiction. The events and characters described herein are imaginary and are not intended to refer to specific places or living persons. The opinions expressed in this manuscript are solely the opinions of the author and do not represent the opinions or thoughts of the publisher. The author has represented and warranted full ownership and/or legal right to publish all the materials in this book.

Cover Design: Natasha Brown

WORLD LITERARY PRESS
PRINTED IN THE UNITED STATES OF AMERICA

A Note to Readers

DREAMING OF LOVE was such fun to write. Italy provided a rich background for Emily and Dae's incredible love story. I loved Emily so much in her brothers' books, and *finally* it was her turn to find her happily ever after. I hope you love Emily and Dae as much as I do.

If this is your first Braden book, then you have a whole series of loyal, sexy, and wickedly naughty Bradens to catch up on, as well as several other hot heroes and heroines. You might enjoy starting with SISTERS IN LOVE, the first of the Love in Bloom series. The characters from each series (Snow Sisters, The Bradens, The Remingtons, and Seaside Summers) make appearances in future books.

DREAMING OF LOVE is the eleventh book in The Bradens and the nineteenth book in the Love in Bloom series.

Melissa Foster

For Lynn Mullan and Alessandra Melchionda who were gracious enough to share their knowledge and their time with me in hopes of bringing you a better story

PRAISE FOR MELISSA FOSTER

"Contemporary romance at its hottest. Each Braden sibling left me craving the next. Sensual, sexy, and satisfying, the Braden series is a captivating blend of the dance between lust, love, and life."

—Bestselling author Keri Nola, LMHC

(on The Bradens)

"[LOVERS AT HEART] Foster's tale of stubborn yet persistent love takes us on a heartbreaking and soul-searing journey."

—Reader's Favorite

"Smart, uplifting, and beautifully layered. I couldn't put it down!"

—National bestselling author Jane Porter

(on SISTERS IN LOVE*)*

"Steamy love scenes, emotionally charged drama, and a family-driven story make this the perfect story for any romance reader."

—Midwest Book Review (on SISTERS IN BLOOM*)*

"HAVE NO SHAME is a powerful testimony to love and the progressive, logical evolution of social consciousness, with an outcome that readers will find engrossing, unexpected, and ultimately eye-opening."

—Midwest Book Review

"TRACES OF KARA is psychological suspense at its best, weaving a tight-knit plot, unrelenting action, and tense moments that don't let up and ending in a fiery, unpredictable revelation."

—*Midwest Book Review*

"[MEGAN'S WAY] A wonderful, warm, and thought-provoking story...a deep and moving book that speaks to men as well as women, and I urge you all to put it on your reading list."

—*Mensa Bulletin*

"[CHASING AMANDA] Secrets make this tale outstanding."

—*Hagerstown* magazine

"COME BACK TO ME is a hauntingly beautiful love story set against the backdrop of betrayal in a broken world."

—*Bestselling author Sue Harrison*

Chapter One

LUSH. VERDANT. HILLY...Amazing. Emily stood on the covered balcony of the villa where she'd rented a room just outside of Florence, Italy, overlooking rolling countryside and the spectacular city below. The sun was kissing the last light of day goodbye, leaving chilled air in its wake. She sighed at the magnificent view, wrapped her arms around her body, and gave herself a big hug. She couldn't believe she was finally here, staying at the villa that her favorite architect, Gabriela Bocelli, built.

Gabriela Bocelli wasn't a very well-known architect, but her designs exuded simplicity and grace, which Emily had admired ever since she'd first come across this villa during her architecture studies. That felt like a hundred years ago. She'd dreamed of visiting Tuscany throughout school, but in the years since, she'd been too busy building her architecture business, which specialized in passive-house design, to take time off. If it weren't for one of her older brothers, she might still be back in Trusty, Colorado, dreaming of Tuscany instead of standing on this loggia, losing her breath to the hilly terrain below.

She pulled her cell phone from the back pocket of her jeans and texted Wes.

You're the best brother EVER! So happy to be here. Thank you! Xox.

Emily had five brothers, each of whom had hounded her about her safety while she was traveling. Or really, *whenever* they didn't have their eyes on her. Pierce, her eldest brother, had wanted to use his own phone plan to buy her a second cell phone with international access. *Just in case*. She'd put her foot down. At thirty-one years old, she could handle a nine-day trip without needing her brothers to rescue her. It wasn't like she ever needed saving, but her brothers had a thing about scrutinizing every man who came near her. Yet another reason why she didn't date very often.

Still, she was glad they cared, because she adored each and every one of their overprotective asses.

Adelina Ambrosi appeared at the entrance to the balcony with a slightly less energetic smile than had been present throughout the day. Adelina had run the resort villa with her husband, Marcello, for more than twenty years. She was a short, stout woman with a friendly smile, eyes as blue-gray as a winter's storm, and wiry gray hair that was currently pinned up in a messy bun. She must have mastered the art of walking quietly to keep from disturbing the guests.

"Good evening, Emily." Adelina brushed lint from the curtains hanging beside the glass doors. Emily was glad they loved the property as much as she did. They rented out only two rooms of the six-bedroom villa in order to always have space available for family and friends. The villa was a home to them, not just a business, as was evident in the warm guest rooms.

"Good evening, Adelina. Any news on Serafina's husband?"

Serafina was Adelina and Marcello's daughter, who had recently moved back home with her eight-month-old son. They'd been living in the States when her husband, Dante, a United States Marine, had gone missing in Afghanistan while out on tour almost three months ago. Adelina had told Emily that she'd begged Serafina to come home and let her take care of her and baby Luca until her husband returned—and Adelina was adamant that he *would* return. Emily, on the other hand, wasn't quite so sure.

"Not yet, but I have faith." Adelina lowered her eyes, and with a friendly nod, she disappeared down the hall in the direction of her bedroom.

Emily turned back toward the evening sky, sending a silent prayer that Serafina's husband would return unharmed.

"It's a beautiful view, isn't it?"

The rich, deep voice sent a shiver down Emily's spine. She turned, and—*holy smokes.* Standing before her was more than six feet of deeply tanned, deliciously muscled male. His hair was the color of warm mocha and spilled over his eyes, hanging just an inch above the collar of his tight black T-shirt. She opened her mouth to greet him, but her mouth went dry and no words came. She reached for the stone rail of the archway she'd been gazing through and managed a smile.

His full lips quirked up, filling his deep brown eyes with amusement as he stepped closer.

"The view," he repeated as his eyes swept over her, causing her insides to do a nervous dance. The amusement in his eyes gave way to something dark and sensual.

It had been so long since Emily had seen that look directed at her that it took her by surprise. She cleared her throat and reluctantly dragged her gaze back to the view below, which paled in comparison to the one right next to her.

Holy crap. Get a grip. It must be the Italian air or the evening sky that had her heart racing like she'd just run a marathon.

Or the fact that I haven't had sex in...

"Awestruck. I hear Italy has that effect on people." He leaned his forearms on the thick stone rail and bent over, clasping his large hands together.

"Yeah, right. Italy." Emily's eyes widened at the sarcasm in her voice. She clenched her mouth shut. She hadn't meant to say that out loud. He probably had this crazy effect on all women, and here she was gushing over him. She didn't gush. *Ever*. What the hell?

He cocked his head to the side and smiled up at her. Emily saw the spark of something wicked and playful in his eyes, like he could be either in a heartbeat. A hint of danger that Emily thought maybe he knew he possessed. A low laugh rumbled from his chest as he arched a brow.

Oh God. She felt her chest and face flush with heat

and crossed her arms. A barrier between them. Yes, that's what she needed, since apparently she couldn't control her own freaking hormones.

"I'm sorry. I just got in this evening and it was a long trip. Eye fatigue." *Eye fatigue?* She held her breath, hoping he'd pretend, as she was, that that was the real reason she was ogling him.

"I just arrived myself." He held a hand out. "Dae Bray. Nice to meet you."

Emily felt the tension in her neck ease as he accepted her explanation. "Emily Braden. Day? That's an interesting name." She shook his strong, warm hand, and he held hers a beat too long, bringing that tension right back to her body—and an entirely different type of tension to her lower belly.

"Maybe I'm an interesting guy. Dae. D. A. E.," he said, as if he had to spell it often, which she imagined he did. "Is this your first time in Tuscany?"

How could he be so casual, speak so easily, when her heart was doing flips in her chest? He didn't have an ounce of tension anywhere in his body. He was all ease and comfort, his body moving fluidly as he shifted his position and leaned his sexy hip, clad in low-slung jeans, against the rail. When he crossed one ankle over the other and set his palms on the stone, his T-shirt clung to his wide chest, then followed his rippled abs in a sexy vee and disappeared beneath the waist of his jeans. Her eyes lingered there, desperately fighting to drop a little lower. It took all of her focus to ignore the heat spreading through her limbs and drag her eyes away.

"Yes." *Why does my voice sound breathy?* She drew

her shoulders back and met his gaze, forcing a modicum of control into her voice. “How about you?”

He shook his head, and his shiny dark hair fell in front of his eyes. One quick flick of his chin sent it off his face, giving her another brief look at his deep-set eyes, his rugged features, and the peppering of whiskers on his square jaw.

“It’s the first for me, too.”

Emily’s phone vibrated and Wes’s name flashed on the screen. She reached for it and read Wes’s message, desperately needing a distraction.

So glad. Be safe and have fun. You deserve it.

“Probably your husband wondering what you’re doing talking to some dude instead of taking a romantic stroll through the vineyards with him.” His eyes narrowed a hair, but that easy smile remained on his lips.

Emily met his gaze. “That would be a feat, considering I’m not married.” Not that she wouldn’t like to be. Recently, she’d watched four of her brothers fall head over heels in love. They hadn’t even been looking for love, and there she was, waiting to love and be loved and trying to keep the green-eyed monster inside her at bay. She was happy for them. She really was. But she couldn’t deny her desire to find that special someone who would cherish her for more than the Braden wealth. She’d come to accept that she wouldn’t find that in her small hometown. She’d buried herself in building a successful business to fill those lonely hours.

“Well, in that case, would you care to join me for a glass of wine?”

Before Emily could answer, another text came through from Wes.

Not TOO much fun! I'd hate to have to come all the way to Tuscany to pound some guy for taking advantage of my little sister.

Emily laughed, taking comfort in Wes's overprotective nature. Somehow, it put her at ease. She slid her phone into her jeans pocket and smiled up at the gorgeous man beside her. She was thousands of miles from home in the most romantic place on earth. Why shouldn't she have *too much* fun? She wondered what Wes considered too much fun and decided that, knowing her brother, holding hands with a guy was too much fun for his little sister. Maybe, just maybe, it was her turn to have fun.

Feeling emboldened, and a little rebellious, she lifted her chin and gave her best narrow-eyed gaze, which she hoped looked seductive, but she was sure it fell short. She didn't have much practice at being a temptress. But a girl could try, couldn't she?

"Sure. That sounds great."

Dae pushed from the rail and reached for her hand. "Shall we?"

"Um..." Was that too familiar of a gesture? Had she given him too *good* of a look?

"I'm harmless. Just ask my sisters. But I'm also affectionate, so it's a hand or an arm. Take your pick."

"You have sisters?" Why did that make him seem safer? He reached for her hand, and damn if their palms didn't fit together perfectly. His hand was warm and big, a little rough and calloused.

"Two. And two brothers. You?" He led her through

the villa toward the kitchen. She was glad he didn't release her hand when they reached the high-ceilinged kitchen, which smelled of fresh-baked bread. He surveyed the bottles in the built-in wine rack that was artfully nestled into the wall, pulling out one bottle after another and scrutinizing the labels until he found one he approved of.

"Five brothers. Um…Are we allowed to just take a bottle of wine?" Emily looked around the pristine kitchen. Colorful bricks formed an arch over recessed ovens and cooktops. A copper kettle sat atop one burner, and on either side of the ovens were built-in pantries in deep mahogany.

"They said to make myself at home." Dae handed her a bottle, then led her past the large table that seated eight and an island equally as large. He reached into a glass cabinet on the far wall and retrieved two wineglasses.

He smiled a mischievous smile. "So…You're a rule follower?" He narrowed his eyes as he opened the bottle of wine and handed it back to her.

A rule follower? Am I? She had no idea if she was or wasn't. She liked to joke and tease. Did that make her a rule breaker? Were there rules for thirtysomethings? A fleeting worry rose in her chest. What if he was a *major* rule breaker? What if he wanted her to do things she shouldn't? She was a Braden, and her family was very well respected, and no matter where she was, she had a reputation to uphold, which somehow made the whole situation a little more tempting.

"Emily?"

Oh no. What if—

His hands on her upper arms pulled her from her thoughts, which were quickly spiraling out of control.

"Emily. Relax." His hair curtained his eyes, but she caught a glimpse of his smile. "I was kidding."

Now I look like a boring Goody Two-shoes. She rolled her eyes—more at herself than at him. Wes's text must have subconsciously made her worry. *Or maybe I really am a Goody Two-shoes who can take banter but not rule breaking. Boring with a capital* B.

"Adelina told me to help myself to anything in the kitchen, including the wine. Day or night."

He snatched her hand again and led her out a heavy wooden door and across the lawn.

"I'm sorry, Dae. I didn't mean to seem like a buzzkill."

"It's okay. If you were my sister, I'd have hoped for that same careful reaction. You had the am-I-with-a-serial-killer look in your eyes." He glanced at her and smiled.

"Yikes. That's not very nice, is it?" She walked quickly in her heeled boots to keep up. Her eyes remained trained on the thick grass to keep from ogling Dae.

"I'm guessing that it has less to do with *nice* than to do with *safety*. Safety's always a good thing." He stopped short, and Emily bumped right into his side.

Their hips collided. Her hand instinctively rose to brace herself from falling, and the bottle of wine smacked against his chest, splashing wine on his T-shirt. He wrapped an arm around her back, bracing her against him.

"Oh my gosh. I'm so sorry." *Crap, crap, crap.* She swiped at the wine on his shirt as she tried to ignore how good his impressive muscles felt.

"I've been impaled by worse." He flashed that easy smile again, but his eyes darkened and filled with heat, and just like that, her knees weakened.

Damned knees. He tightened his grip on her. *Damned smart knees.*

Just when Emily was sure she'd stop breathing, he dropped his eyes to her boots. "Heels and grass don't mix."

She was still stuck on the feel of his arm around her and the quickening of her pulse.

"You okay?" he asked.

I don't know. "Yes. Fine. Yes."

He ran his thumb along her cheek, then licked a dash of wine that he'd wiped off with his thumb. "Mm. Good year."

Holy crap.

His eyes went smoky and dark. She liked smoky and dark. A lot.

"Let's sit. It's safer." He nodded toward his right.

Emily blinked away the crazy unfamiliar desire that had butterflies nesting in her belly and followed his eyes to an intimate stone patio built at the edge of the hill. Her eyes danced over the wisteria-laced trellis. Purple tendrils of flowers hung over the edges, and leaf-laden vines snaked up the columns.

"This is incredible." Tree branches reached like long, arthritic fingers from the far side of a path at the top of the hill to the wisteria, creating a natural archway. Rustic planters spilled over with lush flowers, lining a low stone wall that bordered the patio.

Holding the wine and the glasses, Dae crooked out his elbow. "Hold on tight. Wouldn't want you to stumble."

She had the strange desire to press her body against his and let him wrap his safe, strong arm around her. Instead, she slipped her hand into the crook of his elbow and wrapped it around his muscular forearm, wondering how a man could make her hot all over after only a few minutes.

DAE COULD PRACTICALLY see the gears turning in Emily's head, and even in her befuddled state, she was sexier than any woman he'd ever met. She was slender, with gentle curves accentuated by her designer jeans and the tight white V-neck she wore under an open black cardigan. He stole a glance at her profile as she took in the patio. She had a cute upturned nose, high cheekbones, and long hair the same dark color as his, which he'd like to feel brushing his bare chest. She wore nearly no makeup, and as his eyes lingered on the sweet bow of her lips, the word *stunning* sailed into his mind. He had a feeling that when Emily Braden wasn't caught off guard by an aggressive demolition expert who rarely gave people time to think things through, she was probably feisty as hell.

He'd felt her body tense when she'd run into him, and unstoppable heat had flared between them. She'd melted a little right there in his arms. *Melted*. That was the only way to describe the way the tension drained from her shoulders and back and brought all her soft curves against him. If he were the type of guy who was into casual sex, she'd be ripe for the taking. But Dae had left casual sex behind and had grown a conscience a few years back.

As he poured them each a glass of wine, he wondered who had texted her earlier and caused her to laugh.

Dae handed her a glass of wine and held it up in a toast. "To Tuscany."

Emily smiled as they clinked glasses, then took a sip of her wine. "Oh, that's really good. It's just what I needed."

Dae watched her as she forwent the long wooden bench and sat atop the wide table.

"I can see better from here," she explained. "I don't want to miss a second of this incredible view."

She could have no way of knowing that Dae almost always preferred to sit atop tables rather than on benches or chairs. Always had.

"A woman after my own heart. I always prefer tabletops to chairs." He sat beside her and rested his elbows on his knees. "So, Emily Braden, what brings you to Tuscany?"

"My brother gave me this trip as a gift for helping him arrange a special night for his girlfriend." She smiled as she spoke of her brother, and he liked that she seemed to like her family. Family was important to Dae. He'd found that he could tell a lot about the generosity and loyalty of a person by how they spoke of and treated their family.

"That's a hell of a gift." Her thigh brushed his, and

when their eyes met and she didn't move hers away, he realized she'd done it on purpose, causing a stirring in his groin. *Down, boy.* Emily was just beginning to relax, and the last thing he wanted to do was to scare her off.

"Yes. It was. He knew I've been dying to see Tuscany, and this villa in particular. Gabriela Bocelli is one of my favorite architects. But if it had been left up to me, I'd never have made it here. Between work and my family, well, I'm not really good about taking time for myself." She finished her wine, and Dae refilled their glasses.

"Life's too short to miss out on the things you really want to do. I'm glad your brothers are looking out for you." Dae was a self-made man with enough money that he could buy all of his siblings trips to Tuscany, but while he and his sisters were close, buying them a trip to Tuscany was so far out of the realm of their relationships that he could barely comprehend the gesture. Leanna never planned a damn thing in her life, and Bailey, his youngest sister, was a musician with a concert schedule that rivaled the busiest of them. Even coordinating dinner with her was a massive undertaking. If he ever purchased a trip for them, Leanna would miss the flight and Bailey would probably have to cancel it. Their gifts to one another were typically as simple as making time to get together and enjoy one another's company.

"My brothers are good at taking care of me. Maybe a little too good." She sighed.

"Overprotective?" Why did he enjoy knowing that?

"Oh, you could say that. They're great, really. I

adore them, but...yeah. They're overprotective." She met his gaze, and the air around them sizzled again. She looked away, pink-cheeked, and pressed her hands to her thighs. "To be honest, I don't hate the way they are. I mean, it probably sounds childish, but I feel the same way about them."

"Overprotective?" She couldn't weigh more than a buck twenty. What could she possibly do to protect a man?

She smiled, and it lit up her beautiful, dark eyes. Her voice softened, and she sat up a little straighter. "Yeah. I know it's weird, but like, when they started dating their girlfriends, I watched out for them. Made sure the girls weren't going to treat them badly, or...well...My brothers are the catch of our town, and girls can be fickle. I didn't want them to get hurt. But now the ones who live in town are all in relationships, so..." She shrugged.

Loyal. He liked that. He wondered if she was the catch of their town, too. "Do you live in the town where you grew up?"

"Yeah, in Trusty, Colorado. It's about as big as your fist. All of us live there except my oldest brother Pierce, and one of my other brothers, Jake. Pierce is in Reno, and Jake is in LA. But they visit a lot. We're all really close. I can't imagine living anywhere else—or living far away from my family. Being away for college was enough. I'm glad to be back in my hometown." She finished her wine and set the glass beside her.

Dae held up the bottle. "More?"

"In a few minutes. I'm a lightweight. I wouldn't want you to have to carry me back up to my room."

Now, there's an idea. "Fair enough." He paused, pushing the thought of Emily in his arms to the back of his mind. "So, what do you do for a living?"

"I'm an architect. I specialize in passive houses, green building." She gazed out over the hillside, and her features softened again.

"Really? The passive-house movement is a good one, but it seems like builders don't understand it well enough to make headway."

Her eyes widened, and he felt the press of her leg against his. "You know about passive houses? Usually when I bring it up, people look all deer in the headlights at me."

"That doesn't surprise me. Most people don't understand heating by passive solar gain and energy gains from people and appliances. It's a concept they just aren't familiar with, so it sounds space-agey to them." Passive houses were the wave of the future, as far as Dae was concerned, and not just houses, but schools and office buildings, too. The technology may seem space-agey, but then again, so had electric cars and cell phones twenty years ago.

"Exactly." She smacked his thigh, and both of their eyes dropped to her hand.

He lifted his eyes to hers, and she swallowed hard. In the short time they'd been talking, he'd seen a handful of looks pass through her eyes: embarrassment, arousal, worry. She had to feel the way the air zapped between them. Her eyes darkened, and her lips parted.

Oh yeah, she feels it.

She licked her lips, and it just about killed him.

"What about you?" she asked, visibly more relaxed now as she leaned back on one hand and turned her body toward him. "Where do you live? What do you do?"

Her question made him think a little deeper about the two of them. *A sexy architect into green building. Figures.* It had been his experience that tree huggers rarely held much respect for demolition experts. He sucked down his wine and went with an evasive answer in hopes of postponing any negative discussion.

"Depends on the week. I don't like to be tied to one place for too long. I get itchy." He'd always been that way. Spending too much time alone in any one of the houses he owned made him edgy. He'd never met anyone he'd liked enough to spend a few weeks with, much less settle down with.

Emily's finely manicured brows furrowed. Clearly he wasn't going to get off that easily.

"So..."

"I'm into construction. I go where the jobs take me."

"Oh. I thought construction workers usually worked around where they lived."

"Some do. I work with larger projects, which means that I travel a lot." He didn't want to talk about his job. Especially not the demolition job he was assessing here in Tuscany. He was enjoying spending time with Emily, and the last thing he wanted to do was talk about why he blew up buildings for a living.

"How long are you here?" His feeble attempt at changing the subject.

"Nine days, and I have every day planned so I don't miss a thing." She held up her empty glass.

"No longer worried about me carrying you to your bedroom?" Their eyes locked, and he couldn't help but think, *Or mine*, as he filled her glass. Although he knew it was just his ego talking. He'd stopped having flings a few years ago—but they were still fun to think about.

"I can think of worse things." Her voice was quiet, seductive. She mindlessly twirled her finger in her hair and lowered her eyes. When she raised them again, she said more confidently, "Besides, you have sisters. I think you'll take care of me."

"That's a lot of trust in a guy you've known for only a little while." He refilled their glasses.

"If you were a serial killer, you'd have stabbed me and hidden my body by now. And if you were going to make a move, I think you'd have done more than talk about family." She moved her fingers over so they were touching his. "Like I said, you have sisters. I think the big brother in you will keep me safe."

Damn. Talk about conflicting signals. The hand. The brother talk. A guy could get whiplash trying to keep up.

An hour and an empty bottle of wine later, they were standing in front of the door to Emily's room. She was tucked beneath his arm, her cheeks flushed, her eyes glassy, and her head nestled against his chest.

Lightweight, indeed. Cute-as-hell lightweight. Dae took a step back, leaned his hip against the doorframe, and crossed his arms, debating. He wanted to kiss her, to feel the soft press of her lips against his and taste the sweet wine on that sassy tongue of hers. *I think the big brother in you will keep me safe.*

"These five overprotective brothers of yours, would they mind if we spent tomorrow together?"

She took a step back and raked her eyes down his body. "That depends. Do serial killers ask women on dates?"

He laughed. "I don't have enough experience with serial killers to answer that."

Emily's phone vibrated in her pocket.

"Maybe that's one of them. You can ask."

Emily pulled her phone out of her pocket and read a text. She trapped her lower lip between her teeth and raised her eyes to his, then held up her index finger before responding.

"Christ, you're not really asking your brother—are you?"

She shook her head, and her hair tumbled forward. "Soon-to-be sister-in-law. Daisy. She's marrying my brother Luke the weekend after I go home."

Dae scrubbed his hand down his face at the prospect of her asking her soon-to-be sister-in-law about going on a date with him. "Great." He didn't even try to mask his sarcasm.

Her phone vibrated again, and her long lashes fluttered as she read the text.

"Well? What does Daisy say?"

"Um..." She lowered the phone and held it behind her back with a coy smile.

Dae rolled his eyes. So much for their date. The words *stranger danger* came to mind. "It was nice getting to know you tonight, Emily."

Her smile was replaced with tight lips and a wrinkled brow as he took a step away. "What? That's it? I haven't answered you yet."

He closed the distance between them, so their thighs touched. Their lips were a breath apart, and her eyes held a seductive challenge. It took all of his focus for him not to lean down and wipe that smug look off her face with a kiss.

"I assumed..."

"Assumed?" Her voice turned low and sexy. "What happened to Mr. Hand or Arm? Wow, you're not quite the man I thought you were if you give up that easy." She touched his chest, nearly doing him in.

Dae clenched his jaw at the challenge. "I'm trying to be respectful. You're the one who gave me the big-brother lecture earlier."

"Oh, yeah." She wrinkled her nose, and her eyes held a hint of regret.

She was so damn cute that he wanted to take care of her as much as he wanted to kiss her. "Yeah." He leaned down and pressed his cheek to hers, then wrapped an arm around her waist, holding her against him. "I honestly don't give a rat's ass what Daisy said," he whispered.

Emily nibbled on her lower lip.

Their bedrooms were located on more of a balcony than a hallway, with wrought-iron railings overlooking the great room below. The villa was silent, save for the sound of their heavy breathing.

"It's your answer I want, not hers."

He leaned back and gazed into her eyes, hoping she'd take a chance on the desire he could see lingering in them.

"Okay," she whispered.

"Great, and just for the record, I'd have kept you safe even if I didn't have sisters, but I can assure you that my feelings toward you are not brotherly."

Emily's eyes widened.

"And I wouldn't mind if you didn't act sisterly toward me, either."

"I—"

"Good night, Emily."

Chapter Two

AFTER A FITFUL night's sleep filled with anticipation, Emily pulled on her favorite black tank dress and stood in front of the mirror. Thinking about last night and the way Dae's stubbly cheek had felt against hers, she stroked her cheek, as if she could bring back the prickly, heated sensation of their skin-to-skin contact. Her lips lifted into a smile. It was mid-July, and the weather during the day was comfortably warm. She had a feeling that she'd be warm no matter what she wore when she was around him.

Dae. Was his name short for something? She slipped her feet into her cutest and most comfortable sandals and read through her overzealous itinerary as she pondered names that could be shortened to Dae. She couldn't come up with a single one.

They hadn't made any real plans for today, other than to spend the day together. Her day was scheduled from nine until six, and she assumed he was okay with following her itinerary so she wouldn't have to miss anything. She didn't even know what time they were meeting, so she planned on eating breakfast early to be ready, just in case he was an early riser.

"Well, Mr. Bray, I hope you're ready for a busy day," she said to the empty room. She drew open the double doors to the balcony and inhaled the warm summer air. Her phone rang and Daisy's name appeared on the screen. She answered on her way outside.

"Hey, Daisy." Her room overlooked the vineyard. She scanned the grounds in search of the patio she and Dae had sat on the evening before.

"Hey, yourself. You left me hanging last night. So? What's the deal? Did you do as I suggested?" Daisy's excitement made Emily smile. Daisy was the Trusty town doctor. Her days were often as busy as Emily's, and when she was working, she was professional and serious. With blond hair, blue eyes, and a killer body, Daisy had more people coming to see her, claiming to be sick, than she'd ever seen before. Emily smiled at the thought of her jealous, protective brother Luke's reaction when he and Daisy had first started dating. He'd made quick work of letting the community know Daisy was *his*. She wondered what Luke would make of Daisy telling her to go for it with Dae.

"Did I...*take, rattle, and roll* with him?" She laughed. "Really, Daisy? No, I didn't. Isn't it midnight there? Why are you still awake?"

"I had to know if you went for it. You deserve a great romp! I can't believe you didn't take advantage of the situation. Em, you never date. You're forever and a day away from the eyes of your prying brothers, and you're in *Tuscany*. You can date, kiss, have a three-night stand, whatever you want, and no one in Trusty, Colorado, will ever know."

"A three-night stand? Do people do that?" She spotted the patio off in the distance, and her stomach fluttered as it had the night before.

"How would I know? I've never even had a one-night stand."

"So you haven't, but I should? Great advice, Dais..." Emily heard voices and leaned over the railing. Dae and Adelina were walking around the side of the villa toward the back patio. Dae's hair was damp, and his jeans hung dangerously low on his hips. *Again*. His white T-shirt clung to his hot body. He was even more smokin' hot in the daylight. Emily's pulse quickened. Now that she knew what it felt like to be pressed against those muscular thighs and that rock-hard stomach, she could barely think of anything else.

She stole another peek over the balcony. Adelina was looking up at Dae with a soft smile. Emily imagined all women would be taken with his good looks and easy nature. Dae said something, then patted her back, and they stopped right below Emily's balcony. She hurried back into the bedroom and sat on the king-sized bed.

"What happened?" Daisy asked.

"Nothing, why?"

"You sucked in a breath. Are you okay? Oh my gosh, he's not still there, is he?"

"No. He's not here." *Do I wish he were here?*

"Oh." The disappointment in Daisy's voice was palpable.

"Daisy! He's outside. We're spending the day together."

"Oh! Good. So, tell me all about him. Name? Age? Looks? What does he do? Is he an Italian stallion?"

"You're relentless." Having grown up with five brothers, each of whom watched her like a hawk, Emily secretly loved having her brother's fiancées and girlfriends around. Having Daisy looking out for her was totally different from the way her brothers watched her. The girls supported and understood her wanting to fall in love, and her interest in men, while her brothers seemed to fear it. It was like she had four sisters now.

"His name is Dae Bray, and he's—"

"Hold the boat! Day? Like *day or night*?"

"D. A. E. Dae. I'm not sure what type of name it is, but…I'm getting all hot just talking about him. He's got this amazing voice that vibrates right through me, and his eyes. Oh gosh, his eyes aren't just brown. They're piercing. They looked almost black last night."

"It's called being horny, Em. Pupils dilate when we're turned on. Tell me more."

Emily sighed. "You're such a *doctor*. Anyway, his hair is kind of longish, and he's at least six feet tall, with broad shoulders and…Daisy, the man is pure muscle. I touched his stomach—washboard abs and all." Emily fanned her face and exhaled loudly. "Oh, Daisy. This is bad."

"No, this is very, very good. Go on…"

"You do remember that you're marrying my brother in two weeks, right?" Emily teased.

"Oh, please. You know no man could compare to

Luke for me, but you're a different story. Your forever love is out there somewhere. Who knows? It could be this guy."

Emily paced the bedroom. Rich, dark woods, cream-colored walls, and hues of peach and mauve brightened the room. A fresh bouquet of flowers graced the bureau, and a plush throw rug covered expensive tile floors in the same peachy hues. There was a throw draped over an armchair in the corner and a stone fireplace on the wall opposite the bed. The room wasn't very large, but the textures and fall colors gave it a homey feel. Her thoughts traveled back to Dae and how easy he was to be with once she got her initial lust-fest under control. Oh shit. She remembered how she'd come onto him when they'd said good night.

"Daisy, don't get your hopes up." Emily wondered if she was talking to herself more than Daisy. "I mean, he's totally hot...and fun. He seems smart and attentive, and—"

A knock at her door stopped Emily in her tracks. *And I hope I didn't scare him off.*

"Someone's at my door."

"So? Answer it."

"Right." Emily rolled her eyes. "I'd better go. Hey, Dais..."

"Yeah?"

"Thanks for checking on me. I wish you or Callie or Rebecca or Elisabeth were here with me. I still can't believe I came all this way by myself." Why had she come by herself? Why had Wes given her this expensive trip in the first place? She'd been so excited by the gift that she hadn't really dissected the reasons behind it. Now she wondered if he'd booked the trip because he wanted to thank her for helping him or if there was something more. Did he think she needed it? *Boy, did I ever need it.* Did he notice how she'd swamped herself with work lately to keep from being lonely? *Did everyone?*

"Em, you've dreamed of this forever. You're an intelligent, successful woman. You can certainly handle a little vacation on your own."

"Thanks, Daisy. I needed to hear that." She'd been so overcome with desire for Dae that she felt like her brain had turned to mush. She needed the reminder that she was smart and successful and that it was okay for her to enjoy a little time off. A vacation. Yes, that's what this was. Of course it was. Wasn't it? Something deep in her belly twisted with the thought. She felt like she'd been searching for something for months. For love? For companionship? Or was something much bigger lacking in her life, and she'd molded it into the hope of finding true love because of watching her brothers fall in love? Had she taken this trip with the hope of finding true love rather than relaxing and simply enjoying a vacation? *Ugh.* She pushed those thoughts as far away as she could. She was not ready to try to reevaluate her life. All she wanted was to have a good time with handsome, sexy, attentive Dae.

"I know. Besides, you're not alone anymore. Hottie is probably on the other side of the door." Daisy laughed.

There was another knock, rattling Emily back into the present.

"I'd better go. Wish me luck."

"You don't need luck. Just be safe."

Emily smoothed her dress, wondering why on earth she was so nervous. It had only been...Oh, jeez. It had been months since she'd been on a real date. She breathed deeply before opening the door, but found no one there. She peered down the empty hall. It had to have been Dae knocking on her door. Or maybe Adelina? Had she taken that long to answer? Disappointment settled around her as she went back into her room and started to close the door.

"Wait!"

Emily spun around at the sound of Dae's voice. He caught the door just before it closed, and when their eyes met, she saw as much relief in his as she knew she had in hers.

"Wow." Dae dragged his eyes down Emily's body, and she knew she was guilty of doing the exact same thing to him. "Emily, you look amazing."

"Thanks. So do you."

He stepped into her room, and the door closed quietly behind him. The room felt ten degrees hotter—and smaller—as he closed the gap between them, settled a hand on her hip, and kissed her cheek.

"I'm sorry I left you hanging at the door. I forgot my wallet and had to grab it from my room."

"Where's your room?"

He arched a brow. "Next door. They only rent out two of their rooms."

"Oh," was all she could manage. *Next door*. Her eyes slid to the wall. She'd known they rented out only two rooms, but she hadn't thought about what that *really* meant in terms of her proximity to Dae's room.

He shifted his eyes to the wall behind her bed. "Other side."

"Oh." Wow. Only one thin wall separated them at night. That was *so* hot.

"Are you ready to roll?" He looked around the room, and Emily followed his gaze to her cami lying in a heap in the center of her bed. The little pile of pink silk suddenly seemed like an invitation. Dae smiled and raised his brows.

He didn't miss a thing, and unfortunately, neither did all her good parts, which were heating up way too fast. Emily grabbed her purse. "Um, yeah. I'm ready." She grabbed his arm and tugged him toward the door.

"I have seen lingerie before, you know," he teased.

"Yeah, but not mine."

"Good point. Maybe we should stay." He stopped and turned back toward the bed with a wicked grin.

Emily rolled her eyes and tugged him toward the door again. "Yeah, that's *so* not happening right now." Later, maybe…but she wasn't about to miss seeing Tuscany.

"Damn. What happened to the tipsy girl I met last night?"

"She sobered up and is starving."

"Well…" He raised his brows in quick succession with a tease in his eyes.

"Really?" She closed the door behind him, enjoying the sexy comments. She liked this playful side of Dae. She liked it a whole heck of a lot, which was exactly why she needed to get as far away from the bedroom as she possibly could. Now.

They found Serafina and Luca having breakfast on the patio. Luca's mop of thick, dark hair stood up at funky angles. The brown shirt he wore mirrored the color of his and Serafina's eyes. Serafina wore a navy skirt that hung to her ankles and a comfortable-looking T-shirt of the same color. While Luca's eyes were wide with amusement, Serafina's were solemn and heavy lidded.

"Good morning," Emily said. She waved at Luca, who gave her a wide, almost-toothless grin. Serafina smiled down at her son, but her smile didn't reach her eyes.

"Good morning," Serafina said.

Dae pulled out a chair at a nearby table for Emily.

"Buongiorno." Adelina joined them on the patio with a flourish of energy. She set down a cup of cappuccino for each of them and opened her arms wide. "It's going to be a beautiful day."

"Yes, it is," Dae said, smiling coyly at Emily.

Adelina said something in Italian to Serafina, then disappeared in the direction of the kitchen again. When she returned with a tray of jam-filled tarts with dough lacing the top like lattice, she set it on their table and eyed her daughter.

"Thank you," Emily and Dae said at the same time.

"My pleasure." Adelina smiled, her eyes lingering on the two of them for a moment. "These are *crostata di marmellata*—sweet, jam-filled tarts. My mother used to make them." She looked at Luca, and her eyes warmed even more. "Good memories. I hope you enjoy them."

Adelina joined Serafina at her table. "Is Luca ready

to go?"

"Mama." Serafina's voice was just above a whisper. "Maybe it's no use. Wishing won't bring Dante back."

"*Tsk!* Serafina." Adelina spoke in Italian fast and with a harsh tone. Serafina dropped her gaze to Luca, then kissed the top of his head and closed her eyes for a beat.

Emily bit into the tart. "*Mm*. This is amazing."

Dae ate half of his tart in one bite. "It reminds me of my mom's comfort cakes. She used to make them when we'd have a bad day. One bite and you forgot all of your troubles."

"I think almost anything my mom makes is comfort food. Somehow everything tastes better when she cooks it."

"You're really close to your family."

You noticed already? She nodded, trying to ignore the heated discussion taking place between Adelina and Serafina.

Emily and Dae finished eating, sharing concerned glances. She was glad that Dae appeared just as empathetic as she was.

"Thank you again, Adelina. That was a wonderful breakfast," Emily said as she rose from the table.

"I'm glad you enjoyed it." Adelina turned back to Serafina.

Emily heard Adelina's tone soften as they left the patio, her words trailing behind them. "We will wish, and he will return, Serafina. I promise you. He will return."

Emily couldn't begin to imagine the devastation

that Serafina was feeling, but she was glad Adelina was there to support her and Luca, even if she worried about keeping Serafina's hopes too high.

They followed a stone path around the house toward the parking lot. Dae reached for her hand. Emily widened her eyes, and he laughed.

"Do you prefer an arm?"

I prefer a lot more than an arm. Calm down, girlie. "This is perfect. I was just thinking about Serafina."

"It's awful." Dae's voice grew serious. "Adelina is so hopeful. I hope they do find him."

"Yeah, me too. I hate to say it, but three months is a really long time. Is it even possible that he's still alive?"

Dae's eyes grew serious. "There have been POWs that have been found years later, so I don't know. Maybe?"

They walked through the front gardens with the sun shining brightly down on them. Emily focused on her hand engulfed by Dae's and pushed aside thoughts of Serafina's husband.

"That's my rental." Dae nodded to a champagne-colored Mercedes.

Emily had a hard time reconciling Dae to a Mercedes. She pictured him in an expensive truck or SUV, but now, watching him open the door and lean casually against the side of the car, she realized there were many sides to Dae Bray, and she looked forward to getting to know them all.

"You haven't asked me what I had planned for today."

"That's because I don't care where we go." He

waited for her to settle into the passenger seat, then closed her door and went around to the driver's seat.

Emily wasn't sure if she should be offended or intrigued. "You don't care? Then why are you coming?"

He reached across the console and squeezed her hand. "I want to spend the day with you. It doesn't matter if we see Florence, Siena, or some remote village I've never heard of."

She couldn't help but smile. He held her hand as he drove away from the villa, and she wondered if she'd ever *stop* smiling.

"You tell me where and I'll take us there."

"Florence. Do you have a GPS?" Emily glanced around the luxurious car.

"No need." He pointed to his head.

Emily rolled her eyes. "No GPS? So, you have been here before?"

"Nope. It's my first time, but I studied maps before I came. I like to know my surroundings."

"Okay, but I hope you brought a map, just in case. First stop, the cathedral complex."

"Ah, yes. The Basilica di Santa Maria del Fiore, located at the Piazza del Duomo."

Emily narrowed her eyes. "You sure you haven't been here before?"

He shrugged. "History buff—what can I say? Besides, like I said, I like to know my surroundings."

Why did she have the feeling that there was much more to Dae than he was letting on? Maybe he was a closet history addict. Emily gazed out the open window as they drove toward the city. The roads were lined with fields and farms. Low stone walls crept along the roadway in front of older villas, and trees and flowers were plentiful. The landscape looked just like the pictures she'd drooled over for so many years, only everything felt richer, more vibrant. Even the air felt cleaner than she would have imagined—and there must be an aphrodisiac among those flowers, because she'd never experienced so much want as she had since she'd met Dae.

Her phone vibrated, and she pulled it out to read the emails that had come through.

Dae gave her a sideways glance, eyeing her phone with distaste, and shook his head.

"What?" She went back to answering her emails.

"You're in Italy."

"It's work." She scrolled through her messages.

Dae covered her phone with his hand and lowered it to her lap. "Take thirty seconds to look at the flowers. They'll be gone before you finish reading your next email."

She sighed and turned toward the windows. *Holy cow*. She was mesmerized by the meadow dotted with her favorite vibrant red blooms.

"Look at all the poppies." Emily heard the excitement in her voice. She'd never seen so many poppies in one place. "They're even more beautiful in person than online."

Dae pulled the car over to the side of the road.

"Why are you stopping?" she asked.

"You'll see." Dae got out of the car and came around to her side, then opened her door and reached for her hand.

"Where are we going?" She eyed the cars speeding

past as she took his hand, and Dae led her directly into the field—and kept walking. She almost allowed her mind to drift back to the idea that maybe sweet, sexy Dae was a serial killer and she was just being naive, but as quickly as the thought came, she pushed it away. They were completely surrounded by a sea of red. What kind of serial killer would *make her* go look at flowers?

"Experiencing life." He released her hand and held his hands out to his sides. "Can you do this in Trusty, Colorado?" He spun in a circle and brushed the blooms with his fingertips.

"There are lots of fields of flowers there."

He leveled her silent with a heated stare. "Yes, smarty-pants, I'm sure there are. But are there Tuscan poppies in Trusty? Are there fields of poppies that you can dance in?"

Before she could process what he was doing, he wrapped her in his arms and spun her around.

"You're crazy." She laughed and let herself get lost in the freedom of being spun in his arms.

"No. I'm just not confined by social norms." He set her on the ground and took her hand in his again. "I'm not sure if that's a good or a bad thing, but it is who I am." He took his phone from the pocket of those sexy jeans of his and draped an arm around her, then pressed his cheek to hers.

Oh, that feels nice.

He clicked a picture, then tickled her ribs. She squealed and he clicked another picture. Emily was a photo hoarder. She had dozens of digital albums of her family and friends. She loved that Dae had taken their picture.

"That's more like it. I like your smile."

"You're not like most guys." Emily liked that he left his arm draped around her and that it seemed so natural to be that close to him. The weight of his arm and the heat of his body in such close proximity made her wonder what it would feel like to be even closer.

Dae ran his hand through his hair. In that second, with his hair pulled away from his face, sunlight caught the sharp angles of his handsome features. Attraction tightened every nerve in her body. How could he be so virile one minute and so playful the next?

He narrowed his eyes and said in a serious voice, "Good. Most guys are douche bags."

"Tell me about it." She laughed. "You don't have to date them."

"Yeah, well, girls can be pretty lame, too."

Emily knew that was true. Women used men as often as men used women. That's why she'd kept her eyes open when her brothers had brought home her soon-to-be sisters-in-law. What she found was women who loved her brothers for the attentive, loving, virile men they were, and not for their wealth or social status. She counted them lucky to have met such wonderful women.

Dae grabbed her ribs again, and she squealed and ran toward the car. She hadn't had this kind of unfettered fun with a man...ever. Maybe her brothers when they chased her around, but that was a whole different type of giddy enjoyment. Having this type of fun with Dae wasn't giddy at all; it was enthralling, intoxicating, freeing. He caught up to her in three long steps and picked her up under one arm. She giggled and wiggled, secretly loving the feel of him holding her.

"I have a deal for you." He set her down by the car and stood with his legs wide, gazing down at her with lust in his eyes.

"A deal?"

"A deal." He stepped closer, backing her up until her back hit the car, and he placed a hand on either side of her, caging her in.

His scent filled her senses again, and when their thighs brushed, her pulse sped up. He leaned down close, pinning her in place with the sheer proximity of his body.

"I'll go wherever you want today, and you go wherever I want tomorrow."

"Okay." He'd surprised her. She'd spent weeks mulling over her detailed itinerary for her trip. The idea of taking a day willy-nilly, not knowing what she was in store for, wasn't something she'd ever considered.

"Okay?" He drew his thick, dark brows together. "Didn't I warn you not to be so trusting?"

She laughed. "Yeah, but I'm at your disposal today. In your car, without anyone other than Daisy, who's thousands of miles away, knowing where I am. If I don't make it back to the villa in one piece, it won't matter what I agree to."

That earned her a smile.

"You're a sassy woman, Emily Braden."

Her insides whirred with delight. *Sassy?* She

thought of herself as organized, determined, focused in everything she did. *Sassy*. He saw a part of her that she'd never given much thought to, and it gave her confidence. She pushed off the car so their bodies were joined from thigh to chest, and holy moly did it feel good. With his compliment driving her, she was beginning to feel like a part of herself was climbing out from where it must have been hiding—and she decided to go with it. "You need to make higher-stakes deals, Mr. Bray."

"Higher stakes." He clenched his jaw again. "Got it."

"Higher. Much higher."

His lips spread into a sexy smile, full of promise and intrigue, stirring all sorts of deliciously lewd thoughts in Emily's mind.

"What's beneath your sweet facade, Emmie Braden?"

Emmie? Emily's gaze didn't waver from his, even as a shudder rippled through her body. What was he doing to her? She liked this side of herself. This sassy, risqué side that was taking her by surprise and filling her with unfamiliar sexual confidence. She hooked her finger in his belt loop and his eyes followed. "Careful, Emmie. We have a cathedral to see." He grabbed her wrist and held tight.

For a hot second they stared into each other's eyes, bound by sexual tension, until he broke the spell and raised her hand to his lips. He pressed a kiss to her palm, then stalked around the car to the driver's seat, leaving her hot and bothered, and once again, uncharacteristically flustered. And he'd called her

Emmie. *Emmie!* No one called her that, but from Dae, she liked it. A lot. She'd never met a guy who was so comfortable in his own skin, and she was more turned on than she'd ever been.

Chapter Three

DAE MANEUVERED THROUGH the busy streets and parked as close as he could to the cathedral, all the while wondering how the hell he was going to make it through the day without kissing Emily. No matter how much he tried to ignore the comment she'd made last night about him being a big brother, it had struck home. Every time he looked at her, he saw her as not just a hot, sexy woman, but as a sister, a daughter, and, from what he could gather, a caring friend. Since when had he begun caring so much about someone else, and how was it happening so quickly?

Emily's phone vibrated for the third time since they'd left the villa.

"Are you really on vacation, or are you one of those telecommuting workers and you just like fancy environments?" He watched her face scrunch up as she read and responded to an email.

"I'm on vacation, but I have to be available for work." Her serious eyes remained locked on her phone.

"Why? Your assistant, or secretary, or partner can't handle your emails while you're away? I just don't get it."

She sighed and finally met his gaze. "My assistant is very capable. Of course she can handle them."

"So..."

"So what?" She crossed her arms, and her dress tightened like she was holding her breath.

"So when do you actually get to relax and take a vacation?" He knew he was boxing her in to a corner and he shouldn't take pleasure in watching her squirm, but something told him Emily was a workaholic and she deserved a break. Besides, he wanted to get to know her better without the confines of dinging notifications and emails.

She looked down at her phone, and her eyes became serious. "I like to keep on top of things."

"Uh-huh." He covered her phone with his hand again. "I'll make you a deal. How about if you let your assistant handle your emails and enjoy your vacation, at least when you're with me, and I'll..."

She arched a brow. "You'll?"

"Hell. I'll do anything you want. I'll be your chauffeur the whole time we're here."

She laughed, and the tension in her eased as she unfolded her arms. "Well, how can I turn that down? Let me send this email." She sent off the email and raised her eyes. "I'll try, but no promises."

"You know, it's really simple to turn off email notifications. That might help."

She rolled her eyes and tucked her hair behind her

ear.

"What? Would it kill you to relinquish a modicum of control so you could actually enjoy yourself?"

She smiled, but he saw the struggle in her eyes as she stared at her phone.

"Scared you'll lose clients? Even the most pompous of clients understands that no one works every day of the year."

"I try to be better than everyone else."

"And I'm sure you succeed in every way. But even Superwoman deserves a break. Especially when she's flown all the way to Italy, and even more especially when she's on a date with a handsome guy."

Emily smiled, washing away her remaining tension, and scrolled through her settings. "Okay. I'm doing it, but only emails, not texts. My family might need me."

"Really?" He couldn't believe he'd won her over that easily.

"Yes, really, but I hope you like your new career, Mr. Chauffeur."

He reached for Emily's hand, and she took it without hesitation. He knew the answer to his question of when he'd begun caring about someone else. *Since Emily.* There was something different about her. In the span of a few hours, she'd knocked him off-kilter. Even the thought of her going home to her family with a heavy heart caused by him made him feel queasy.

Holy hell. What am I thinking? A heavy heart? What the...?

He shook his head to clear the strange thoughts

from his mind. One thing was for sure. He needed to be careful around her. It was true he was an affectionate guy, but he got the sense that it would be easy to move beyond affectionate and fall for sassy, seductive Emily Braden. But he was all too aware that a tree-hugging architect and a demolition expert would probably not play well in the sandbox for long. Still, when he looked at her wide eyes as she gazed up at the cathedral like a kid faced with a penny-candy store for the first time ever, his chest constricted in an unfamiliar way. He couldn't restrain himself from capturing the moment.

"Hold up, Em." He pulled her close, slipped his phone from his pocket, and snapped a picture with the impressive cathedral in the background.

"Why do you keep taking our picture?"

"I don't know. It feels right. Does it bother you?" Why *was* he taking their picture so often? He had never been a photo guy, but there was something about Emily that had him cataloguing their time together. Maybe it was because he knew they had only a few days, or that she had him confused as hell and thinking new thoughts that scared him a little. All he knew was that he liked being with her and wanted to remember every detail of her beautiful face. Other than that, he had no idea what the hell he was doing.

"No." She searched his eyes and then said softly, "I like it."

The way her eyes darkened and her lips curved into a sweet smile made his stomach feel funky. He knew he was playing with fire, but he had no interest in dousing the flames.

"Good, then the picture taking will continue. Now that that's settled, what's your cell number?"

"*That's* your smooth line to get my number?" She arched a brow.

"No. That's my way of sending you these pictures so your friend Daisy can show your brothers that you're alive and well."

"Oh." She dropped her eyes and smiled.

He pulled her against him, loving the feel of her soft curves. He lifted her chin with his finger, and when he was sure he had her attention, he said, "Did you really expect me to admit that lame line was my way of getting your number?"

She pushed at his chest and rolled her eyes. "You're impossible."

"Impossible is definitely *off* the table where you're concerned. Possible, Emmie. All this…" He ran his hand up and down his body with a teasing smile, though he was anything *but* teasing. He didn't have time to play games with Emily, and he didn't want to, but he didn't want to scare her off, either. "All this is totally possible. *If* you give me your number."

"That's pretty high stakes. You learn quickly." She gave him her number and he sent her the pictures.

He hadn't realized how much he'd wanted her number, but now that he had it, he wanted more. *A lot more.*

BETWEEN DAE'S STRONG grip on her hand and the artful nuances of the rosette and rose windows, the statues of the apostles and Mary, coupled with the intricate architecture and meticulous details of the cathedral, Emily's heart was racing. Or maybe it was caused by the way Dae smelled like strength and heaven wrapped into one, or the way he was looking at her, like she held all the answers.

"You're staring at me."

A smile played across his lips. "Am I?"

"Uh-huh. You're making me nervous."

"Oh, come on. You must be used to guys staring at you." He stepped closer and bent his head forward. His hair curtained their faces from the rest of the world—and Emily's pulse kicked up again.

"You're..." She swallowed to gain control of the urge to rise up onto her toes and kiss his full lips. "You're looking at me different from the way most guys do, and you're supposed to be staring at the cathedral." She tried to shift her eyes to the magnificent cathedral towering before them, but she couldn't. Her eyes remained trained on the very masculine, very real man standing an inch away, who was making her head and heart go crazy, stealing her ability to focus one second at a time.

His dark, penetrating gaze seared through her, warming her from the inside out. Anticipation pulsed around them. Every second he remained silent felt interminable. His scent, the look in his eyes, the way his hair shielded them from the rest of the world—it all wound together and drew Emily up onto her toes, unable to resist him for a second longer.

I'm going to kiss you. That new side of herself was guiding her, stretching her comfort zone to new places. She felt the earth shift, the world close in on them, as if only the two of them existed—and she wanted to stretch a little more.

I have to kiss you.

Her eyes began to close as she felt his grip on her hand tighten. This was it. Their lips would finally meet. She felt his breath whisper across her cheek as he leaned closer.

"Shall we go inside?"

She sank to her heels and stumbled backward on shaky legs. *What?*

"Inside. Yes. Definitely yes." *Holy crap!* She'd misread everything? Him? The air around them sizzling? She moved as if in a daze, feeling foolish and nervous as they joined the line for the cathedral.

Thankfully, the line moved quickly.

"Want to climb to the top of the dome first?" He looked...normal.

Why didn't he look as flustered as she felt? He was glancing around at the other people, looking up at the cathedral; his eyes even danced over Emily. They danced, they didn't drag or get hung up on her like hers were to him. Stuck on his freaking Adonis-like muscles.

"Uh-huh." Emily couldn't get past the awkward feeling of nearly kissing Dae and having him jerk her back to reality. Was she really that out of practice in reading men? He'd held her hand, called her nicknames, and stood close enough that she could feel heat rolling off him. She might not have dated much recently, but she knew when someone was attracted to her. What was he doing? Why was he keeping his distance? Or was this all a stupid game to him? Was she so swept up in his attentive nature and good looks that she'd allowed herself to believe it?

She glanced at his warm eyes, the sincere smile that curved his lips—and now she was more confused than ever. She saw the interest in his eyes. No woman could misread the way the air sizzled between them. Not even her. Not even out of practice. Maybe she was just overthinking things.

Dae kept a tight grip on her hand as they followed the arrows toward the dome. Emily focused on counting each of the four-hundred-plus steps as they climbed the stone stairs. It was easier than trying to decipher the fast and furious emotions coursing through her. The steps were spiraled, though squared off. They were wide and stable—a blessing in disguise, as she felt Dae's eyes on her. As the steps went from steep to shallow and became narrower, Emily felt Dae's hand on her back, steadying her, ensuring her safety, while completely oblivious to the fact that every touch made her legs less stable.

"You doing okay?" he asked softly.

Confused out of my mind, but... "Yeah. Fine." The walkway was darker and in some places, colder, than she'd imagined it would be, and still, with Dae walking behind her, it also felt romantic and a little dangerous—in a good way. She lost count of the steps the third time his hand touched her back. His touch was a much more interesting distraction, and she began counting how many times he touched her.

He pulled her close and wrapped his arms around her waist as a group of people descended the narrow stairwell. "You're awfully quiet for *fine*," he whispered, sending a shiver down her spine.

Emily couldn't answer. What would she say? *Why didn't you kiss me? You confuse me?* Even in her head she sounded like either a petulant child or a horny adult, and she wasn't sure either was appropriate for whatever was brewing between them.

After the group passed, they began their trek up again.

"*Fine* is what women say when they're really not fine."

She heard the smile in his voice, and damn if he wasn't right. She was kind of annoyed at him for that, but he touched her again, and that sexy smile of his turned that unwarranted annoyance back into desire again.

Ugh. She was hopeless.

He placed his hand on her back for the thirty-eighth time as the walkway opened up and they came to a balcony that overlooked the stained-glass windows. The narrow balcony went partially around the circumference of the dome. The balcony was surrounded by a clear plastic shield, so there was no chance of falling. Above them were the magnificent frescoes climbing all the way up the dome.

"I knew the stained glass would be spectacular, but look down." Emily pointed to the intricately inlaid marble floors below.

"The view doesn't change for me. No matter how high we climb, it's always spectacular."

She turned and found his eyes locked on her. Her pulse soared and her stomach twisted. He wasn't just sending mixed messages; he was the king of mixed messages. He was the master of them.

"You know what we need to do..." Dae's eyes lit up with that wicked, playful grin of his as he draped an arm around her.

"Kiss?" She slapped her hand over her mouth. Holy Christ. When did she lose her filter? *Ever since I met someone I really wanted to kiss.*

His eyes darkened, and his face grew serious as he withdrew his phone from his pocket and snapped a picture.

OhGodohGodohGod. What was she thinking? Emily wondered if she could scale the plastic barrier and use her dress as a parachute on the way down to the floor below.

"Now, that was priceless." Dae ran his finger down her cheek. "So, you think we should kiss, huh?"

She was sure her cheeks were beet red. She couldn't even think of a snappy comeback.

"Shut up." She pushed him away and focused on the gorgeous colors coming through the windows across the balcony. She imagined him laughing inside. *Kiss? You?* Mortified, she tried to make herself feel better. *I'm hot, aren't I? Warm, at least. And smart. Definitely smart.* If she needed to chase a man, he wasn't the right man. How many times had her mother told her that? Well, not many, but enough that it had stuck.

She felt his presence behind her before he touched her or uttered a word. Goose bumps raced up her arms and—embarrassingly—she felt her nipples harden.

"Impossible," she mumbled.

"Totally possible," he whispered as he took her

hand and led her back to the stairwell without saying another word.

What. The. Hell?

They continued climbing the stairs in silence, save for the sound of Emily's heart thumping against her chest. *Possible?* What did he mean by possible? Who says something like that but doesn't kiss the object of possibility?

This time when a group of tourists passed on their way down, Dae moved to the step behind her, his hands fastened to her waist. This did all sorts of crazy things to her head. His face would be close to her butt, or maybe his head was at her hips. She hoped for hips rather than butt, but she couldn't be sure. There was no way she was turning around on the steep stairs to find out. All she could do was pray he wasn't thinking she had the butt of a twelve-year-old boy. She'd never been particularly curvaceous, which she'd always been a little self-conscious of. And now, with her brothers' fiancées around more often, she was even more aware of her slender frame. She didn't have an hourglass figure like Pierce's fiancée, Rebecca. Heck, she wasn't even as curvy as Daisy, who drew every man's eyes in Trusty. And Callie and Elisabeth were, well, they were perfect all over. Emily felt plain and simple, with understated curves and a lean body that, thanks to good genetics, she barely had to work for.

A couple came barreling down the stairs, and Dae's hand snaked around to her belly. *Yup. Hip height.* She felt his neck press against her ass as the couple raced by them, and her body reacted as if he were the key that revved her engine. She got hot and tingly all over.

She really needed to stop thinking. Just the thought of him anywhere near her butt was making her stomach quivery—and his neck pressed against her? Well, she should go straight to hell for the thoughts she was having about Mr. Impossibly Possible.

Emily needed a distraction, and began weeding through facts as they made their way up the stairs. *When it was originally built, technology hadn't progressed enough to construct the dome. In the early fifteenth century, Brunelleschi designed and built the dome. To this day, it's the largest brick dome ever constructed.* The last part of the climb brought them into a narrow area between the inside walls of the dome, where the frescoes were painted, and the outer walls. Emily was caught up in the complexity of the structure and the incredibly talented minds that had designed the cathedral.

Dae squeezed in beside Emily on the narrow stairs. His arm circled her shoulder, his hip brushed against hers as they ascended the staircase toward the final steps to the cupola. He stopped on the landing before the last set of steps—the famed ladder—that led outside and gazed down at her. His thick brows drew together as he brushed her hair from her shoulder. Her breathing hitched at the intimate gesture.

"I just want one second with you. Right here."

His whisper slid over her skin and nestled deep inside her chest. How could she have only just met him? Even with the hot-and-cold messages he was sending, he still felt strangely familiar and safe, like she'd known of him forever but they simply hadn't met face-to-face before last night. Light spilled into the dark corridor from above. Her back hit the cold, hard stone, and she pressed her hands flat against it, trying to stabilize her shaky legs.

"Hi," he whispered.

"Hi." *Gulp.*

"Is the cathedral everything you hoped it would be?"

This was what he wanted to ask her? Emily was vaguely aware of the people who had been behind them on the stairs. People were barely squeezing by, excited to get outside, and he was holding a conversation as if they were standing in the middle of the street. Except they were in the cathedral she'd dreamed of forever. She was out of breath from climbing the steps in her aroused state, and he was doing that thing he did—where he invaded her personal space. And, sweet mother of all things hot and delicious, she liked it. She tried not to focus on the feel of his entire lower half pressed against her as he placed his hands on her hips and flattened her against the wall to allow a rather large man to pass behind him. She tried her best to ignore the impressive steel rod against her belly. She tried, *oh, how she tried,* to ignore the strength of his masculine scent, more pungent, more alluring, after the exertion of the climb.

He touched his forehead to hers, reminding her that he'd asked her a question. *The cathedral. Right. Was it everything she'd hoped?*

"More," was all she could manage.

"More." The word left his lips like a secret. One of his hands slid up to her rib cage, and his thumb brushed the side of her breast, sending a shiver through her. "How much more, Em?"

She swallowed hard again, suppressing her urge to swallow *him* whole. He pressed his lips to her forehead, then slid them lower, brushing the outer shell of her ear.

"How much more?" he whispered again.

Her legs turned to jelly, and she grabbed his waist with both hands to remain upright. *Holy cow*. What he did to her with words alone should be against the law.

"Impossibly more." She smiled at her own cleverness and felt the muscles in his sides jump as he laughed under his breath. The hand on her rib cage tightened, and his other hand cupped her cheek as people continued to walk past them. Irritated scoffs and romantic *awws* flitted around them as his thumb brushed over her lips, pulling the air from her lungs.

Warmth filled every crevice of her body as his lips settled on her cheek and he pressed a warm kiss to her skin. Her eyes fluttered closed in anticipation. His cheek grazed hers as his hand slid behind her, and he pressed their bodies even closer together and whispered again.

"I can't have a fling with you, Emily Braden. But I desperately want to kiss you."

"Yes." The plea was out before she could process his words. "Kiss me."

He lowered his lips to hers and whispered against them, "Did you hear me?"

"Yes. Kiss me. No fling. Want kiss." The words

tumbled fast and hard. She couldn't think past knowing their lips were about to meet.

A smile played across his lips as he lowered his mouth to hers. With the first sweet press of his lips, she inhaled a shaky breath, swallowing the taste of him. Her body melted against him as he tightened his grip and deepened the kiss. It wasn't a tentative, getting-to-know-you kiss. It was a claiming, possessive kiss that branded her as his. Sealing the intention of his heated glances and furtive touches. Never before had lips and tongues felt so perfectly matched as they collided hungrily, then slowed to explore, gliding over one another. His heartbeat matched the eager speed of hers. These feelings of her emotions being out of control was unfamiliar and scary territory, but Emily was powerless to resist the desire to be closer to him, to touch him and be touched by him. She slid her hands beneath his T-shirt and felt his powerful back muscles bunch as he pressed his body harder against her. His hand slid down her side and around to her backside, where he held on tight. The sexy new side of her purred with delight, stifling the more reserved Emily that she was quickly losing grip on.

"I love your ass," he whispered as they drew apart.

Oh, sweet Lord, she was going to tear his clothes off right there on the concrete steps of the dome.

Chapter Four

HOLY HELL. DAE had no idea that one kiss could completely rock his world. But kissing Emily had left him feeling like denim that had been worn thin. It had been hours since they'd kissed, and he still got hard every time he thought about how sweet she tasted and the way her body responded to every stroke of his tongue. The feel of her sweet curves against him had sent a bolt of lust to his groin that still tugged at his mind, making it difficult for him to concentrate on much else.

They'd spent hours looking around the church, the baptistery, and the campanile, which was the most amazing bell tower he'd ever seen, and still it all paled in comparison to their one and only kiss.

Now it was late afternoon, and the sun had started its descent. Soon the day that had blown him away would be over. It would come down to just the two of them, staring into each other's eyes in the villa where they were staying, separated by only a thin wall, and he'd have to make a decision. His body was begging him to take her to bed, but his mind waved a flag that read, *No flings.* Nothing about being with Emily felt like a fling. He knew he needed to take it slow, to allow his mind to figure out why she had such a powerful effect on him before his body clouded his thoughts. Knowing what he should do and following through had never been an issue for him. He always did the right thing. The trouble was, he wasn't entirely sure that taking it slow with Emily *was* the right thing to do. Emily was making him do and feel things he never had before with or for any other woman. He'd never in his life felt compelled to arrange a romantic surprise for a woman he'd just met, and yet he'd done just that. He'd phoned Adelina while Emily was in the ladies' room, and his romantic plan was set in motion.

He watched Emily eating a cup of gelato as she gazed out at the Ponte Vecchio, the "Old Bridge" that spanned the Arno River at its narrowest point. Jesus, she was beautiful. Her slender hips were pressed against the stone. Her long, silky hair cascaded over her perfect breasts, and when she opened her mouth to eat a bite of the sweet treat, her eyes slid to him and she smiled around the spoon. Jesus. Ever since they'd kissed, she'd radiated happiness. Her movements were fluid instead of coiled tight with that will-we-or-won't-we phase where all couples began. Will we or won't we? It was like their kiss had set her free, and he couldn't deny that it had done the same for him. She was like a vibrant light, trailing a sparkly veil in her wake, which drew attention from every man who passed, and Dae was unable to look away.

"I think I could stay in this spot all night and be perfectly happy," she said as she leaned over the stone wall and looked out over the river.

"We could buy you one of the shops. I'm sure the locals wouldn't mind." He nodded toward the far end of the bridge, where goldsmiths, jewelers, and art galleries lined the interior. "You could practice architecture from here, convince people to tear down their homes and build passive houses."

Emily tilted her head back and laughed. She had a glorious, sweet, musical laugh, and he hoped to hear it more often now that she didn't seem as nervous around him. Funny how a kiss had a way of easing tension. He hadn't planned on kissing Emily in the duomo. He'd been intent on spending a reflective moment with her, hearing her thoughts on the climb up the stairs, and finally reaching the dome. But when he'd looked into her eyes, he'd nearly drowned in desire. It was as if she were a lantern in the darkness and he were a moth, drawn to her despite the danger of being burned. He hadn't known her well enough to figure out if she was a fling type of girl, even though he wasn't a fling type of guy. All he could do was follow his gut, and his gut told him that Emily wasn't anything like a fling type of girl. In fact, she was nothing like any woman he'd ever known.

"As much as I would adore being on this medieval stone closed-spandrel segmental arch bridge—"

"Look at you going all *Architectural Digest* on me."

She laughed. "Sorry. As much as I would love to be right here on this bridge, day in and day out, people around here don't tear down their homes." She ate the last of her gelato, and when she licked her lips, he wished it was his tongue swiping across them.

"Are you trying to wow me with your architectural prowess?" *And should I worry that when you find out I tear things down, your architectural prowess will be the death of us?*

"Possibly." She smiled up at him. "No, really. People here don't even tear down chicken coops. They make them into houses and cottages. History and architecture are very important to the people here, and they do everything they can to preserve it. Unlike our society, where people think everything is disposable. Houses. Barns...Relationships."

Guilt threatened to strangle him. He knew he should tell her about the villa he'd been hired to demolish, but he could tell by the passion in her words that it would slay her to hear it. Instead, he focused on the other part of what she'd said that caught him off guard.

"Relationships? Is that based on opinion or personal experience?"

She leaned her hip against the wall and searched his eyes with a look that gave nothing away.

"You tell me." She hooked her finger in his front pocket. "Now that my brain is properly functioning, I remember you saying something about not wanting a fling."

"So, your mind wasn't functioning when you kissed me? Should I chalk up our one and only kiss to bad judgment? Because if that's your bad-judgment kiss, I'd give my left arm to experience a dedicated I-want-you-so-badly-I-can't-think-straight kiss." He loved playing with her, leaving her wondering what the hell he was really all about. That's what he knew, what he did best. It was easier than talking his way out of flings. Women didn't usually appreciate him turning them down for a quick roll in the hay. He'd had to adapt a defense in order to stay true to himself. With Emily he had the urge to shed that camouflage and just be himself.

"That was my testing-the-possibilities kiss." Her lips quirked up in a smile again, and she poked him in his chest. "Nice try, by the way. You're not getting off that easily. Is your desire to not have a fling with me based on personal history or...?"

"Or?" He couldn't help but grin.

"*Tsk!* I don't know. Or something else. Ugh. You are maddening. You know exactly what I mean."

She turned away, and he spun her around and pulled her close—losing the battle to keep his camouflage in place. One look into her trusting eyes and he was a goner. The truth spilled from his lips like a waterfall.

"I know what you mean. The reason I don't want a fling with you is that you're not *fling* material." He didn't *do* flings anyway, but if he did, she definitely wouldn't be fling material.

"What...?"

He touched his forehead to hers and breathed deeply. "It means that the way I feel when I'm with you is like nothing I've ever experienced before. It means that I have a feeling that if we were to get together, *really* get together, that I may not be able to walk away without leaving a piece of me behind."

"Oh." She dropped her eyes and twirled her hair around her finger.

Jesus, why did he get turned on every time she did that? "You kill me when you do that."

"When I do what?" Her hands splayed across his chest as she gazed up at him.

"When you do that adorable, sexy thing you do. Your *ohs* make me wonder what your bigger, sexier, *O*s will sound like." He held her gaze, hoping he didn't scare her off but unable to restrain himself from telling her what he was feeling.

She fisted her fingers in his shirt. "Oh."

"Em..."

"Oh." Her eyes widened, as if she couldn't even believe she'd said it again. "No, no, no. Oh God." She banged her forehead against his chest with the cutest little groan.

He folded her in his arms and knew he was in big trouble. Like a fish on a line, everything she did reeled him farther in.

Chapter Five

THEY PASSED THE poppy fields on the way back to the villa, and Emily couldn't believe it had been only a few hours since they had danced through them. It felt like they'd been gone a week. She stole a glance at Dae as he drove down the tree-lined road toward the villa. He really did have striking features from every angle. She wondered what he would look like when she was lying beneath him. How it would feel to have his naked, muscular body on top of hers, his hip nestled against hers. She shifted in her seat with the emotions that were becoming more familiar with every minute she spent with him. She looked out the window. She couldn't even pretend that these were feelings of a crush or infatuation. They were too all consuming, too powerful, too different. Never before had she turned every glance into something sexual. What was it about him that had her brain scrambling to remain unfettered from dirty thoughts?

Dae reached across the console and squeezed her

thigh. "Tell me something I don't know about you."

Something you don't know? Her mind raced, searching for something fun, sexy, or even interesting to tell him. She wasn't exciting enough to have secrets. Darn it, why didn't that slinky new side of her show up a month ago and gather some secrets? "Gosh, like what?"

He narrowed his eyes and smiled. "I don't know. What were you like as a little girl?"

A little girl? Had she ever been a little girl? It seemed like she'd been a grown-up forever. "What I think I was like and what I was really like are probably two very different things. I think I was a normal kid, but my dad left us when I was a baby, which is probably why my brothers are overprotective and why I'm a little protective of them and maybe a little headstrong." She had never been particularly bothered by people knowing her father had abandoned them, but it wasn't something she typically offered up out of the blue. For some reason, she hadn't even thought about keeping it from Dae.

His eyes filled with compassion. "I'm sorry, Em. I didn't realize your father left you."

"He didn't leave me. He left our family." She saw him flinch. She didn't mean to sound like she had a chip on her shoulder. She didn't, did she? She'd dealt with her father's leaving years ago. "I'm sorry. I don't know why I reacted so strongly."

"It's okay. I understand. It probably still hurts."

"It really doesn't, except when I think of my mom. I mean, I didn't really know my father. But I know my mom loved him, and I guess it makes me sad, and apparently angry, to think of her being hurt."

"Is she remarried?" Dae parked beneath the umbrella of a tree in the parking lot and turned off the car, waiting for Emily's answer. Moonlight filtered in through the windows, and when he turned in his seat to face her, he brought her hand to his lips and kissed the back of it.

"She's not, but she's happy. She's not the kind of woman who needs a man in her life." Emily loved the way his entire focus was on her. He wasn't rushing her to get out of the car, or trying to make a move despite the seriousness of their conversation. He wasn't trying to avoid the uncomfortable subject, and if his eyes were as honest as they appeared, he seemed sincere in caring about her answers.

"I get the feeling that you're not the type of woman who needs a man in her life, either."

Emily opened her mouth to answer and realized that she didn't know how to respond. Was she the type of woman who needed a man? She certainly had been hoping to find love for a long time. But did she *need* a man? No, surely she didn't. She looked away, and Dae reached over and gently brought her face back toward him.

"I don't know you that well, but I get the feeling there's a lot going on in that beautiful head of yours. All day I've wondered what you were thinking, and right this very second you have a look that makes me want to pull you into my lap and hold you."

Yes, please. That would feel so nice.

"If you want to share your thoughts, I'd really like to hear them."

She couldn't form a response, overwhelmed by what she was just now realizing, much less admit it to a man she'd known only a day, but the longer she stared at him, the clearer the sincerity in his eyes became. They drew her words from her heart.

"I haven't ever felt like I needed a man in my life. But lately I've felt like something was missing. Or like I was missing out on something, I guess. Maybe it's because my brothers have all recently fallen in love, and I haven't. They were dead set against relationships whereas I was completely open to one. I don't really know why I feel like something's been missing. Maybe I'm too wrapped up in work. Maybe, like you said, I need to grab the happy moments when I can and enjoy life a little more. I don't really know. But if you want to know what's going through my mind right now, this very second, I'm wondering why today—why *right now*—I feel like I'm not missing a darn thing."

Dae placed his hands on her cheeks and lowered his forehead to hers. "Because you may not need a man in your life, Emily Braden, but sometimes it sure is nice to find someone who makes each day a little better." He sealed his lips over hers and took her in a deep, mind-numbing kiss. When their lips finally parted, he ran his thumb over her lower lip and gazed into her eyes.

"Yeah." It came out in one long breath. Her lips tingled, and she felt dizzy with desire. "That must be why."

"Or maybe it's because you got to see the places you've been dreaming about and eat Italian gelato while looking out over the Arno River." He stepped from the car, and when he came around to her side, he reached for her hand.

She grabbed her purse with a grin she had no hope of restraining. "I think it was that first thing you mentioned."

He slid his arm around her waist, and they followed a slate path toward the two-story villa. The porch was illuminated by yellow lights on either side of the large arched windows, highlighting the dips and grooves of the rough stone walls. Set against the backdrop of the midnight-blue sky, broken only by the branches and foliage of large trees set off to the west, the villa looked like it belonged on the cover of a romance novel.

Dae pulled her closer. "Smells like Adelina and Serafina have been busy baking."

Emily was so focused on Dae that she hadn't noticed the smell of fresh-baked bread. "I love that they bake together. Are you close to your parents?" She didn't want the night to end. She wanted to walk a million miles by Dae's side, feeling the strength of his grip and hearing his deep, sexy voice as they got to know each other better.

"I am."

They sat on a wooden bench on the porch. It felt natural for Emily to snuggle beneath the crook of his arm, and with the realization came surprise. Emily mulled over that surprise, dissected it, turned it until she began to see herself with a little less reservation. The part of her that had been pushing her in ways that were new and scary, but also sensually exciting, somehow knew that being with Dae felt right in all the best ways. And now she knew it, too, which took away some of that fear but left all of the good stuff.

"My parents adopted me when I was a baby. My birth mom is Korean, and my father was American. He was in Korea on business, and well…Then came me." He ran his hand through his hair and shrugged, a there-you-have-it shrug.

"That's how you got that dangerous sex appeal. Your looks are so intriguing. It must be the combination of Korean and American heritage. I bet your parents were both very beautiful. Now I know your secret."

"*Dangerous*, huh?" He kissed her temple.

"That's what you picked up on? Yes, dangerous enough to make me fumble for words, and I *never* fumble for words. Do you know your birth mom?" She ran her finger along the seam of his jeans, wanting to be closer to him but also wanting to get to know him better first.

"I have access to who she is and I can reach out to her, but from what I've been told, she isn't really interested in meeting me. She was shamed by the pregnancy. Her family actually shunned her for months." The muscles in his leg tensed beneath her touch.

"Oh, that's horrible." She couldn't imagine being shunned by her family, but worse, she wondered what it did to Dae to know it was because she had conceived him.

"Yeah. I was pretty mad when I found out, and then I went through this guilty phase. Like I'd ruined her life or something. But my family helped me realize that I didn't ruin her life. I was just the product of her emotions. I mean, people have sex; women get pregnant. You can't blame the child for that. Human emotions are what they are. My biological father and my birth mother's family are the ones who made her feel bad about getting pregnant, which is really sort of sick and definitely mean."

Emily curled her legs up beneath her on the bench and turned her body toward him. "I can't imagine what she must have gone through."

"People can be assholes." He tucked Emily's hair behind her ear, and in return, she ran her fingers through his, brushing it away from his face. Her hand came to rest on the back of his neck, and she felt him tense a little under her touch.

She wondered if it was from her touch or the topic of his parents.

"I've been wanting to do that since last night," she admitted.

"I've wanted you to do that since last night."

"Oh."

His lips quirked up in a half smile.

She remembered what he'd said about her saying "Oh" and pressed her lips together. She'd never been with a man who had been so open about how she made him feel, and knowing that a simple word could have such an effect on him made her happy and confident and nervous all at once.

He cupped her cheek and pressed a kiss to her lips. "What am I going to do with you, sweet Emily?"

She shrugged and answered by bringing her lips

to his again, kissing him softly at first, then matching his desire as he deepened the kiss. He buried his hand in her hair and held on tight. His other hand lifted her legs over his so she was sitting half on his lap. His hand came to rest on her thigh.

"I like what you're doing with me right now." She brushed the back of his neck with her thumb, and his eyes darkened.

"You do, do you?" He kissed her again, and the heat of his hand spread up her thighs and between her legs. Until last night, it had been a very long time since she'd felt the tug of desire. She couldn't remember ever longing to be touched and tasted as she was with every stroke of Dae's tongue. She'd never had the urge to kiss every inch of a man's body. Those were things she'd talked about with girlfriends as if she'd felt them, too, even though the mere act of pretending had made her feel like she was missing out. Her girlfriends probably really did have those urges. Heck, according to them, they'd had them since they were teenagers, while Emily had played along so she didn't feel left out. She'd never really understood what she was missing until now. She'd never felt the avalanche of lust that was breaking down every barrier she never even realized she'd constructed.

This is it. This was what had plagued her these last few months. Something in her heart must have known she was missing this. Needing this. Needing him. *Dae.* Heat filled her veins as Dae's lips slid to the corner of her mouth, then trailed kisses down her neck to the crest of her shoulder. A moan escaped her lips, and she closed her eyes against it. She desperately wanted to give in to this feeling, to let her body get swept away and devoured. But something in the back of her mind nagged at her. It was these feelings that had caused Dae's birth mother to experience such heartache. These overwhelming desires could drive her to make bad decisions.

But his lips felt so good on her skin. And his teeth, as he nipped at her skin, sent shivers right through her.

Dae drew back, and she clutched the back of his shirt, keeping him close. She opened her eyes and met his heated stare.

"You didn't eat dinner," he half whispered.

What? "Not hungry."

He pressed his lips together in a hard line. "It's late. I should let you get some sleep."

"Not tired." *What are you doing?*

"Emily," he breathed.

Anything.

He searched her eyes as he brought his hand from her thigh to her cheek.

No! Put it back! She wanted to feel him close to her most private places, even if they weren't taking things further—or maybe they would. Either way, she wanted to feel the heat of his hand crawling up her thigh.

"It's late." He shifted his eyes to the empty yard. "We're on the front porch."

He lifted her legs off of his, rose, and drew her to her feet. Her heart thundered in her chest as he folded her into his arms. She wrapped her arms around his neck and went up on her toes to kiss him again, even though he'd tried to sever that connection. He met her halfway in a tender kiss that ended way too soon. She should stop trying to kiss him, but her mind and body were reeling out of control. Before she could process what he was doing, he grabbed her purse from the bench and led her inside and up the stairs toward her room.

He wasn't even trying to sleep with her, but in her head she was trying to figure out if she was really ready for what she wanted—which was to be beneath him. Naked. Her thighs pressed against his hips. She took stock of her emotions. Oh hell, she couldn't take stock of anything. She was too amped up to think of anything other than making out with Dae. At the door to her room, she fished her keys from her purse.

Her mouth went dry at the thought of going further with him, and he wasn't even *trying* to go further. She felt like they were on the cusp of something real, and she worried that rushing into sex might somehow tarnish that.

Dae took the keys from her hand and wrapped his arms around her again. His hair fell around their faces, and the air beneath it warmed.

"Emily, I'm so attracted to everything about you."

"Me too, you." *OhGodohGodohGod.*

"If I go in that room, we're going to get to know each other very, very well."

"Yes."

"I want that with you. I want to know every inch of you."

Her body hummed with anticipation. "Yes."

He touched his forehead to hers. "I'm so glad you

didn't say, *Oh*."

She managed a smile, but nerves had stolen her voice.

"Em, I don't want a fling with you because I'm not a guy who has flings. I can't. I mean, I can. I'm capable, and I did when I was young and stupid, but..." He closed his eyes for a beat and shook his head.

His eyes were as apologetic as they were sincere. He was a gentleman at heart, which made him even more attractive.

She swallowed past her nerves as the pieces began to fall into place. She forced herself to speak. "Because of your birth mom?"

"Yeah," he whispered. "It didn't sink in until I was in college. I suddenly realized that I could cause the same pain my mother experienced, and I don't want to do that. I know that makes me sound strange, or weak, or some shit like that, but..." He shrugged. "It's who I am now."

"Oh, thank goodness." The words slipped out before she could stop them.

His brows knitted together. "Not the reaction I was expecting, but okay."

"No, not because I don't want to sleep with you. I do. But...I'm out of practice." *Out of practice? What am I doing, playing golf?*

"Out of practice?"

"Not practice. Dae, you make me flustered." She sighed. "It's been a long time, and I'm really enjoying this. Us. And I was worried that sleeping together tonight might change things." She pressed in closer, feeling less flustered now that she'd told him how she felt, and knowing the kind of man he was made telling him, and moving in closer, that much easier. Better. More meaningful. She pressed her hand to his chest and smiled up at him.

"Dae, I like that you don't want to cause any trouble for me, even though I'm a big girl and know how to protect myself against pregnancy."

He pressed his hands to her cheeks again and kissed her again, nearly pushing her hesitation out of the way completely.

"So do I, but that's not the point. There's more than one way to hurt a person. Sometimes the worst pain comes from things you can't see. It's not about pregnancies. It's about what's in here." He placed his hand above her left breast, covering her heart, and it made her pulse speed up even more. "Let's see what tomorrow brings."

Tomorrow. "I promised you tomorrow, didn't I?" *I'm so glad we have tomorrow. I want a lot of tomorrows with you.*

"Yes, and I intend to take full advantage of every minute."

"Promises, promises." She smiled to let him know she was teasing. Sort of.

"There are two things I never do. The first is break a promise. The second is the wrong thing."

"That's impossible. Everyone does the wrong thing at some point in their lives."

"Not if I can help it." He lifted her hand to his lips and kissed it. "*Buonanotte bella. Lo sogno di voi.*" He dropped her hand and bowed before walking away slowly.

"You lost me after *good night, beautiful.*"

"Sleep well. I shall dream of you."

She had the urge to run to him and leap into his arms, but her legs wouldn't move. She was swept up in the essence of him. If she moved, she'd surely fall.

He blew her a kiss as he unlocked his door. "Good night, sweet Emily."

"Good night, Dae."

She unlocked her door and willed herself to step inside. After closing her door behind her, she leaned against it and closed her eyes. *What a day! What a night! What a kiss!* She tried to calm her racing heart, but even breathing deeply didn't lessen the excitement she felt.

She opened her eyes with a dreamy sigh and turned on the lights. Her keys and purse dropped to the floor at the sight of vases and planters filled with beautiful, vibrant red poppies. They covered the dresser, the bedside table, and from where she stood, she saw that there were planters in the bathroom as well. Nothing was left undecorated. Rustic, heavy planters lined the floor by the glass doors that led to the balcony, spilling over with bright red blooms. Emily's eyes filled with tears as they swept over the petal-covered bedspread, where a white envelope sat nestled on her pillow.

"Dae," she whispered. She reached for the card and opened it carefully, wondering when he'd had time to ask Adelina to help him pull this off. She realized that he couldn't have written the note, but she didn't care. It was his voice she heard as she read the words.

My sweet Emily,

It was the light in your eyes that first attracted me to you last night, but it was the energy radiating from you that drew me closer. And it was you, Em, who kept me there. Thank you for the wonderful day. I can't wait to spend tomorrow with you.

—Possibly yours, Dae

Emily fell back on the bed, clasping the card to her chest. She squealed and kicked her feet up and down with glee, then bolted upright. He was right beyond that wall. She could bang on his door and thank him. She should do that. She wanted to do that. But he'd given no indication that he'd planned anything like this. Maybe he didn't want her to say thank you.

Well, then, what could she do? What might he want? She stared at the wall that separated them and smiled. *Dae Bray, you are so impossibly wonderful.*

She remembered that he had texted her the pictures from earlier. *Perfect!* She snagged her purse from the floor and dug her phone out. She had several missed texts. She scrolled through them. Daisy. Wes. Elisabeth. Callie. Luke. Ross. Rebecca. Pierce. Jake. And finally, Dae. She rolled her eyes, surprised her mother hadn't texted, too. Daisy must have told someone about Dae, which must have sent the Braden grapevine into motion. She wondered how loud the buzz was around Trusty, where gossip spread faster than wildfire—and how long it would take for her brothers to call out the armed forces if she didn't respond to their texts. She stared at the phone, and as she decided what to text to Dae, she texted Daisy. It was late afternoon in Colorado and a weekend, so she was sure to get the text.

Someone can't keep a secret. Tsk, tsk, tsk. After hitting send, she scrolled through the pictures that Dae had texted earlier in the day. Dae's gorgeous dark eyes stared back at her. In every picture he had his arm around her, and she looked happy. Happier than she'd seen herself look in ages. *Ever*. Even in the picture he'd snapped when she was out of sorts, she had a dreamy look in her eyes. When she reached the picture of them in the poppy field, she wondered if he'd known then that he was going to fill her room with them. She still wasn't sure how he'd pulled it off. There were so many flowers!

She scrutinized the pictures again, wondering if the relaxed, happy look in her eyes was from being away from the stresses of everyday life: work, keeping up with family, which wasn't really a stressor but still added pressure to her days. The stress of wondering if she'd *ever* meet a man she'd want to go out with. She sighed at how often she used to wonder just that and mused at how true it was that people met at the least expected times.

She scrolled through the pictures again, and she knew the sparkle in her eyes and what had her heart doing a little happy jig in her chest had little to do with where she was and everything to do with the handsome, sexy, playful man staring back at her from the tiny iPhone screen.

She texted Dae.

The poppy fairy visited my room. I think he's about six two with bedroom eyes and hair any girl would die for. I love them. The flowers, that is. Well, and your eyes and hair. The only thing that would make them (the flowers) better is if you were here with me. Xox.

She reread it before sending and realized that maybe she wasn't so far off her game after all.

A minute later her phone vibrated, and she smiled, hoping it was Dae. *Daisy*. She groaned as she read her text. *I ONLY told Elisabeth. But Margie might have heard us because she was serving us coffee at the time.*

"Margie!" Emily shook her head as she typed in another response. Margie had been the waitress at the Trusty Diner forever. She was the eyes and ears of the town, and if she got whiff of a rumor, the whole town knew about it within minutes. Or at least it seemed that way. Emily loved Margie despite her gossiping ways. Margie was protective of the people who grew up in Trusty. She was witty and motherly, and when Emily was near her, she felt loved.

Her phone vibrated again while she was typing her message to Daisy. *Daisy! You just gave candy to a baby at my expense! It's a good thing I love you, because I'd like to hate you right now. Xox.*

Shaking her head, she scrolled to Dae's text and opened it.

If I were there with you, the beauty of the poppies would be forgotten.

Heck yeah, they would. She bit her lower lip as she thought up a cute response. Her phone vibrated again. She glanced down and read Daisy's message. *In all fairness, I didn't give it to her. She has sonic hearing. Hope he's worth every bit of the juicy gossip. I might have embellished a little.*

"Oh no." She texted Daisy back. *He's def worth it, and hopefully soon you won't have to embellish! Going to bed. Please text my intrusive and adorable family members and tell them I'm alive and well for me? Xox.*

After sending the text to Daisy, she texted Dae with what she hoped was the perfect response to keep him thinking about her all night long.

Oh.

Her phone vibrated a few seconds later with his response, which she read with an ear-to-ear grin. *Unfair. You're impossible!*

"Oh dear Dae, you have suddenly switched me into competitive mode. I have no idea how or why, but here goes." Emily felt herself morphing into the confident work persona she filled so skillfully. Becoming the woman who rose to the challenge to be wittier, sharper, and more in control than her male colleagues. Having grown up with a slew of brothers had its benefits. A mischievous grin spread across her lips.

She texted her response to him. *Totally possible. Good night. Xox.*

Emily plugged her phone into the charger and carefully cleared the poppy petals from her bed, wishing Dae were right there with her.

Chapter Six

DAE WALKED THROUGH the yard of the villa he'd been hired to demolish with his cell phone pressed to his ear, listening to Frank Corrington, the man who'd hired him, rattle on about another project. Dae had gotten up early to come out and take an initial assessment of the property. There were several different approaches to demolition, from wrecking ball, to explosion, to felling a building into an empty lot, to full-on implosion. Dae was an expert in implosions and was one of only a handful of skilled demolitionists qualified—or willing—to handle them. As far as he could see from the front yard, there wasn't much to this particular job. He was way overqualified for this simple project, but he'd known that when he'd agreed to assess the job. Frank was a friend of a valued business associate, and Dae had taken on the assignment as a favor to him.

He gritted his teeth, listening to Frank, whose typical demeanor was snapping off curses like adjectives, and allowed his thoughts to shift to Emily. He'd much rather be with her at seven in the morning, but he'd committed to the assessment. And doing it at seven in the morning in order to spend the rest of the day with Emily was well worth it. She was probably sleeping in. At least he hoped so. One of them should get some rest. He'd been up all night fantasizing about her sexy little body and those intelligent, sensual eyes that burned a path straight to his heart.

He trekked across the lawn and stopped at the crest of the hill, where the land gave way to rolling hills flecked with thick patches of red, yellow, and white blooms and the olive grove down the road. His thoughts drifted back to Emily. Adelina had been so excited to help him arrange for the floral delivery, and it had taken all of his restraint not to follow Emily into her bedroom just to see her reaction.

She was so damn cute with her frisky text. *Oh*. How could one simple word make his entire body vibrate with desire? Knowing she was just on the other side of his bedroom wall last night hadn't helped. He'd kept envisioning her in that silky material he'd seen on her bed the day before and wondering what she'd look like stripped bare, the silk tossed to the floor.

He felt a tightening in his groin. *Jesus*. He was hard again. He ran his hand through his hair and breathed deeply. He hadn't had this many erections in a twenty-four-hour period since he was a teenager.

Frank's voice grew louder, and he returned his attention to the phone call he'd been ignoring. Frank was reiterating his plans for the one-hundred-and-twenty-seven-acre estate. He supposed he should be thankful Frank had contacted him. If it weren't for him, he never would have met Emily. And even after knowing her for just a short while, he knew she was worth the trip.

Dae turned at the sound of voices and noticed two women who looked to be in their early twenties stepping off their bicycles at the end of the driveway. The villa had been empty for years, and as he watched the women walk up the driveway and around the side of the house, he wondered what they were doing there. He headed in that direction as he listened to Frank.

"In any case, I'll be out of touch for a few days while I'm on this godforsaken trip with my wife," Frank complained. "Why do women feel like anniversaries are meant for sucking the life out of their husbands?"

In the months since Frank was referred to him, Dae had come to see him for the manipulative, selfish bastard that he was. Those weren't unfamiliar traits, as many of Dae's wealthy clients felt the world should be at their beck and call. Dae was used to dealing with those types of people, but it didn't mean he enjoyed working with them. He loved what he did for a living, and he was a leader in the industry, which meant that Dae's skill set and expertise earned him six figures for every job he took on. That type of paycheck didn't come to the weakhearted. He knew how to play the game, when to let clients rant and when to shut them down or rein them in.

Dae bit back his initial reaction: *Do the woman a*

favor and leave her. Let her find a man who would give anything to spend a few nights alone with her instead of an old curmudgeon like you.

"Who the hell knows. I'll send you an email when I've concluded the assessment, and you can respond when you get back." He rounded the corner of the house, walked around a group of sizable empty ceramic pots, and stopped cold. The women were standing with their arms splayed wide, their bodies pressed to the largest olive tree he'd ever seen.

"Holy shit."

"What's that?" Frank asked, jerking Dae back from the distraction.

"Uh...Nothing. There's no rush. I'm assessing on this trip, not demolishing." Even as he promised again to assess the villa—something he'd been excited about when he'd first booked the trip and accepted the assignment—Emily's words sailed through his mind. *People here don't even tear down chicken coops...Unlike our society, where people think everything is disposable. Houses. Barns...Relationships.*

As he stared at the massive tree that was growing smack-dab in the center of the rear wall of the house—and the women clinging to it—he knew this particular job needed more than just an average assessment. Were there laws in Tuscany about taking down certain trees? In the States there were all sorts of certifications for trees and locations. He had already scheduled meetings with the local building and zoning officials and was traveling to the records department tomorrow. He added *check on tree certifications* to his mental checklist.

"I received your request for the history report on the property," Frank said. "I gave you what I had. Two owners prior to me. That's all I've got. I have no idea about this other bullshit you've asked for, and frankly, I can't see why it matters. Why the previous owners sold? Who gives a damn? What's done is done. It's mine now, and that's all that should concern you. Is there a problem I'm not aware of?"

"No, no problem. When are you going to be back in Tuscany?"

"Back in Tuscany? Hell, Dae. I've never been there in the first place. Bought the damn place sight unseen. The wife needs a hobby to get her off my back. We're going to tear that sucker down and put up a grand resort with all the fixin's. She'll spend five or six months a year there, feeling like she's got a new project, and I'll be a happy man. I've got guys from my LA crew lined up to run it. They know the plan. She'll think she's making all the decisions. You could learn from a guy like me, Dae." Frank laughed. "The secret to a happy marriage is to stay the hell apart."

Learn from you? No, thanks.

Dae wrapped up the call and shoved the phone in his pocket. He didn't approach the women but watched them as they stumbled back from the tree, both wiping their eyes as if they were crying. He was too far away to see if they really were, but he watched, mesmerized by the enormity and the sheer beauty of the tree. One of the women withdrew something from her skirt pocket and went around to the other side of the tree. Dae couldn't make out what she was doing, as his vision was blocked by the tree's gnarled and twisted trunk. He walked back toward the front of the house, and only moments later he heard the women giggling as they ran down the driveway and hopped on their bikes, then pedaled away.

Once they were gone, he returned to the rear of the house. There were acres of clear ground. Why would anyone choose to build around a tree that stood the chance of growing this large? Olive trees became gnarled and wider with age. Anyone around this area would surely know that. It looked as if the tree had been halved and plastered against the house, but he knew this wasn't the case. No tree would survive that type of cannibalism.

The tree must have been at least twenty feet in circumference with multiple wide trunks that were gnarled and twisted like ancient lovers that had fused together. He stepped around the impressive breadth of the trunk and followed it up toward the roof, realizing there were pieces of paper and fabric stuck in the holes of the bark. He reached out and touched his index finger to one of the flecks of paper. It crumbled to the ground like dust. He took a step back and around the tree, where he saw a pristine piece of paper shoved beneath the bark. He reached for it, then thought it better to leave it be. Whatever those women were doing was none of his business. Maybe they were leaving love letters for their boyfriends.

The side of the tree that was free from the stone walls grew healthily, with multiple long branches that billowed rich and plentiful with ripe foliage above the roof. Substantial branches snaked up the stone, to tangles of more healthy branches. He took out his phone and snapped pictures of the tree, then moved to the other side of the wide trunk.

He glanced up at the massive tree and was struck by its beauty. He had to bring Emily out to see this. He couldn't tear this down without her ever seeing it, even if she'd disapprove of him demolishing it. It was too special of a sight for her to miss out on. He'd Googled Emily's name last night, stalked her Facebook page for about an hour, and noted the impressive number of architectural awards and passive-house and other building conferences where she'd been a keynote speaker. It appeared that the sweet, sensual woman he was enthralled with was also quite the businesswoman. And after he reviewed several of the houses she'd built and remodeled, it was apparent that her design skills were impressive as hell.

The pictures he'd seen on her Facebook page were mostly of Emily and her family, all smiles and love that jumped off the page and smacked him in the chest. The whole you're-a-brother thing had come around full circle. She was right. He would take care of her and keep her safe, but he'd have felt that way about her even if he hadn't had any sisters. And now, after spending yesterday with Emily, the urge to protect her was even stronger, but not at all in a brotherly fashion. Not even close. He wanted more with Emily. He wanted to know what made her body quiver, where she liked to be touched, how she'd feel beneath him when he was buried deep inside her. He wanted to wake up and see her looking at him with the desire that had filled her beautiful dark eyes last night. He wanted to watch her face light up when she took time out of her busy schedule to enjoy something as simple as a poppy field. He wondered what she'd be like in her own territory, back in the States, with work and family both vying for her attention.

Places like this drenched people in romance, and he wondered again how much of his mounting emotions were stronger because he was here. There was definitely something about being in a place where textures and colors were vibrant and family was the center of people's worlds that made his mind travel to unfamiliar places. He had a great family, and they saw one another fairly often, and kept in touch via email and phone calls, but having his own family had never been something he longed for. Hell, as far as he knew, his siblings hadn't longed for that either. They were free spirits brought up by hippyish parents who believed life experiences should outweigh book knowledge. While they all had found successful careers that offered the ability to travel and allowed them not to feel hemmed in, none of them had settled down until a few years ago, when his older sister, Leanna—the most restless of them all—had fallen in love with Kurt Remington, a bestselling thriller writer. Before meeting Kurt, Leanna had been his only sibling who hadn't at least settled on a career. Colby was a Navy SEAL, and Wade was a world-traveling artificial-intelligence guru. And Bailey, the youngest, was an incredible rock star, which often worried the shit out of Dae. Celebrities were often the target of stalkers, but he knew she was strong willed and stubborn as a mule. And Colby had ensured that she had a host of ex-SEAL bodyguards watching out for her at all times.

When Leanna had first settled down with Kurt, it had made Dae's head spin, because it was so unexpected. She'd been so happy since that it caused Dae to take a long, hard look at his life. He owned houses in Denver, Boston, and Chicago, and he never stayed in any of them for a very long stretch, but Leanna? She'd never remained in any one location for very long. He'd never thought he'd see her settle down in a job or a relationship, and now he'd never seen her happier. She had a successful jam-making business on Cape Cod, and she was engaged to a solid man who worshipped the ground she walked on. The stability that Kurt provided seemed to have been exactly what Leanna needed, and ever since, Dae'd wondered if he was missing out by not allowing himself to really connect with someone. And now that he'd met Emily, he wanted to try.

He couldn't wait to bring her here. He could only imagine the way her face would light up when she saw the way the tree had engulfed this villa—and how fast her smile would fade when he told her that he was there to assess its demolition.

Chapter Seven

PERCHED ON HIS mother's knee with a piece of toast clenched in his little pudgy fist and crumbs dotting his lips, Luca watched Emily, wide-eyed, from across the portico. Emily heard Marcello's voice, and she turned and searched the grounds, hoping Dae might be with him. He'd texted her earlier to say that he'd meet her around nine o'clock. It was eight forty-five, and she was anxious to see him. He'd told her to go ahead and eat breakfast, as he had a busy day planned for them and he was tied up this morning. She was excited to see where they were going and surprised at how perfectly happy she was to give up her intended schedule in order to spend the day with Dae.

She didn't see anyone on the grass or near the gardens. Disappointed, she turned back to Luca and wiggled her fingers in a silent wave. Luca giggled again. Serafina glanced at him with a smile on her lips without missing a beat in her conversation with Adelina. They were speaking Italian. Emily couldn't understand what they were saying, but she caught Dante's name a few times. She really should have taken a course in Italian before coming on the trip, but her schedule had been hectic as she'd prepared to be away for nine days. Not to mention that Daisy had wanted to make sure everything was in order for her wedding, which, of course, it was. Between the two of them, Callie's excellent organizational skills, Rebecca's and Elisabeth's meticulous planning, and Emily's mother's ability to see through chaos, they'd worked closely with Daisy's mother and planned the perfect wedding. Luke and Daisy were getting married at their ranch in Trusty, with about a hundred close friends and family. Emily was Daisy's maid of honor, and her dress was pressed and ready, hanging in her closet at home. She was excited to see the first of her siblings get married. She'd struck it lucky with her brothers' significant others. She'd heard stories about sisters-in-law not getting along, and she adored each of the women her brothers had fallen for. She wondered, briefly, what they'd think of Dae. He was easygoing and very manly, like her brothers. She was sure they'd all hit it off.

She hoped so, and immediately caught herself moving too fast. It had been only one evening and one day. That did not necessarily equate to a meet-your-family relationship. Although she'd already gone without checking her email for longer than she had in the last ten years. Dae was definitely having an impact on her life. The best impact she'd ever experienced.

She turned her attention back to Luca, waving, and he giggled again, then shoved the toast into his mouth. Emily's thoughts went right back to her family. She wondered if Daisy and Luke would have kids right away. She knew they both wanted a big family, as she did. She and the girls conjured up all sorts of fun scenarios of raising children together. *First comes love, then comes marriage, then comes Emily pushing a baby carriage*. She sighed. Yeah, she might have to be late to that little party.

Adelina filled her coffee cup. She wore a gray skirt and sweater with flat leather shoes. After spending the day around so many tourists yesterday, Emily noticed the differences in styles between tourists and locals. She glanced across the room at Serafina, who was wearing a cream-colored dress belted at the waist. She looked down at the outfit that she had on, skinny jeans and a red short-sleeved shirt, black flats, and dangling earrings. Yes, there was definitely a difference in styles.

She met Adelina's gaze and realized that Adelina was staring at her. Was she thinking the same thing? That tourists dressed differently?

"Thank you, Adelina. The croissant was delicious."

"Grazie." She leaned closer to Emily and lowered her voice. "And the poppies?"

Emily felt her cheeks heat up. "The poppies were beautiful. Thank you."

She smiled and nodded. "You have a handsome gentleman trying for your affection. You should visit Casa Dei Desideri."

"Mama!" Serafina snapped, then said something quickly in Italian, to which Adelina responded just as adamantly. Serafina frowned, then said something else in Italian. Luca's head swooped from side to side, following the heated discussion between the two women.

Adelina patted Emily's back and said something just above a whisper in Italian. Whatever it was, it caused Serafina to blush, too.

"Careful, Emily," Serafina said with a warm smile. "My mother is a matchmaker at heart."

"What is Casa Dei Desideri?" Emily asked. *And why did it make Serafina blush?* "I don't remember seeing that on any of the tourist maps."

Adelina's lips curved into a smile. Her gaze softened, and when she spoke, her voice was smooth as butter and filled with wonder. "This is not a tourist destination. This is something passed secretly from mothers to daughters. Women to women."

Emily leaned in closer, wanting all of the juicy details she smelled coming her way.

"It is known as the House of Wishes. You want true love? You make your wish there. You want a baby..." She turned a loving gaze toward Luca. Serafina blushed again. "You make your wish there."

"So, it's like a wishing well?"

Adelina shook her head. "No, *bella*. There is no well. Just an old house and a tree. Women come from all over and leave a piece of their heart there, and their wishes have come true. I found my Marcello that way. Serafina became pregnant with Luca after wishing."

"Mama!" Serafina followed that up with something in Italian that made them both smile; then she turned a shy smile toward Emily.

"Ah, Serafina. That is how the wishes work. We

will continue to wish every morning and every evening for Dante's safe return, and you mark my word. He will return." She made a *tsk* sound with her tongue and shifted her eyes to Emily.

"Only wishes of the heart will come true. Wishes that cannot be bought or sold. Wishes that cannot be manipulated, but can only be felt." She pressed her hand to her heart and looked up at the ceiling as Marcello came around the side of the porch with Dae. Adelina lowered her eyes and smiled at her husband. "Wishes of love, *bella*."

Wishes of love. Tuscany was overwhelmingly romantic. Emily's pulse sped up when her eyes met Dae's. His hair was tousled, as if he'd run a hand through it while it was still wet. He was clean-shaven and somehow still managed to look rugged and edgy. The top buttons of his white shirt were open, revealing a patch of his tanned chest and a sprinkling of chest hair. His sleeves were rolled up and pushed above his elbows to the base of his bulging biceps. He looked even more handsome than he had last night.

"Il mio amore." Marcello spread his arms wide. "Are you filling our guest's mind with silliness?"

Adelina shook her head and mumbled something as she headed back into the house.

"Ah, *il mio ometto*." Marcello swept Luca into his arms and kissed him on both cheeks. Luca squealed with glee. Marcello turned a smile toward Emily. "My little man. That's my Luca."

Emily's heart warmed for the baby who was so loved and for the grandfather who adored him. Luca's father might not be there, but there was no shortage of love toward the little boy.

Dae strode across the floor, all edgy confidence and sultry eyes. His deep voice slithered over her. "*Il mio dolce* Emily."

My sweet Emily. The endearment sent goose bumps up her arms. He leaned down and kissed her on each cheek. She assumed this was out of respect for Serafina and Marcello, and she wished they'd been alone. The butterflies in her stomach had awakened with the sound of his voice, and she wanted nothing more than to be in his arms, to have his lips on hers again.

She could not be trusted around this tantalizing creature, and instead of that freaking her out, as it probably would have a week ago, she welcomed it. And she didn't want to be trusted.

Marcello spoke animatedly to his grandson as he left the room in the direction of Adelina. Serafina stood quietly, smoothed her dress, and smiled at Emily as she followed her father into the house.

"Hi."

He pulled out the chair beside her and sat down, his knee brushing hers. "Did you sleep well?"

"I did." *Fibber!* She'd tossed and turned all night, thinking about him. *Wanting* him. "Thank you for an amazing day, and the flowers were the most romantic thing anyone has ever done for me."

"I'm glad you liked them. I only wish I were there to see your face when you first walked into your room, but I knew if I were, I'd never leave."

She forced herself to concentrate on anything but the idea of him in her bed. It didn't work.

"Did...Uh...Did you sleep well?"

Dae put both hands on her thighs and leaned in close. "It took every bit of restraint not to come through that wall." Then he slid his hand to the nape of her neck and pulled her into a deep, delicious kiss. They both came away dizzy. He touched his forehead to hers and breathed her name. "Emily."

"I know," was all she could manage. She did know. She could feel the air palpitating around them. Her body felt heavy with desire. Every inch of her yearned for him in a way that she'd never known and had no desire to fight.

An hour later they were driving toward the town of Poppi to see the medieval Poppi Castle. Dae drove with the windows down, one hand holding Emily's, which she realized, as she stared at his thick wrist, she'd come to expect. *Wow, that happened fast.* There were a few things she'd come to expect from Dae. His furtive glances when he thought she didn't notice. It was like he had a direct line to all the sensitive nerves between her thighs, which took notice every time she fell under his heated gaze. She knew he'd kiss her every time he greeted her, and when they had to part, for even a few minutes, he squeezed her hand and searched her eyes, as if to say, *Don't disappear on me.*

"What made you pick the Poppi Castle as our destination? Did you already have a trip to it planned?" She loved the way the side of his mouth kicked up as her question registered. He looked like he was conjuring up a mischievous response.

"To be honest, when I came to Tuscany, I didn't have anything planned except work. But then I met this adorably sexy woman who just happened to be an architect, and I was lucky enough to gain her attention and the promise of an afternoon together, which I hope to turn into many more before I have to return to the States. I chose the castle mainly because of the architecture. For you, sweet one. But I have to admit, I was intrigued by the history, too."

She tucked her hair behind her ear and sat up straighter, trying her best to look a little less like she was swooning, which she totally was. "Mr. Bray, might you be referring to the legend of Lady Matilda?"

He squeezed her hand. "The one and only."

"So you have a thing for women who commit adultery and then slaughter the men they've slept with?" The legend of Lady Matilda had always fascinated her. Lady Matilda was supposedly the most beautiful maiden in the land. She was forced to marry the most powerful man in Poppi at a young age, whom she felt no love for. She envied the carefree lives of the commoners who lived outside the cold stone walls, and eventually, that envy led to her demise.

Dae's laugh rumbled through the car. "Actually, I currently have a thing for a petite brunette who I hope doesn't sleep with men and then lead them over a trapped door, where they fall to horrible, bloody deaths, landing on razor blades and broken glass."

Emily cringed at his impeccably accurate and gruesome description. She gazed out the window as the car darkened. The trees that lined the narrow street leading to the castle had formed an arch over the road, stealing their sunshine.

"I'd never do that," Emily said quietly. "I'd go for a

quick, less bloody death, like poison."

He laughed. "Then you'd probably design an immaculate crypt for the bodies. Remind me to check my food from now on."

"You know the castle is haunted, right? The townspeople noticed that men were mysteriously disappearing after spending a night with Matilda, and they stormed the castle and locked her in the tower to die. Supposedly, tourists have seen her ghost."

Dae parked the car in the lot at the top of the old town of Poppi. The view was magnificent, spanning beyond the castle to the rooftops of villas and shops, and farther still, to miles of fields and farms.

"I've heard of the sightings, and you, my lady, are about to find out for yourself if it's true. I booked us a private tour." He stepped from the car, leaving her looking after him with a slack jaw.

A private tour?

She watched him walk around the car. She should be ashamed at the way she was practically drooling over his broad shoulders and amazing ass. And the way his hair shielded his eyes was almost too sexy.

He opened the car door and folded her into his arms. She already felt like she belonged there, resting against his chest, gazing up at his stubbly jawline. She wanted to kiss it. Rise up on her toes and kiss a path from one side to the other. Her hands found his waist, and she felt her stomach flutter.

Okay, Emily, chill. She tried to distract herself with thoughts of the tour.

"But they don't do private tours," she said. "I tried to book a small tour group and was told that during this busy tourist season, they only gave standard tours."

Dae kissed her softly. "Obviously, you don't have the right connections."

"Connections. Right. I thought this was your first time here."

"It is." He turned her in his arms so she had a full view of the castle, her back nestled against his chest. "Stop worrying about logistics and look at that view. Think you can scale the castle walls?"

"Maybe," she lied.

He kissed her neck. "I doubt there's much you can't do."

"Flattery will get you everywhere. How did you really get a private tour?" she pushed.

He pulled his phone from his pocket and turned with her in his arms, so their backs were facing the castle. "Smile, baby."

She did, despite wanting an answer to her question, and he clicked a picture.

"I can't tell you all my secrets." He took her hand and led her out of the parking lot. "Come on. Let's go explore."

It was amazing how cobblestone streets could change the way a place felt. If these same streets were paved instead of cobblestone, Emily was sure she wouldn't feel like she'd been plunked down in a fairy-tale land of romance. It was stupid, really. They were nothing more than stones, and yet she felt even more swoony than she had at the car. She glanced at Dae, and he caught her looking and flashed a smile.

Okay, maybe it has nothing at all to do with the

streets and everything to do with you.

The wide, hilly walk to the castle opened into a grass and stone courtyard. Emily and Dae held hands on the way up to the entrance. There were people milling about on the lawn, but it wasn't as crowded as the cathedral had been. Emily shielded her eyes from the sun and looked up at the bell tower.

"I can only imagine how lonely Lady Matilda must have been. I know I shouldn't, but I kind of feel sorry for her. Look at this place. It's magnificent, but can you imagine being left alone with only your thoughts while your disinterested bastard of a husband was away on military assignments? With no one to talk to, no one to share meals with or..." She turned toward Dae and was struck by the intensity of his gaze.

"She killed men. Dozens of them."

"Yes, I know that. Obviously, she was crazy, and she probably deserved to be bricked up in the bell tower to die a lonely death, but come on. She was stolen away to sleep with a man more than twice her age. A cold, angry man who was part of the family that ruled this area with an iron fist. She was left with only the guards to watch over her. Maybe that's what drove her over the edge. Knowing that outside these thick stone walls life went on for people. They laughed and loved. Women kissed the men they fell in love with. They slept beside their husbands, hugged their children. What must it have been like for her?"

Dae pulled her close and kissed her temple. "We'll never know what it was that drove her over the edge, but I love that you have such a big heart that you want to find a redeeming quality in her."

"I don't think it's a redeeming quality. I think part of who we are and how we act comes from what we know. We are products of our families and our surroundings. How we spend our days definitely has an impact on how we act, don't you think?"

At the entrance to the castle, Dae stopped and touched her cheek. She loved how often he touched her. He had said he was affectionate, but she'd rarely met any man as affectionate as her own family was. Dae was every bit as touchy-feely.

"I do think that's true," he said. "Especially after spending time with you."

She wrapped her arms around his waist and hugged him close. "I feel the same way."

THE PRIVATE TOUR Dae had arranged turned out to be the perfect way to spend the day. Without throngs of people around, they were able to take as much time as they wanted in each area of the castle and were able to focus more on getting to know each other. Dae loved watching Emily take in the architecture and listening to her explaining the history and significance of the designs throughout the castle. Emily was in her element, and her face lit up as she stroked the cold stone, rattling off facts as if she were reading from a book specifically on the architectural design of Poppi Castle. Their tour guide, a short, heavyset man, was more than happy to let Emily share her knowledge. Watching her speak with confidence and enthusiasm, Dae found it easy to imagine her speaking at conferences and quickly earning the respect of the attendees.

They spent hours inside the castle, toured the bell tower and the grounds. They examined the areas that were used as the castle's prison hundreds of years ago and took pictures in most of the rooms. Dae's favorite picture was the one they took in front of the grand stone stairwell, which Emily deemed *too impressive for words*. He knew the image would relay the excitement in her voice. She was so easy to be with. Every little thing she did made him want her even more. It was all those things—her Emilyisms—that were coiling themselves around his heart. The adorable way she trapped her lower lip between her teeth when she accidentally made a double entendre. The way she touched his side when she wanted to show him something. Hell, even the way her eyes grew serious as she explained the history of the castle captured his attention. But what he liked most about Emily was that she was real. She didn't pretend to be something she wasn't, and she didn't try to impress him. She was as vulnerable as she was strong, as witty as she was serious, and after watching her roll her eyes at her brothers' texts, which she graciously checked only once—her love for them overrode the irritation in her exasperated sigh—he sensed that she was loyal to the core. By the time they left, Dae was completely and utterly enthralled with her.

After eating a late lunch in Poppi and exploring the city until the sun began to set, they headed back toward the villa. Dae wasn't ready for their date to be over, especially since he'd have to spend most of the day tomorrow doing research on the property he was there to assess. The idea of being away from Emily made the muscles in his neck cord up. He glanced at her, resting against the headrest, her eyes closed. A slight smile curved her lips. She looked relaxed and happy, and she was stunning.

"Tired?"

"No," she said softly, eyes still closed. "Just relaxed. I think it's been years since I've felt so relaxed."

"Are you up for a stroll by the river?"

Her eyes opened wide, like he'd offered her a pot of gold. "Definitely."

Fifteen minutes later they'd parked in a quaint town that bordered the river, and with the sun kissing the horizon, they headed across the cobblestone street toward a tree-lined path along the river.

"Thanks for an amazing day," Emily said as she gazed up at him.

Dae put his arm around her and pulled her close. "Thank *you*. But the day's not over yet." He kissed her temple, inhaling her floral and feminine scent. *Pure Emily*.

She leaned her head against his side as they walked along the water.

"Do I get to choose our day tomorrow?" Emily asked.

"I'm sorry, Em, but I have some things I need to do for work tomorrow."

Her grip on him eased. "Of course. I shouldn't have assumed..."

Dae stopped walking and turned her in his arms so she was facing him. Then he pulled her close and used his index finger to lift her chin so he could look into her disappointed eyes.

"You should assume. I want you to assume. I just need to do some research to decide if I'm taking on this job or not, and that's going to take a few hours. Why don't we try to get together in the evening?" Damn, he wished he could blow off his meetings. He felt a twinge of guilt not telling Emily that the meetings were about a demolition job. He needed to talk with her about that and was waiting for the right opening to do so.

"Sure, but don't feel pressure. I don't mean to monopolize your vacation."

"Em, this wasn't a vacation. It was a work trip, and then I met you. And you are far more interesting than my work could ever be. Please, monopolize me." He pressed his lips to hers and smiled against them as her arms circled his neck.

"That's better." He deepened the kiss, loving the way her body softened against him.

They reluctantly parted. He ran his hands up her back, then down her rib cage, as he touched his forehead to hers and sighed her name.

"You make me feel all sorts of things I've never felt before," he admitted.

"I feel them, too. Your touch, your voice, it's like sensation overload."

Hearing her confession amped up his arousal. Knowing that he had the same effect on her as she did on him was making it hard for him to restrain the desire spreading through him like wildfire.

They walked a little farther and sank onto the riverbank. Dae pulled Emily's body against his, and they sat in comfortable silence, listening to the sounds of the river flowing and, in the distance, the sounds of a city slowing down for the evening.

"Tell me about your work." Emily slid her hand along his thigh.

Work. Right. They were alone on the riverbank. He tried to focus on something other than how much he wanted to put his hands all over her and how she might not let him after he revealed what he did for a living. But he realized that he couldn't hide it any longer, and with Emily, he didn't want to. "I'm into real estate investments and demolition, primarily."

"Demolition, as in blowing things up?"

He laughed, but it was more to ease his worry about what she really thought about his profession. "You could say that. Sometimes tearing things down means blowing them up."

"So are you here for investment purposes or demolition?"

Her hand slid up and down his thigh, and damn, if he wasn't aroused again. He tried to concentrate on her question rather than what she was doing to him. He had to be honest, even if it meant she might back away. He cleared his throat, trying like hell to regain his focus. "Demolition."

She nodded and leaned in to him. His hands slid down her shoulder to her upper arm. She felt too damn good, smelled too damn sexy. They were alone on the riverbank, just off the beaten path and sitting beneath the shadow of a large tree. The scent of the river mingled with the scent of Emily, and Dae couldn't hold back any longer. He lifted her chin and pressed his lips to hers. One slip of his tongue, and she opened to him, allowing his tongue to sweep over hers. She met him stroke for eager stroke, deepening the kiss and making him hotter than hell. Damn, she could kiss. He fisted his hand in her hair and tugged gently, arching her head back, giving himself better access to her sweet neck. He kissed his way along her jaw to the tender spot just beneath her ear, where he nipped at her skin and drew a sensual moan from her lungs. She arched in to him, pressing her breasts against him as he rained kisses along the curve of her neck, then tugged her shirt off her shoulder and sucked her warm skin.

"Dae, you're driving me crazy."

Their eyes met, and in the next second their lips crashed together. He palmed her perfect, firm breasts, groaning with need.

"Holy hell, you feel incredible."

He leaned in to her, gently laid her on her back, and took her in another kiss. He wanted to kiss her until she couldn't think, until tomorrow afternoon passed and they were together again. He slid his thigh over hers, blanketing her body with his, breathing air into her lungs as his hand traveled under her shirt to the lacy bra beneath. He squeezed the taut peak between his index finger and thumb, wanting so badly to take her breast in his mouth. She arched up and wrapped her leg over his so they were coiled together like mating snakes. Her hips pressed against his, and she moaned into his mouth. He wanted to take her right there beside the river, to feel every inch of her naked body beneath him as he claimed her as his own.

He couldn't resist her any longer. He couldn't get enough of her, feared he never would.

She drew back, her body trembling, her breasts heaving. Her eyes held his lusty gaze.

"Take me home," she whispered.

She didn't need to ask twice. They walked quickly toward the parking lot, kissing every few seconds, until they reached the car. He lifted Emily easily into his arms and set her on the hood of the car, spread her legs with his thighs, and kissed her again. Her center pressed against his hard length, their tongues thrusting, tasting, memorizing the feel of each other's mouths. He pulled back to clear his mind enough to drive. He could barely think past the need to be inside her.

He set her back on the ground and helped her into the car. "Home. Now."

She tugged his shirt and dragged his lips back to hers, his body half in and half out of the car. She was driving him out of his freaking mind. Would it be wrong to recline the seat and make love to her right here and now? *Fuck.* What was he thinking? He reluctantly pulled back, out of breath and hard as steel. He stared into her eyes, which had gone nearly black, and grabbed the sides of her head harder than he'd meant to as their lips collided again. She fisted her hands in his hair and held his mouth to hers as aggressive as he'd been with her.

Holy. Hell.

"We're never going..." He kissed her again. "To get out..." Another steamy kiss. "Of here."

She laughed against his lips. "Go. Drive. Hurry."

Twenty minutes later he was fumbling for his room key, one arm around Emily, the other hand flipping through the ring of keys. Emily settled her lips on his neck and sent a bolt of heat to his already throbbing erection. He shoved the key into the lock and kneed the door open, then kicked it closed behind them. Moonlight spilled in through the balcony, drizzling light over the bed. With one swift move, he had her back against the door as he turned the lock and tossed his keys and her purse to the floor. His hands moved without any thought. He wanted to touch all of her. Now. He made quick work of lifting her shirt over her head and—*holy hell, she's going to push me over the edge*. Her black lace bra exposed the mounds of her breasts and barely covered her nipples. She looked sexier than a Victoria's Secret model. His hands fondled the perfect, supple mounds as he thrust and kissed her, probing, devouring. She moaned into his mouth and pulled his hips to hers, holding him against her. She clawed and grabbed and pushed at his shirt. He reached behind him and pulled his shirt over his head, sending buttons flying across the room. Her eyes rolled over his chest to his tattoos, and her lips curved up in appreciation. He lowered his mouth to her breast, laving his tongue over her tight nipple through the scratchy lace. She smelled amazing, and he couldn't get enough of her. She gripped his head, holding his mouth to her breast.

"Oh…yes," she panted.

He pulled her bra straps down, freeing her breasts. Still supported by the bra beneath them, they were full and beautiful and too much for him to forgo.

He licked long, slow strokes around first one nipple, then the other, as he kneaded their fullness. She thrust her hips forward, and he took her in another passionate kiss. The feel of her hard nipples against his chest sent his body into overdrive. He had to have her. He tugged her jeans open, hesitating for a minute, searching her eyes for approval. Without a word she nodded and the edges of her lips curved up. He sealed his lips over hers while he slid his thumbs into the waist of her jeans and tugged them down, biting her lip as he drew back. He released her lip, and air left her lungs in a rush.

His hands slid down her ribs to the gentle curve of her hips. She was bare from the thighs up, save for her panties and her bra, bunched up between her breasts, and she was hotter than any centerfold could ever be.

"Emily, are you sure you want this? I can't promise to stop if we go one minute further." He held her gaze.

"Yes. I'm not...I don't..." She paused, her eyes grew momentarily serious. "I don't usually do this so early on in a relationship, but yes, Dae. I want you. This. Us. More than I've ever wanted anything."

That was all he needed to reach behind her and unclasp her bra. It fell to their feet, and he took her glorious breasts in his hands.

"You have the most amazing body." He pushed her breasts together and licked and kissed her nipples, then ran his tongue between her breasts, first up the center, then down the center of her body, all the way south to her belly button. He kissed her there, slipping his tongue in and out, circling the center, then probing in again, before shifting lower and dragging his tongue along the edge of her black lace panties. She arched forward and reached for her jeans, trying to push them down. He gripped her wrists.

"Not yet," he whispered.

She groaned.

He licked her through her damp panties, then settled his teeth on her inner thigh. Emily squirmed beneath his touch, her thighs straining against the denim as she tried to widen her stance. He slid his hand between her thighs and stroked her wetness. She squirmed and panted, growing wetter by the second. Her body was so responsive to his touch. He throbbed with need as he drew the top of her panties down. She was waxed bare, which nearly did him in.

"Emily," he groaned, resting his forehead against her lower belly.

"Going-away present," she panted. "From Daisy. Hurt like hell. Don't get used to it."

"Oh, baby. I'll make you feel better."

He licked up the crease of her leg beside her sex, inhaling her sweet scent and drawing another sexy moan from Emily. He moved to the other side, letting the room's cool air brush over her wet skin, and felt goose bumps travel up her thighs. Using only his index fingers, he looped them under the hips of her panties and drew them down her thighs.

"Dae," she whispered as she buried her hands in his hair and drew his mouth to her center.

His tongue stroked her lightly, loving the way her body shuddered against him. He spread her thighs with his hands and buried his tongue inside her, using his thumb to circle the sensitive bundle of nerves that caused her legs to stiffen and her body to quake and quiver as his name sailed from her lips. He remained there, loving her, drinking her in, until the last tremor moved through her body. Only then did he reach down and remove her shoes and pull her jeans free from her trembling legs. He kept one hand on her hip to steady her. Her eyes were closed, and she still had one hand fisted in his hair.

"You okay, baby?"

"Oh God, yes." Her eyes fluttered open, and a sated smile parted her lips.

Dae stepped from his jeans and pressed his naked body to hers.

"You feel so good. I could devour you from morning until night."

"I can't...think."

He kissed her, hard and deep, and she melted against him. "Then don't."

He lifted her into his arms and kissed her on the way to the bed. Their hair tangled together, curtaining their kiss from the moonlight. With one hand, he stripped the blanket from the bed and laid her down. Her hair spread across his pillow, and the sight of her in his bed stole his thoughts.

She reached for him, her eyes dark and her voice husky. "Make love to me."

He sealed his mouth over hers. Christ, he loved her mouth. He reached into the nightstand for a condom.

"I'm on the pill," she said.

"Ninety-nine percent effective. When you're one

hundred percent sure that I'm the man you want to spend your life with, then we'll take the one percent chance." He kissed her as he rolled on the latex sheath. "I never want to do wrong by you."

Their lips met as their bodies came together, and he drew away to take a moment. She felt so good he had to stop, to revel in the feel of her thighs against his, her tight, wet center swallowing every inch of him, and her chest meeting his. Their foreheads touched as he began to move. Fuck, she felt good. Their bodies moved in sync as their lips met again in a deep, passionate kiss. He quickened his thrusts and felt her heartbeat quickening, her muscles tightening. Her head fell back, lips slightly parted. Her fingernails dug into his lower back as he pushed faster, deeper. He felt the rise of an orgasm and tried to hold back, but as her inner muscles tightened around him, a rush of heat swamped him and he couldn't. They spiraled over the edge together in a heated, sweaty, intense release as he ground out her name through gritted teeth. His head bowed as he tried to remember how to breathe, and when she whispered, "Again," he thought he'd died and gone to heaven.

And there was no one he'd rather be there with than his sweet Emily.

He wasn't sure he could recover that quickly, but her delectable mouth slid to his neck, sucking and licking, teasing him into submission, and within seconds, he was ready to give sweet Emily the loving she deserved again.

Chapter Eight

EMILY FELT THE softness of Dae's lips on her cheek and smiled as the memory of last night returned, kiss by sumptuous kiss. Her eyes fluttered open as she remembered the way he'd wrapped her in his arms after they'd made love the second time and whispered, "Stay with me."

He was fully dressed now and smiling down at her with wet hair and a worried look in his dark eyes. She reached up and stroked his unshaven cheek. Her body responded to the feel of his scruff. She probably had whisker burn between her legs, but she didn't care. She'd do it all over again right now if he didn't have to leave. She'd never felt so loved, so much like she was in the right place, with the right person, as she had last night.

"Morning," she said.

He kissed her lips. "I don't want to leave you."

She gathered the sheet over her chest and sat up against the headboard. "Then don't." She knew she shouldn't ask him to forgo his work for her, but the words slipped out before she could check them. Where had the request even come from? It felt wrong coming from her, a woman who lived to succeed. Or at least she had, until meeting Dae. Now she was questioning her drive to work harder than everyone else. To be better. To excel no matter what the cost.

His lips curved into a smile. "I wish I could. Tonight, though. Let's meet here. What are your plans for today?"

"Let's see..." She peeked beneath the sheets. "I think I'll get dressed and go to my own room so I can shower."

He lowered his body onto hers and kissed the tip of her nose. "Now I have the image of you naked in the shower in my mind. How am I supposed to work?"

She laughed. "It's not that great—trust me."

"Oh, now I know how untrustworthy you are, too, Miss Braden, because you have the most incredible body I've ever seen." He pressed his hard length to her hips and kissed her.

"Oh." *Maybe I can convince him to blow off work. Or maybe I should just blow him. I have got to stop. It's so unfair. Work comes first, and of all people, I should know that.*

He lowered his forehead to her chest. "You kill me."

She laughed again, remembering his comment about what her big *O*s looked like. "Sorry. Sort of."

"Yeah, I bet you are." He kissed her again and brushed her hair from her face.

"I'm going sightseeing, but I'm not sure it's going

to be much fun alone."

"Yes, it will. You'll have a great time. Why don't we meet back here for dinner? And if you're having too good of a time, just text me and I'll meet you wherever you are."

"Really?" Wow. She'd never been with a guy who had been so amenable to her.

"Absolutely. I only have another few days before I have to fly out, and I want to spend as much time as possible with you."

Her stomach sank. "When do you leave?"

"Well, let's see...Today's Monday, and I leave Thursday. So if we include today, I leave four days from now."

Only four days. *Only* three more nights. Why did that seem so tragic? She swallowed against the desire to beg him to stay longer. She had so many questions. He'd never even told her where he lived. She glanced away, taking in the tidy room. His clothing from last night was folded neatly and set on the chair in the corner. A hairbrush sat on the dresser, his leather wallet beside it. She realized that she didn't know that much about him, and she desperately wanted to know more. Everything. She wanted to know everything about him.

"Four days," she said softly. "Where will you go when you leave Italy?"

"Denver. I have a business meeting about a property I own out that way." He glanced at his watch. "I have to run. I've got a meeting in an hour. Text me throughout the day? Send me pictures of all the great places you go?"

She smiled. "Sure." She suddenly felt a little funny. He was trusting her to be alone in his room. "Don't worry. I'll get out of here in a minute and lock up when I leave."

"Em, I wouldn't care if you stayed all day. Make yourself at home." He kissed her, then rose from the bed. "Adelina said to tell you good morning."

Emily cringed. "You saw her already? And she knows we were together?"

"With only two rooms rented in the villa, I'd imagine not much gets past her. I've been up for hours. She and Serafina had just come back from wherever it is they go to pray for the safe return of Serafina's husband when I got downstairs. We had coffee together this morning."

"Hours?" *Oh my gosh.* "You should have woken me up."

He touched her cheek. "You're adorable when you blush."

She felt her cheeks flame even more.

"You looked so peaceful. Besides, after last night, I assumed you needed the rest."

She fluttered her lashes. "I would have totally been up for getting up early to mess around before you left."

"I…You…" His jaw clenched, and he closed his eyes for a beat, clearly struggling with having missed out on an opportunity—or maybe debating it for another day.

"You're cute when you're befuddled," she teased.

"Jesus, I adore you." He pressed his lips to hers. "Actually, it was partly selfish. I love seeing you in my bed. Naked."

"You're impossible. You're just trying to make me blush again."

"I think you know by now that I'm not impossible where you're concerned. I'm a sure thing. And you're right. I love to see you blush, but I really love to see you in my bed." He grabbed his wallet, blew her a kiss, and reached for the door. *"Ciao, bella."*

Emily stared after him, feeling lonely already. She dressed and then wrote a note on the back of one of her business cards from her purse.

Dear Sure Thing,

Miss you already and you've only been gone a minute.

Xo,

E.

She made the bed and placed the card on his pillow, and then went to her room and showered and dressed for the day. Downstairs she found Adelina on the porch, carrying Luca on her hip.

"Good morning, Adelina. Good morning, Luca." She tickled his feet, and he giggled.

"Ah, Emily. Good morning." She held Emily's gaze a beat too long, reminding her that she knew she and Dae had spent the night together. Emily felt her cheeks heat up again.

"Your handsome man has left you a gift." She pointed to a small package wrapped with a red ribbon beside the plate on the table.

"Thank you." Surprised, she picked it up and glanced back up at Adelina. Her embarrassment was swept away, replaced with excitement over the thoughtful man who was leaving her gifts and opening up her heart in ways she'd only dreamed of.

"He has love in his eyes when he speaks of you." Adelina pulled out the chair for Emily and poured fresh coffee into her cup while murmuring something in Italian to Luca.

"Casa Dei Desideri," Adelina sang as she poured fresh coffee into Emily's cup.

House of Wishes. Emily smiled. "I want to see the Casa Dei Desideri, Adelina, but today my schedule is very tight."

Adelina kissed Luca's cheek three times. "Casa Dei Desideri brought us Luca. Write your wish and then visit. You'll see. Your wish will come true." She looked off into the distance and sighed. "*Albero di amore*."

Emily settled into her chair, once again wishing she had taken a refresher course in Italian.

Beneath the wrapping she found a small memo pad. Inside, handwritten in a way that reminded her of Dae—easy, curved letters that glided over the page, the way he'd glided into her life.

Sweet Emily, when we're together, nothing is impossible. I thought you might enjoy seeing this villa if you can fit it in your schedule. Until tonight, Dae.

He'd drawn a map, including sketched landmarks along the way. The final destination was marked with a big heart instead of an *X*.

Dae's directions were perfect. Emily drove past the olive grove that he had sketched, and a mile or so later, she pulled into the driveway of the only house in sight, the front of which Dae had also sketched perfectly. In true Tuscan style, the house boasted shallow roof tiles, many of which were missing or broken, arches above the doors and windows, and beautiful, ornately designed columns. She stepped from the car and crossed the lawn, noticing that the columns were cracked and chipped, and some of the windows were broken. The house was covered in ivy, obviously abandoned. She wondered how Dae knew of this place, and what, if any, significance it had to the area.

Emily followed a cobblestone walkway to the top of the driveway, where it forked toward either side of the house, and walked to the far side of the property. As she rounded the corner of the house, a beautiful pergola capped by lattice and crawling with vines, similar to the one she and Dae had sat beneath the first night they were together, came into view. She stepped inside and enjoyed the view, overlooking miles of rolling hills and giving her a perfect view of the olive grove she'd passed on the way there. She turned, taking in the expansive yard, and smiled when she noticed an old hand pump off to her left. She loved the antiquity of metal hand pumps. The gentle curves of the handle, the spouts, which were often quite simple and rustic, like this one was, even the pole that held it in place, all added to its charm. Well pumps conjured up images of families coming together, sharing chores, and cooking together like Adelina and Serafina did. She felt a little nostalgic and wondered if it was too late for her mother to teach her how to cook. Catherine Braden was a talented cook and had always enjoyed preparing their family's meals. As a girl, she'd striven hard to keep up with her brothers. Whether with grades or outside horsing around, Emily had never wanted to be left behind, and it seemed she'd never slowed down enough to do girlie things. With five active brothers, there was always someone to keep up with. Then she'd gone away to college and was busy with grades and a social life. She wondered now how much she'd missed out on by not taking the time to learn to cook with her mother.

She tucked away the thought to revisit another time and looked across the yard at the house. She spotted an alcove toward the rear of the house and stepped beneath the arched entranceway into the cozy enclosure. Old planters hung on the wall to her left, their contents dead and brittle. A broken wooden chair lay on its side, and the cement floor was littered with leaves and dirt. A waist-high wall faced the yard, with three arched openings spanning the length. Emily imagined how beautiful the area would look with colorful blooms and green plants decorating the unique iron and clay planters. There were two wooden doors at the far end. She tried the handle of each and was bummed to find them both locked, of course. She went back outside the way she'd come and scanned the backyard.

"Holy cow." The largest olive tree she'd ever seen was growing in the wall of the house. She'd never seen anything like this. Her eyes trailed the left side of the wall to where it disappeared into the bark of the tree, engulfed by years of growth. And then, as if the wall had been built straight through the massive trunk, it continued on the other side of the trunk. As an architect, she could see the unique value in building a house *around* a tree, as in inside a particular room, but why would anyone want to build the wall of a house *into* a tree? What stymied her even more was the fact that the wall had not cracked or shifted as the tree grew. This house was built so many years earlier that the tree must have been at least half its size at that time. *Walls don't adapt to the increasing girth of trees. This is not possible.*

No wonder Dae wanted her to see it. Mr. Make the Impossible Possible. How had he even found this house? She wished he were with her. She pulled her phone from her pocket and stood far back so she could capture the entire tree, then clicked a picture and texted it to him. *This is impossible and nothing short of amazing!*

She gazed up at the leafy branches snaking out from the middle of the tree and arching out, thick and tangled, far above the roof.

Her phone vibrated with a text from Dae. *I knew you'd like it. Be sure to walk down the east side of the property. The view is incredible. Heading into another meeting. See you tonight. Miss you.*

She shoved her phone into the pocket of her shorts, feeling as if she were walking on air. He missed her. *He misses me!* She felt good all over knowing that he was feeling the same connection as she was.

She walked toward the trunk. She loved the gnarled and twisted trunks of olive trees. She'd never seen them up close, but she'd studied photos of them and they'd always intrigued her. No two were the same, and she found even the most gnarled trunks lovely. Knowing that she'd found this place only because of Dae made her admire the trees even more.

It took a moment of staring at the lacy bark to realize what she was looking at. There were pieces of paper, fabric, and ribbons sticking out all over the trunk. She stepped closer, wondering what they were. In the distance, she heard a car door slam and then another. She stilled.

I'm trespassing. Crap.

She had visions of being arrested. That would really give her brothers something to worry about.

She hurried toward the front of the house and made a beeline for her car. The car she'd heard was parked across the street. Three women were holding hands and gazing at the house. Emily climbed into her car as fast as she could before the women could spot her and drove back toward Florence, loving the fact that Dae had thought of her when he'd seen that house.

LATER THAT EVENING Dae and Emily had dinner at a quaint restaurant on the Arno River. Dae couldn't take his eyes off of Emily. She looked radiant in a short summery dress with her hair falling loosely over her breasts. They'd already finished eating a delicious meal of *zuppa de arselle,* soup with bread, tomato, and mussels, and *tagliatelle ai funghi,* tagliatelle pasta with mushrooms, and were sharing a bottle of wine as Emily told him about her afternoon.

"It was nice just to stroll through the city and

people watch. But the highlight of my day was definitely seeing the villa you gave me directions to. Your map was perfect, by the way."

He reached for her hand. "I wish I could have seen your face when you saw the tree." He was trying to figure out how to tell her that he might have to demolish the house, but she looked too happy to ruin the moment.

"I didn't get to look for too long. There were three women who showed up, and I was worried about trespassing, so I took off. Can you imagine if I called home to tell my brothers that I'd been arrested? They'd never let me out of their sight again."

"I would have been there to bail you out." He shifted his seat closer and draped an arm around her. "Did you see all the things that were on the tree? It looked almost as if it had been decorated."

"I saw that, too, and it made me think of this place Adelina told me about. The House of Wishes. She called it something else today. Something about love."

"Well, that tree would have to be called *albero di amore*, tree of love."

"That's it! That's exactly what she called it." Emily's eyes widened, and her jaw dropped. "That's got to be the place she was talking about. She said the women around here go there and make wishes for matters of the heart. Relationships, fertility, that sort of thing."

She leaned forward and stroked his cheek. He loved when she did that. Hell, he loved when she touched him anywhere.

"Dae, I think you sent me to the House of Wishes.

She said that's how she met her husband, by wishing for him. *There*. At that house, I think. And Luca? She said Serafina wished for him, too. It's got to be the same place. I wonder if it's where they go every morning to pray for Dante's safe return. If it is, it's probably also the place she told me I should go." Emily gazed out over the water and sighed with a dreamy look in her eyes.

"I wonder why she thought you should go there." Dae thought he knew the answer to that. Earlier that morning, when he'd had coffee with Adelina, she'd told him that he had the *look of love* in his eyes. She said that Tuscany had a way of bringing lovers together, but not all lovers. Only the ones who were destined to be together. Dae wasn't sure how he felt about the notion of destiny, much less that a geographical location could have anything to do with two people finding each other. Although now, as he sat with Emily pressed against his side, looking at him like he was more special than the Florence Cathedral, setting all sorts of unfamiliar emotions free in his heart, he began to reconsider his belief.

"She said she saw something in your eyes." She blinked up at him and nibbled on her lower lip. He knew she was holding back.

"Something?"

"Mm-hmm." She fiddled with the ends of her hair in that adorable, nervous way she had.

Dae paid for dinner; then they walked beneath the star-spotted sky. After a few minutes of comfortable silence, Dae said, "She was right."

"Who?"

He stopped by the water and gazed into Emily's eyes. He could drown in those sensual dark pools of emotion. He felt himself slipping down a slope toward her, and he didn't know how to put on the brakes—or if he wanted to.

"Adelina," he answered. "I do have feelings for you, Emily, and not just the kind driven by thoughts of the dirty things I want to do with you. I have real feelings for you. Big ones that are sort of knocking me for a loop."

She dropped her eyes, and worry passed through them. When she met his gaze, the worry was gone, replaced with sincerity. "I feel that way, too."

A simple, honest answer. No promises of more, no pleas for more details on his feelings. She wasn't needy or clingy, and that made him like her even more and drove home how real and different Emily was.

They strolled along the water for a while longer, letting their admissions settle in and bind them together. Then they drove back to the villa, and Dae swore everything felt different. Where the air had felt electrified before, now, with their feelings out on the table, that electricity was sharper, heavier, more substantial and meaningful.

At the villa, they sat on the back patio overlooking the grounds. Emily cuddled up against him and curled her legs onto the bench they shared.

"How did you find that villa you sent me to?" Emily asked.

He'd been worrying about this moment, and now that it was here, he was ready to face it head-on. At least he hoped he was.

"That's the house I came here to assess." He watched as understanding dawned on her.

"To demolish or to purchase as an investment?"

He heard the worry in her voice and wished he had a different answer to give her, but all he had to offer was the truth. "I'm here to assess its demolition."

Emily nodded. Her lips pressed into a serious line. "And if it's the same house that Adelina told me about? What if it's the House of Wishes?"

"I honestly don't know, Em. I only just learned of this tonight. We don't even know if it's the same house she's talking about. And besides, it's a myth. A legend."

"But that's what dreams are made from. If it's the same house, it's where Serafina prayed she'd have Luca. Where Adelina left her hope of meeting Marcello. What if it is the same place? I know how this sounds, Dae. I know it's silly and maybe childish, but what if it's the same one? Adelina said women have been wishing there forever. Will you tear it down?" She crossed her arms, and his gut twisted.

How could a house and a tree form a barrier between them?

"I haven't thought that far ahead." He put his arm around her and felt her resist. "Baby, you can't seriously be mad at me for this, can you?"

"I'm not mad," she said quietly. "I don't know if I even believe in this myth, but that's not the point." She leaned in to his side. "*They* believe in it. Isn't that what matters? For generations women have believed in something. It makes me sad to think that if that is the House of Wishes and you tear it down, all those women who believed their love stemmed from what they did there will have part of their history obliterated. And what about poor Serafina? If that's where she prays every morning for her husband's safe return, won't you feel like you're letting her down?"

This conversation was a lot harder than he'd anticipated. "Aw, babe, there's so much to process about this. So what you're suggesting is that if it is the same place, then I should walk away from it." *Can I even do that?* He never walked away from jobs unless they were too dangerous or there were legal complications that made it impossible for him to do the work. Then again, he'd never had a girlfriend who wasn't totally captivated by what he did for a living. Or who cared so much about something she didn't own.

He'd never dated Emily Braden.

"No. It's your job." She cocked her head and looked up at him. "I guess…I don't know. Maybe?"

He leaned down and kissed her softly. "You know that if it's not me who demolishes it, they'll just hire someone else to do it."

"*Ugh*. Well, there's only one thing to do. We have to find out if it is the place she told me about. Maybe it's not even an issue. We can ask Adelina tomorrow."

"That sounds good."

"How did your meetings go today? I forgot to even ask."

The last thing he wanted to do was talk about work any more than they already had. "They were fine, but I'm more interested in how *we're* doing. Work is just that for me, Em. It's work. I love what I do. It pays the bills, and most of the time it's interesting and fun, but when I'm with you, I feel like everything else is secondary. Promise me tomorrow."

"Tomorrow." She smiled.

"Good. I have something planned."

"I guess since I gave up checking email for you, I can give up my itinerary, too." She spoke sweetly and softly, without a hint of disappointment.

"First of all..." He touched the ends of her hair and kissed her. "I would never think about making you miss out on a thing. Second, we have three more days together, and I want to make the most of them."

She banged her forehead against his chest. "Three days. I hate that."

"I know. But even after we leave, we'll make sure we see each other." He pulled her onto his lap and gathered her hair over her shoulder. "You can't cut me off cold turkey. I'll have Emily withdrawal."

"I have no interest in cutting you off. I want you to stay for the whole nine days I'm here; then I can put you in my suitcase and carry you home."

He laughed at her serious tone. "That would be quite a feat, you carrying me in a suitcase." He lifted her arm and shook it. "You're in great shape, baby, but you've got to build some muscle to carry all this around." He ran a hand down his chest, then took her in a passionate kiss.

"I love to kiss you," he said against her lips.

"Then take me upstairs and show me how much."

Done.

Chapter Nine

EMILY LAY ON her back, one arm across her stomach, the other arced over her head, resting on the pillow. Her room was silent save for their heavy breathing. Even in the darkness she could see the red blooms of the poppies surrounding them on every surface. *He* did that for her. *For us.* Everything he did was romantic and thoughtful, from the little map he'd drawn to the way he was touching the outside of her thigh with his fingertips. Feathery flutters fanned her leg and made her excited all over again, even after they'd made love until they both fell to the mattress, sated and spent.

"Wow." Dae reached for her hand.

"Wow? That's what you say after you have sex?"

"No. That's what I say after I have sex with you." He leaned up on his elbow and grinned down at her. "It wasn't *wow* for you?"

"Oh, it was *wow*, all right, but *so* much more than *wow*." She scooted closer, pressing her side against him. She'd come so close to giving up on finding this type of connection. She didn't know how to verbalize what she really felt. She didn't even understand it herself. She was so happy, but in the back of her mind she worried about what he'd told her. He was a demolitionist. Okay, well, she could deal with that, but she was having trouble thinking about him demolishing that beautiful house with the tree. And what if that really was the House of Wishes?

She couldn't process the conflicting emotions. She pushed them away and reached for him instead, dragging her finger down his cheek, and loved that he closed his eyes, looking peaceful and happy. "I love your face." She ran her fingers through his hair and fisted her hand in it. "And your hair. It's insanely sexy."

"Well, it's a good thing you love my face. It's the only one I have, and I guess I'll cancel my crew-cut appointment." The tease in his eyes made her smile.

"I can't even imagine you with short hair."

"Oh, there was a time when I tried to conform. When I was in college, I was Mr. Clean Cut for the first semester, until I realized that fitting in with others was highly overrated."

"I thought your parents were hippies."

He lowered his lips to hers and kissed her softly. "They were hippyish. My father's in the military, but he's not at all what you'd expect. He's not regimented and it's like he *expected* that we would stray from the rules. He was like the anti-military man, and my mom was definitely a free spirit, like my sisters. They just have different ideals, you know? They were all about life experiences, owning our feelings and our personalities, even if it made us different from everyone else. They never hounded us or grounded us, like most parents do. My mom always said life was about experiencing the moment, not controlling it. I'm sure that's why I believe in working hard but enjoying life instead of working myself to the bone and missing out. And...it's why I thought I should try to fit in and conform. I thought that when I went to college, fitting in was important, conforming to the norms." He flicked his hair. "You know, trendy haircuts and clothing? It's no different from girls wearing the right shoes or owning the right purse."

"I guess. Your parents sound like they just wanted to be sure their kids were happy."

"Yeah. I'm pretty lucky in that regard. It sounds like you are, too, though, with your mom and your brothers."

"Yes, definitely. Although my mom made sure we made the grades, so to speak. I think she always worried that coming from a single-parent family, we might fall short or something might fall through the cracks. But she has always put family above all else." She looked off into the distance, strolling down memory lane, remembering the way her mother used to check each of their backpacks, make their lunches, take her brothers to sports practices, and attend every game. She was very present in their lives, and Emily loved that. She still did.

"What are you thinking?"

"Just that I really had a great childhood. Even without my dad around, I don't feel like I missed out on anything. And I'm really glad that you made me see that I didn't need to do work every second I was here. Thank you."

"Em, what's it like for you back in Colorado? Are you the same person there as you are here?"

Am I the same person? She thought about what she was like at home, how many hours she worked, how she was in almost daily contact with her family. "I'm not sure. I mean, I'm basically the same person, but I work a lot, so..."

"So, do you date very often?" He drew his brows together.

"Do I hear a hint of jealousy?"

"Maybe."

She arched up and kissed him. "No need to be, but I love that you are. The town I live in is so small, and gossip spreads really fast, so I kind of lie low on the whole dating scene. To be honest, I haven't met many guys in the last few years that I've *wanted* to date. What about you?"

"About the same as you. On and off, but nothing serious. I was thinking that after you went back to Colorado, I'd come visit. I'll be staying at my house in Denver. How far away is Trusty? A few hours?"

Her heart soared. *Denver*. He had a house in Denver! She hoped they'd last beyond Italy, but this made it all seem very real and possible. "I forgot you were going to Denver. It's only two hours away. When will you have time to see me?"

"That depends on how soon you want to see me."

She pushed him onto his back and climbed on top of him. Her hair shielded their faces. She stretched her lips into a big, cheesy smile. "The day I get home."

He gripped her hips, and his laugh vibrated through his chest. "Don't you think you want some time to settle in?"

"Nope. Meet me at the airport. I get into the Denver Airport Saturday at two thirty in the afternoon Colorado time. It's going to be so weird to be back home."

"You mean the jet lag?"

"Forget the time difference and jet lag; it's going to be weird being there instead of here with you. Although being there with you will be just as good." She leaned down and kissed him, then drew back quickly, too excited to stay still.

"Will you really come see me?" She felt him getting hard beneath her. Worry fought to overtake her elation and desire. How would they piece together their lives when their fundamental beliefs were so very different?

"Even your overprotective brothers couldn't keep me away." He wrapped his arms around her and shifted her beneath him again, so his hips claimed the space between her thighs. "By the way, can you cook?" he asked against her lips.

Could he read her mind? "That's a weird question. Not very well."

He kissed her again. His hand slid down her side and gripped her hip, and thoughts of their conflicting careers slipped away.

"Hmm. A guy has to make sure of these things." He nipped at her jaw, then kissed his way to her breasts. "Can you clean?" He licked her nipple, and she gasped.

"Yes," she whispered.

"Yes, you can clean, or yes..."

She chuckled. "Both."

"Then maybe I'll even stay overnight."

She lifted her knee and rolled him onto his back again, feeling bold and brave and wanting to continue unleashing and exploring this new side of her that she hadn't realized was tethered. And she wanted to explore it with him. "I have other talents that are far more important than cooking or cleaning." She splayed her hands on his rippled abs and traced the lines around his muscles with her tongue. "You can choose one room for me to excel in. *One* room." She kissed a path between his hips, then followed the vee of muscles down to the crest of his thigh. Her body shivered with delight at the way his body reacted to her touch, all his muscles tensing, his eyes darkening to nearly black.

"One room," he said in a gravelly voice.

She wrapped her fingers around his hard length and licked the tip. "Choose carefully," she whispered.

He sucked in air between gritted teeth as she swallowed him deep.

"Holy hell, Em."

She teased and licked, then swallowed him deep, over and over again, her hand wrapped securely around him, following her mouth up and back down. She squeezed as she reached the tip, then eased her grip on the way back down. He groaned and grasped her shoulders.

"Em."

She opened her eyes and met his gaze as she licked him from base to tip.

"Fuck." He closed his eyes and dropped his head back to the pillow.

Heat seared through Emily's body. She loved knowing she had this effect on him. She licked and stroked until he fisted his hands in the sheets. His thighs tensed and his hips bucked as he reached for her. She crawled up his body and he rolled her onto her back and reached for another condom. He was perched on his knees between her thighs, every muscle in his gorgeous body corded tight with need. His hands shook as he tore open the condom, pinning Emily to the bed with a dark, hungry stare. She rose and helped him with the thin latex sheath. He lowered her to the bed and followed her down, taking her in a greedy kiss as their bodies joined together in a hard collision of hips and mouths. She'd been with only a few men and never before had she felt so full, had she fit together with a man as if they were two halves of one whole. He plunged and thrust, taking her right up to the edge of coming apart, and then he withdrew slowly, tearing a whimper from her lungs. He pushed in equally as unhurried as his tongue swept over hers in lovingly long and slow strokes, until her entire body trembled with need. She pressed on his hips, urging him for more, arched to meet each careful thrust.

He smiled against her lips. "In a rush?"

"You're driving me insane. Please, Dae, I need more of you."

She ran her fingers lightly up the curve of his back and felt him shiver against her. Still he didn't quicken his pace. She clutched his ass and pulled him to her.

"You took me right to the edge," he whispered,

then bit down on her earlobe and sucked it into his mouth.

She was going to lose her mind. "Please," she whispered.

He kissed the dip below her earlobe, and she heard amusement in his voice.

"Please what?"

"Go faster. Harder. Please."

He rocked his hips, probing deeper, until she felt every blessed inch of him; then he undulated in a slow, rhythmic motion, sending shocks of fire down to her toes.

"Oh...Ah..."

"Faster isn't always better, baby." He took her in another kiss, robbing her of her thoughts as her toes curled under and her hips shot up off the bed.

His kiss turned relentless, penetrating and rough, and God help her—she loved the hell out of it. She clawed at his back, tangled her hands in his hair, pulled him to her, and returned his passion. She lifted her hips and wrapped her legs around his waist. A moan of desire escaped her lips.

"That's it, baby," he coaxed against her mouth. "Let go. Let me hear how much you want us."

Holy. Cow. She couldn't stop the sexy moans of sluttiness escaping her lungs if she tried. And she didn't want to. She was loving her new sexiness as much as she loved how he reacted to it.

"Holy hell, you turn me on," he whispered.

His hand slid down and cupped her ass, lifting her hips as he drove in deeper, bringing her right up to the edge again. She couldn't breathe, was lost in the tightening in her lower belly that was racing lower, and finally, blissfully, consumed her. She was vaguely aware of his other hand fisted in her hair. He tugged her head back, opening her mouth to him as he sealed his lips over hers. Every inch of her body throbbed, overstimulated and sizzling with ecstasy. He plunged his tongue into her mouth and—*thank the heavens above*—he breathed for her as his own powerful release tore through him. His body shook and thrust until the last pulse of his orgasm subsided.

He rested his head on her chest. Emily ran her fingers through his hair, trying to gain control of her emotions, her limbs, her brain. Dae not only made her feel beautiful and respected her needs and desires, but he knew how to make her body sing in all the right ways. She could get used to falling asleep in his arms. She wanted to get used to sleeping with him and waking with him and everything in between. She craved him like a drug and knew she was at no risk of overdosing—but would enjoy trying.

"Every room," he said.

"What?" She laughed.

"You said I could choose one room for you to excel in. I want to choose every room in the house. I don't care if you cook and clean. I was kidding about that, but I'd love to devour you in every room."

She wrapped her arms around his back and squeezed, loving his playfulness. "How do you know I don't have roommates?"

"Blindfolds work wonders."

She felt him smile against her chest. "You're a naughty, naughty boy, Mr. Bray." She imagined Dae at the bottom of a steep hill, arms wide open, welcoming her, accepting her, caring for her—but behind him, the world was crumbling down in a shower of concrete and stone, with plumes of dust billowing into the air. Her earlier worry pressed in on her again. *How can we piece together our lives when our fundamental beliefs are so very different?*

"I was talking about blindfolds for the roommates." He lifted his warm dark eyes and met her gaze. "I like to see your eyes. They tell me exactly what you're feeling and sometimes what you're thinking."

She shifted her eyes away, and he rolled off of her. Emily turned away from his gorgeous body as he walked, naked and completely comfortable, to the bathroom to dispose of the condom. She gazed out the glass balcony doors into the starry sky. What was she going to do? She'd never felt this much for anyone before, and she didn't want to, couldn't, wouldn't, turn her back on those feelings.

The mattress sank, and Dae's arm curled around her, pulling her against him. He kissed her cheek and whispered, "I already saw your eyes, babe. You don't need to look away from me. I know something's on your mind."

Why did she suddenly feel like she was going to cry? She turned toward him, their foreheads touching, and she settled her hand on his cheek. He wrapped his strong arm around her again and tucked her body against his.

"You blow things up. I preserve them." She hated the way her voice cracked.

"Those are our jobs, Em." He pressed his lips to

her forehead. "No one said a relationship between us would be easy, but you can't deny the connection you feel when you're with me." He tipped up her chin and looked lovingly into her eyes. "You can't deny it, because I feel it, too, babe. When I think of you, when I'm with you, when I hear your voice...You have already become a part of me. It's like the moment our eyes met, my heart decided you were the missing piece I never knew I needed."

She couldn't deny the connection, and she didn't want to. "I'm not denying it. But how...?"

"I don't know. Somehow."

Somehow. She wanted to believe in *somehow*.

"I told you that I won't do the wrong thing by you. Trust me."

She did. She would.

She closed her eyes and absorbed the comfort he offered, and as he pressed his lips to her forehead again, she seared the feel of him to memory.

Just in case.

Chapter Ten

EMILY AWOKE TO bright sunlight streaming across her face. She turned away from the sunlight, and Dae came into focus, sitting on the corner of the bed with her itinerary beside him and a map spread across his legs. He turned as the bed dipped with her movements.

"Good morning, beautiful." He reached for her hand and brought it to his lips.

She couldn't stifle her dreamy sigh. *I've got it bad, despite my niggling worry about our jobs conflicting.* She watched his eyes shift back to the map.

"I'm making sure I've got you covered for today. I've packed my backpack with everything from first-aid supplies to water and protein bars."

"First-aid stuff? Power bars? Are we going on a mountainous trek?"

"No." He laughed.

"Don't you think you're overpreparing for an afternoon in Italy?"

"That would be no, thank you very much. Besides, this from the girl who had every second planned for her entire trip?"

"I planned where to go, not how to survive the wilderness."

He laughed. "I've got my girl to look after. And now..." He waved her itinerary. "I'm making sure I've got all the things on your itinerary covered."

Of course you are.

"You're very good to me."

"You're easy to be good to."

So this was how love happened. Her brothers had fallen in love so fast with their fiancées, and she'd never questioned it. The love they shared exuded from every touch, every glance, every stolen kiss. She felt so completely taken with Dae that she wondered if it was as obvious from them as it had been in her brothers' relationships.

How could it? Our jobs are so different. Surely that was what people would see when they were together. From what she'd seen, her brothers and their significant others hadn't ever had that type of strife.

Then how did Adelina see love in Dae's eyes?

And why did she tell me to go to the House of Wishes?

The House of Wishes. That's it.

"I want to add something to my itinerary." She pulled the sheets up to cover her chest and sat up beside him. He was wearing a pair of black boxer briefs, and he looked entirely too edible.

"Anything you want, babe."

"The House of Wishes." She tried—and failed—to

restrain her smile as he slid his eyes to her.

He brought a hand to her cheek and kissed her lips before sighing loudly.

"House of Wishes."

"Yes. I don't care if it's the same house you gave me directions to or not. I want to go, and I want to go with you." She didn't know why, but all of a sudden it felt very important that they do this together.

"This will throw a hitch into my perfectly mapped-out bike tour." His words were stern, but his eyes were bright and good-humored.

"Bike tour?"

"Yup. You promised me today, and I promised you that you'd see everything on your itinerary. I want to experience the outdoors of Italy with you, not just the sites, and that means compromising." His lips spread into a wide grin. "Still game?"

She hadn't ridden a bike in ages, although that didn't worry her. But she'd kind of been looking forward to those long drives where he held her hand. The idea of pedaling her heart out between sites didn't exactly thrill her.

"I see the gears turning in your beautiful head again." He set the map aside and pulled her onto his lap. The sheets fell, leaving her bare to her waist. She felt him get hard beneath her bottom. "You're amazing." He draped the sheet around her and lifted her hand, curling her fingers around the two ends of the sheet so she was holding it up. "Trust me?"

She nodded, sidetracked by his arousal, hard and very present, beneath her and the planes of exposed masculinity before her. He'd already showered, and he smelled like a very delicious fantasy waiting to happen.

"I would never ask you to do something you couldn't handle." He raked his eyes down her body in a way that made her shudder. "Well…that's not entirely true. I did enjoy teasing you last night, so there is *that* kind of torture."

She drew in a shaky breath. "If you keep insinuating dirty things, I'm not going to agree to leave this bedroom."

AN HOUR AND two overwhelming orgasms later, they'd finished breakfast and confirmed with Adelina that the House of Wishes was indeed the very house that Dae was supposed to demolish. The color drained from Adelina's face. She reached for a chair to stabilize herself, as if they'd just told her that she had a terminal disease.

"Oh, no, no, no." Adelina looked up at the ceiling and began speaking in Italian. *"Questo è terribile. Demolire? Demolire!* No."

Dae mouthed, *praying,* to Emily. Pain stretched across Emily's face. She reached for Adelina's hand.

"Adelina, Dae might not tear it down." She glared at Dae, urging him to ease her distress.

Fuck. He'd give anything to appease Emily and wipe that worry and sadness from her beautiful face, but he couldn't lie to Adelina. He knew that one way or another, she was going to have to face the truth.

"I don't know what will happen to the property," he explained. "But the man who bought it does have plans to tear it down, and it may be too late to stop him."

Dae reached for her and she leaned out of his reach, focusing on Adelina instead.

"Adelina, I'm so sorry. Dae didn't know anything about the House of Wishes when he came here."

Damn it to hell. Emily was trying to shield him from being the cause of Adelina's sadness. He didn't need protecting. He believed in truth and honesty. He believed in dealing with shit head-on.

Adelina was mumbling in Italian under her breath when Serafina walked into the room. Serafina's eyes widened at the sight of her mother's distress.

"Mama!" She ran to her side. "What happened? What's wrong?"

Adelina's eyes filled with determination as she spoke rapidly in Italian. Emily glanced at Dae, obviously recognizing the name Casa Dei Desideri, as he did.

Serafina gasped a breath and covered her mouth with her hand. Adelina patted Serafina's cheek.

"What can we do?" Serafina asked.

"Now we wish," Adelina answered.

Chapter Eleven

DAE AND EMILY walked down the grassy hill toward the shed where Adelina kept bikes on hand for guests to borrow. Dae had the backpack he'd packed over one shoulder. Emily stomped through the grass, and she hated herself for it. All Dae had done was tell the truth, but damn it...did he have to do that? Couldn't he have softened the blow a little? He didn't even really know if he was going to tear the place down or not. Or did he?

"This is good." Dae walked beside her. He hadn't even reached for her hand. Probably because he saw smoke rising from her ears. "Stomp it out, babe, and when you're ready to talk about it, I'm all ears."

Damn him. How could he be so nonchalant about this? She was upset. And she didn't care if she had a right to be or not. She thought that he might reconsider tearing down the place after seeing how much it meant to Adelina and Serafina and learning that it had so much history. But she was even more upset that he hadn't at least cushioned the blow with Adelina. He didn't have to tell her so bluntly that the man who owned it had plans to tear it down. A little fib while he figured things out wouldn't have been so bad, would it?

Or maybe there was nothing to figure out. Maybe his mind was made up.

When they reached the shed at the bottom of the hill, Dae pulled the heavy wooden doors open. "The silent treatment never solves anything, Em. Don't you think we should talk about this?"

"Maybe." She sounded like an angry child and it even annoyed her.

Dae leaned his shoulder and hip against the wall and crossed his feet at the ankle, reminiscent of the first night they'd met. It was unfair how sexy and casual he looked when she was tied up in knots. He reached for her hand, and when she didn't let him take it, instead of getting mad, he smiled, pushed off the wall, and gently took her hand in his, as if nothing could ever *really* come between them. Then Dae repositioned himself with his back against the wall, feet planted in a wide stance, and he guided her until she stood between his legs.

"Two days, babe," his voice was tender. "That's all we've got until we're forever and a day away from each other. Talk to me. Tell me the good, the bad, and the hurtful. I'm a big boy. I can take it."

Two days. Her eyes welled with tears. Damn it. She never cried. She didn't even know why she was crying. Because of the House of Wishes or because he was leaving? She had no idea, but the fact that she was acting like a brat didn't help.

She pressed her hands flat against his chest, stuck between wanting to pound her fists on him and the desire to melt into one of his smoldering kisses, which would make her forget all of the bad stuff.

"Emily." He said it so sweetly that she felt herself softening toward him. "I told you that I try not to do the wrong thing. That means telling the truth even when it's hurtful."

"Well, it was hurtful."

"I know." He brushed her hair from her shoulder. "Not just to her but to you, too."

"Then why did you do it?"

He arched a brow, and the side of his mouth kicked up in a cockeyed smile.

She rolled her eyes out of frustration. "I know you don't want to lie, but come on. Couldn't you have said—"

"That I wouldn't tear it down? That I'd walk away from the job? That I'd try to stop him from carrying through with his plans?"

"Yes."

"No."

"But—"

He exhaled loudly. His eyes turned serious. "I respect Adelina. How can I look in her eyes and lie to her? How can I say I won't do something that I might end up doing?"

"I don't have the answer, but it bothers me."

His gaze softened, and Emily thought she saw a flash of sadness wash over his face.

"I'm sorry. I would never hurt you or even Adelina

purposely, but, Em. Babe. You don't want a boyfriend who lies, do you?"

Boyfriend. The word wrapped around her heart and squeezed. Why was she arguing about this? It wasn't her house. It wasn't her history that might be torn down. And she loved him. She really, really loved him, despite this issue.

"How would you ever know if I was trying to protect you from something or lying for other reasons? How could you ever trust me again?"

"Damn it, Dae." She couldn't even say it with conviction. *I hate it when you're right.*

"I get that you're upset and hurt. Obviously, this is something that means a great deal to Adelina. I saw that the minute she realized the villa was in danger of being torn down. And my client bought that property sight unseen. I can almost guarantee that he has no idea this myth even exists. And I can guarantee that he won't give a shit. He's a mean bastard."

He touched her cheek, and a little more anger slipped away.

"Babe, tell me what you want me to do. If it's reasonable and within my comfort zone, I'll do my best to make it happen." He wrapped his arms around her waist and held her closer.

Emily sighed. "You can't do what I want, so it doesn't matter. You have your career. I just need to get over this."

He touched his forehead to hers. "I wish I could tell you that I would walk away from the property, but I don't know if I will or not. Besides, if I walk away, someone else will come along and tear it down for

Frank, and at least if I do it, I'll know it's done right and it's done safely. I have a lot of thinking and researching to do before I can make any decisions. But if we're going to be a couple, and I sincerely hope we are, then we need to find a middle ground."

An unexpected sarcastic laugh bubbled out of her before she could stop it. "A middle ground between preservation and demolition? Right."

"You're willing to give up that easily?" He drew back and searched her eyes.

"Not on us," she answered quickly.

"This *is* us, babe. It's what we do, and it may not be who we are, but it's part of who we are. So...yes, a middle ground between what you feel and what I feel is right."

Emily wanted to believe him, that they could find this esoteric middle ground. Could they? Or would they always be at opposite ends of the spectrum?

"Emily, I'll never judge you for what you choose to preserve." He took her hands in his as he spoke. "I know that whatever you do, you do for reasons that are right for you and for whoever is impacted by what you're doing. This hang-up over our beliefs, that's your thing. I understand it, but it's not my fight. I accept you for who you are and what you believe."

Oh great, so this is all on me? "So you blame me for this?"

"Blame? No, babe. What's there to blame?"

"That I'm worried about our beliefs being so far off from each other." *How come this doesn't bother you?*

"That's not something to blame you for. I get it, Em. You don't like what I do for a living. You don't like that I take pleasure in demolishing certain things. That's okay. You're allowed to feel that way, but it doesn't have to be something that comes between us."

"How can it not?"

"Easy." He shrugged. "As I said, I'll never judge what you do with your career. As long as you're happy and at peace with your decisions, what right do I have to judge that?"

She shook her head, unable to form a response.

"I have an idea." Dae took her hand and led her into the shed. He turned her in his arms and sealed his lips over hers.

Emily resisted at first. Or at least she tried to, but within seconds her lips opened to him and her tongue slid over his. When they were intimate, everything else fell away. All it took was one brush of his lips and the tension in her body eased, but the intimacy was just a reminder of how much they had together. This was a bump in the road. A big one, but she could focus on finding a middle ground. Couldn't she?

When their mouths parted, he smiled down at her. "I could do that all day."

"Middle ground," she managed.

"Right." He wheeled a bike over to her and then wheeled one out for himself. "I think we should go on our bike tour—including the stop at the property we're talking about—"

"The House of Wishes." She wanted him to recognize it for the myth the property carried, like showing a serial killer that a potential victim was a living, breathing person—hoping it might change the outcome.

"Yes, that one." He smirked. "And we should debate the viability of some of the places we pass along the way. We'll keep a list, and when we come back tonight, we can review the list and see where we stand."

"How can that possibly help?" She pushed her bike out of the shed.

"I think we can learn a lot about each other, and our own thoughts, by writing down why we think things should be demolished or preserved."

She had little faith that this would do more than make their differences very clear. "What if we come back and we're still at a standoff?"

"Then we're no worse off than when we started."

Emily wanted to close her eyes and miraculously transport back to last night, when all that mattered was that they were in each other's arms, making love without any real-world issues sucking up her thoughts. Then again, if she had a time machine, she'd find a way to dial back ten years so she could have that much more time with Dae.

BY THE TIME they left the villa, Emily wasn't quite so mad, and as much as he hoped she understood where he was coming from with regard to Adelina, Dae knew it was still a sore subject. He could only hope that this strategy of his would prove something to them. He'd adapted the idea from something his parents did when he and his siblings were younger. His parents had always encouraged open communication. They felt that opinions were vital to developing a person's sense of self, and because of this, he and his siblings often engaged in heated debates. Colby was a bullheaded aggressor, while Wade was even tempered and happy to state his opinion and ignore everyone else's, which just pissed off Colby even more. Eventually, instead of trying to mediate the arguments, his parents had derived a system. No matter what the debate was about, they'd have each sibling write down five to ten reasons why they believed their opinion was right. More often than not, they found a number of commonalities between the opposing sides. He could only hope that he and Emily would also find similar commonalities.

A middle ground.

Emily's itinerary had included spending the day in the Greve in Chianti. The bike route was scenic and fairly easy without many steep inclines. They'd been cycling for a while and had already stopped twice to make notes on preserving or demolishing houses they'd seen. One looked like an abandoned cottage, and the other was a very large villa in almost pristine condition. He wasn't sure why Emily had chosen that as a property to debate, but hey, she was game, and he wasn't going to knock it.

Dae spotted a field of sunflowers up ahead and sped up so he was riding beside Emily.

"Let's stop up there."

Her cheeks were a soft shade of pink from the sun and from the exertion of riding for so long, but she looked stunning and cute as hell in her bike helmet. Dae was glad to see her smile reached her eyes again. He knew the afternoon was salvaged, and the discomfort from the morning had been set aside until they chose to deal with it again.

They laid their bikes at the edge of the sunflower field and took long swigs from their water bottles.

"This is incredible," Emily said, a little out of breath.

"The sunflowers? I know. Have you ever seen so many in one place?"

"Everything, Dae. The bike ride, the rolling hills and views of the farms and valleys. All the different types of villas and farmhouses. It all looks so different from a bike than it does from the confines of a car. Thank you for convincing me to do this." She leaned over and kissed him.

"If it earns me kisses, I can think of many things I'd like to convince you to do." He raised his brows and she swatted his arm. "I'm kidding. You weren't hard to convince. You never fought me on the idea."

"Not aloud, anyway," she admitted.

He pulled his phone from the pocket of his shorts and smushed his cheek to hers. "Smile pretty, Emmie." Dae had faith that they'd figure out this blip on their radar screen, and even if it was more than a blip, Emily was worth fighting for.

She made a face, and as he clicked the photo, he kissed her cheek.

"That's a keeper." He laughed. "Look at that tree up on the ridge. The tallest one, standing sentinel over the patch."

She wrinkled her nose at him, then turned to look over the sunflowers. They were almost as tall as she was, and the look of wonder in Emily's eyes was something he never wanted to forget. He took a few pictures of Emily while she was mesmerized and unaware of his trigger-happy finger. He loved to look at her, and he knew that once he left Italy, those pictures would have to hold him over.

"It's amazing. Do you know how much I would have missed if we'd driven?"

"Yes, and if we have it my way and we stay together…" He paused, hating the way *if* tasted. "Then I'll make sure you never miss a thing again."

She wrapped her arms around his waist and hugged him. "I think I've needed you in my life for a very long time."

"Me too, baby. Me too. It's not the things that slap us in the face that are the most impressive. It's the things that we have to look a little harder to find. Look down." Dae slipped his phone back into his pocket and folded her into his arms, reveling in the comfort of knowing she felt the same way he did.

"What do you see?"

"Our feet."

He kissed her forehead. "Okay, now let's pretend you're in a really gorgeous field of sunflowers and you're not looking at our feet but you're looking for something smaller." He paused long enough for her eyes to shift away from their feet.

"Tiny white flowers?"

"The truth of beauty is in the smaller things. The things most people never see."

"I notice things," she said sweetly.

"You sure do. But your mind is always working, worrying about what's next or how pieces fit together. It's one of the things about you that fascinates me. But

I hope that one day you'll allow yourself to really relax and realize that the rest of the world can wait while you enjoy the subtler, silent things in life."

She rested her forehead on his chest. "Okay. You got me. I'm a little neurotic about getting things done."

"There's nothing wrong with that, but while you're getting things done, you might be missing the smaller things that aren't squeaking so loudly."

He kissed her again and spoke just above a whisper. "Do you know how much I'm going to miss you when I leave?"

She buried her face in his neck and groaned. "Do you have to remind me? I'm pretending that you're not leaving. Just for now. I don't want to think about waking up without you."

"Oh, you like that, do you?" He nibbled on her ear, earning him an adorable giggle that made his chest constrict in a way that was becoming familiar.

"I like it more than I should after such a short time. I think my brothers would have my head on a platter—or yours—for us getting so close so fast! And their girlfriends would be celebrating that I'm so happy. There's a *thick,* dark line between male and female reactions."

"Oh, come on. Your brothers would be happy for you if you're happy. I know I was for my sister Leanna when she found Kurt." He took off his helmet and ran his hand through his hair. It felt good to get out and exercise. Walking around and sightseeing was one thing, but it couldn't compete with the daily rigorous workouts he usually put himself through. But just like Emily needing a break from her work, he, too, needed a reprieve from his normal schedule. And even if he didn't, he'd give up his workouts to spend time with Emily.

"Honestly, I have no idea how they'll react. They've never really seen me in a serious relationship. I think they'll be happy for me, but I do think they'll scrutinize the heck out of you." She laughed a little, and her whole face brightened. "They won't make it easy for you. That much I know."

He kissed the corners of her mouth. "Well, whatever they want to do is fine by me. I still want to meet them. I wasn't kidding about coming out to see you."

"And I wasn't kidding about you picking me up from the airport." She reached into the backpack Dae had tied to the back of his bike and withdrew the two small memo pads and pens they'd been using for their *preserve or demolish* lists.

"Sunflower meadow. Demolish or preserve?" She handed him a notebook and pen.

"That's not even a question." He swatted her butt, earning him another flirty smile.

"It is a question. You like to demolish things. Can you demolish something as gorgeous as this without hesitation?" She tapped her pen on the seat of her bike.

"I see where this is going. Okay, write down your thoughts, missy. I'll pick the next stop."

"Impossible." Emily shook her head.

He pressed his cheek to hers and whispered, "Three times in the last twenty-four hours, Miss Please More Harder, proves I'm a sure thing." He felt her cheek heat up against his and took her in a greedy kiss without giving her time to respond—though he knew she couldn't by the way her jaw had gone slack and her eyes had filled with a mixture of embarrassment and lust. And now, just as he'd hoped, she was kissing him back with as much passion as she had earlier that morning. It took all of his concentration to stop kissing her when a car horn sounded. They both laughed as they mounted their bikes.

Dae had mapped out a stop at Strada and another visit at a vineyard near Chianti, but the sky was beginning to turn gray, and they opted to ride past the colorful buildings of Strada and the thick rows of the vineyard straight into Greve in Chianti instead. As they approached Greve, traffic thickened. They weaved their way toward Piazza Matteotti, the main piazza in Greve, and were surprised to find a small festival in full swing. The triangular piazza was lined with a number of colorful aged medieval buildings in vibrant shades of yellow and muted creams. In front of each building was an arched stone entranceway to the shop below, and above each archway, terraces were decorated with bountiful plants. Vines and blooms in various shades of red, yellow, purple, and white spilled over the iron railings. In the center of the crowded piazza was an impressive statue of the Florentine explorer Giovanni da Verrazzano, and a handful of tented booths lined the square.

They locked up their bicycles and walked hand in hand toward the booths. Dae wondered if the euphoria that was sweeping through him was caused by the commotion of the crowd, the beauty of the piazza, or the woman he was falling in love with.

"We're so lucky to stumble across this," Emily exclaimed. "Listen to that music." She inhaled and closed her eyes.

It's you. It's definitely you.

"And that aroma is insane. Everything smells so...Italian."

"It smells almost as amazing as you do." Dae draped an arm around her and kissed her temple.

"I didn't see a festival in the brochures. Did you know about this?" she asked.

"No, but I'm glad we stumbled upon it." He led her beneath a tent, where a woman was selling handmade baskets. "Excuse me, is this an annual arts festival?"

"The annual music and wine festival is in September. This was an impromptu festival that was put together a few weeks ago. To be honest," the woman explained, "I can't even tell you why it was thrown together, but I'm glad it was. I'm visiting my aunt, and these baskets are her handiwork. I would have never gotten to experience any of this if they hadn't put it together. I'm leaving tomorrow to return to California."

They talked with her for a few minutes before making their way through the other booths. They were offered bread with thick olive oil at one of the booths, which they gladly devoured, both famished after their rigorous trek. The elderly Italian couple at the next booth offered them tastes of wine from a local winery. Dae could watch Emily for hours as she *ooh*ed and *ahh*ed over fine artistry and furniture made from olive wood. He was able to purchase a scarf she had been admiring in the next booth without her noticing. He tucked it into the backpack and circled her waist with his hands. He loved the way she snuggled in close and pressed her hand to his side when she wanted to show him something. Hell, he was beginning to realize that he loved everything about her, even her struggle to accept the possibility that the House of Wishes might come down. She was stronger than any woman he knew and was not afraid to speak her mind. He admired that, and so many other things about her, that he was already letting his mind fast-forward to a few months from now, to Thanksgiving and Christmas. He'd love to bring her back here again, when they were firmly entrenched in coupledom, without his leaving looming over their heads.

They had lunch on the patio of a restaurant at the piazza, where they could people watch as they ate. It was customary to eat the largest meal of the day at lunch, and after eating mozzarella, tomato, and fresh basil, all of which tasted heavenly, they shared a plate of tortellini that melted in Dae's mouth. From the moans of appreciation coming from Emily, he knew she was just as delighted with the delectable assault on her senses as he was.

After they ate, an attractive brunette waitress offered them tiramisu and coffee.

"I'm too full to move, thank you." Emily patted her stomach.

The waitress's eyes lingered on Dae, pushing past politeness to uncomfortable. Dae set his eyes on Emily and reached across the table for her hand.

"Just the check, please," he said without taking his

eyes off of Emily. Dae was used to attention from women, and he took it in stride. Until now. He didn't want Emily to feel the least bit threatened by any other woman. *Ever*. She made him feel things he'd never imagined he would, and he'd never met anyone with the ability to slay him with a glance, or a whisper, or a touch, the way Emily could. He was beginning to understand how Leanna had felt when she'd fallen for Kurt so quickly. And like his sister, he wasn't going to let anything get in the way of the feelings that were becoming more intense with every second they were together.

"I guess I should get used to that, huh?" She bit her lower lip.

He debated playing it off like he had no idea what she was talking about and quickly decided against it. *Head-on*. That was the only way to handle things. The next two days would go by in the blink of an eye, and by the time he left, he wanted no question in Emily's mind about how he felt about her.

"What you need to get used to is knowing, and trusting, that it won't matter who looks at me. I only have eyes for you." He brought her hand to his lips and kissed it, holding her eyes with a steady gaze that he hoped translated how deep his feelings were taking root. "Never doubt that as long as we're a couple, whether you're with me or if you're a million miles away, there's not another woman on the planet who could draw my eyes, much less my heart, away from you."

"Oh, Dae." His name came out as one long breath.

He shook his head and leaned across the table.

"Now that I know what your other *O*s feel like, when I hear you say it, my body remembers, too."

She flushed, and he kissed her softly on the lips.

"I know it's a lot to take in after knowing me such a short time, but, Em, it's how I feel. And when I leave on Thursday, I want you to know, without a shadow of a doubt, exactly where I stand."

EMILY COULDN'T BEGIN to form a response to Dae professing his feelings for her. She was sure her heart had swelled so large it would burst. He'd said everything she could hope to hear, but she was afraid to reciprocate. Wouldn't it just make it that much harder when they both realized that they might never find a middle ground? Would he ever see her side or understand her love of preserving culture and history—even if some of that culture and history was intangible? Or was she just being stupid to worry and think about this stuff at all? Was this what relationships and love were really like? Did people pretend their way through life, giving in when they didn't really want to, accepting each other regardless of their own beliefs?

How would she ever know for sure?

She needed to talk to someone, but over the past year she'd become closest with her brothers' girlfriends, and they weren't going to tell her those things. Not when she was loyal to her brothers and there was a chance it would get back to them. Family always came first. And yes, when she was with Dae, he was first. Above family. Above her brothers when they texted her. Her priorities had shifted so fast and without any warning. She never knew the heart was so powerful, so all important.

"Babe?"

One look at Dae and she understood, could feel the difference from her scalp to her toes and everywhere in between. He was her priority. She blinked past her confusion, bringing Dae's handsome, concerned face back into focus.

"I'm sorry. I spaced out a little."

Dae paid the bill and took Emily's hand as they walked back into the crowd. He didn't push her for a response after laying his heart out on the line, and she knew that had to be killing him. But she was afraid that the minute she started to explain—again—what she was feeling, sadness would hit her and tears would rob her of her voice. They made their way to the statue in the center of the square, and while Dae read the plaque, Emily tried to sift through the roller coaster of emotions that were confusing her to no end. She knew what she felt for Dae. She should tell him that, at least. He deserved to know that he'd opened her heart in a way that no man ever had, and that whether they were together or apart, she thought about him every second. He deserved to know that when they made love, her world came together in a blissful state she never wanted to leave.

He deserves to be with someone who doesn't think that blowing up the House of Wishes is one of the worst offenses he could commit. The thought made her throat close up.

"You had the museums on your list. Do you want to head over that way?"

She met his warm, loving gaze. She expected to hear a grating in his voice over her lack of response, or to see a lessening of emotion in his eyes. She didn't expect him to simply accept her for who she was and for what she had to offer at this very second, which wasn't much more than silence. Guilt settled around her as heavily as the gray clouds that were moving across the sky.

She stepped in closer and pressed her cheek to his chest, taking comfort in how naturally, and willingly, he folded her into his arms. His heart beat strong and sure beneath her cheek.

I love you, Dae. I love the way you treat me. I love how thoughtful you are and how you're eager to do the right thing. I don't care that it's fast or that we're both thousands of miles away from anything familiar. This. You. Me. It feels right. This feels real. And I never want it to end.

He kissed the top of her head, and she knew that she didn't have to say any of the things she was thinking. Somehow, he knew.

The good. The bad. And the conflicted.

Chapter Twelve

THEY FOLLOWED THE Chiantigiana Road back the way they'd come. The blue sky that had smiled down on them on their way to Greve had clouded over during the long afternoon. The wind had picked up, and Dae worried about Emily getting caught in the rain. Her sheer top and shorts weren't exactly rainproof, and he didn't want her biking on slippery roads. He hadn't even thought to bring a slicker in case the weather changed. Damn. And he thought he'd been so prepared. He cocked his head to the side and shifted his eyes up to the ominous gray above, which was darkening by the second.

He flagged Emily over to the side of the road.

"Is something wrong?" Her skin glistened with the sheen of her exertion.

"It looks like the rain is moving in fast." He spoke loudly so she could hear him over the wind. "We should find a place to get you under cover."

"*Pfft.*" She waved her hand. "What's a little rain?

I'll be fine. I really want to make it to the House of Wishes. It's not that far from here."

He glanced up the hillside at a weathered farmhouse. Maybe they should consider finding shelter until after the storm. "Em, I'm not sure I want you on the roads when it's wet and windy. It's dangerous."

"You worry too much, and you sound like my brothers. I'm fine."

"See the farmhouse up there?"

She nodded, brows drawn together.

"See the barn off to the right?"

"Yeah. It looks like it's ready to fall down."

"Preserve or demolish?" He grinned, knowing this was the last thing she'd expect—and he'd put his money on her tearing down the lopsided structure, which had a roof that dipped by at least thirty degrees on one side and walls that sagged like skin on a shriveled old woman.

She rolled her eyes. "Really?" A gust of wind howled over the meadow. "In this wind, with the rain about to pour down on us, you want me to assess a barn?"

He didn't say a word, just raised his brows as he dug out the memo pads and handed her one. She scribbled fast, her face pinched in irritation. She shoved the pad back into the pack, and he glanced up at the farmhouse again, hoping that standing in the path of the gusty wind might soften her resolve.

"Em—"

"Don't even say it. I'm not going to ask some stranger if I can sit out a little rain in their house.

Besides, aren't you the one who said life's too short to miss out on anything?"

She climbed on her bike, and he had no choice but to admire her determination. And her hot little body as she sped away.

The clouds darkened even more as they neared the House of Wishes. When the first droplets of rain dotted Dae's skin, he glanced up at Emily. She was pedaling fast and hard. He couldn't help but be impressed. She was fiercely determined in everything she did. It was no wonder she was having such a difficult time with what he did for a living. She was probably used to reasoning her way through with clients—and winning. He had to wonder if she'd be as disturbed by his love of things that go boom if the latest object of his demolition skills weren't the House of Wishes. She was an intelligent, reasonable woman. She was an architect. Surely she knew that certain structures were dangerous if not torn down. He thought back to the things she'd said about preserving culture, family, and things that weren't tangible, like myths and legends. She had a heart as big as the moon, and he couldn't really fault her for that. He only wished he knew how to get that heart of hers to be more accepting of his ability to make the right decision.

As the villa came into focus just over the ridge, the clouds opened up, sending a torrent of rain like a wall of water down upon them. The wind howled across the fields, picking up speed with the hammering rain. Dae barely had time to think as he pedaled faster to reach Emily. Her foot slipped from the pedal, and her bike keeled to the left. He pedaled faster, coming up behind her as she skidded over a rut in the road. As if in slow motion, Emily's front tire stopped and the rear of her bike lifted off the ground and jerked to the side, sending her flying over the handlebars.

Dae jumped from his still-moving bike. "Emily!" His voice was drowned out by the storm. His heart shattered in his chest as she landed on the grass in a heap.

"Em!" He hovered over her, trying his best to shield her from the pummeling rain, which now felt like a smattering of bullets against his skin. Mud streaked her cheeks, forehead, and hair. He ran his hands down her arms and legs, feeling for broken bones. *No breaks. Thank goodness.* Her pain-filled eyes opened, tears mingling with the rain and mud covering her face.

"Emily. Baby, are you okay? Where do you hurt?" He wiped her tears with the pad of his thumb, but the rain just slicked her skin again. Her body trembled and shook as he shifted his body to try to cover her head to toe from the rain. "Can you move your arms and legs? I don't want to pick you up if something's broken."

"I..." She wiggled her fingers, then shifted her legs. "Damn, that hurts."

"Where?" His heart slammed against his chest. He knew he shouldn't have let her ride. He was supposed to protect her, not let her determination sway him.

"Everywhere. My shoulder and hip are sore from landing on them, but I think I'm okay—just shaken up." She rolled onto her back and blinked at the tears in her eyes. The side of her cheek was laced with scratches and pitted with pebbles. She pushed up onto her elbow.

"Don't get up. I'll carry you to the house. It's not far." He brushed the loose pebbles from her cheek and took off her helmet, then removed his own and tossed them aside.

"Carry me?" She pushed up to a sitting position. "I'm okay, Dae. I might be sore as heck tomorrow, but I can walk."

"Like hell you will. I'm not taking any more chances."

She slid her knee up so her foot was flat on the ground and gasped a sharp breath.

"Ankle?" He slid his hand down over the bones, again feeling nothing broken.

"It's okay. Just twisted or something." She tried to flatten her foot again and cried out in pain.

Dae didn't hesitate. He scooped her into his arms and held her shivering body against his chest. Her skin was ice cold. His only thoughts were to protect her from the driving rain, check out her injuries, and get her inside. He imagined that, like with everything else Emily did, she'd try to muster through the pain, wanting to be strong and needing to feel like she was in control. He knew her well enough to see that although she loved the way her brothers protected her, she was driven by a daily need to prove she was just as strong and successful as they were. When she rested her head against his chest and closed her eyes, he felt a wave of gratitude roll through him. He knelt with her in his arms and unhooked the backpack from its tether to the forgotten bike. He tugged his bike off the road. He'd come back later to retrieve it. Right now he had to get Emily out of the rain. He hooked the pack over his shoulder, shifted Emily in his strong arms, and with her nestled firmly against him, rose to his feet and crossed the field toward the property that had stolen a part of Emily's heart, which he hoped to reclaim, or at least share.

DAE'S BODY WAS warm despite being drenched. Emily bumped against his muscular chest with every determined step as he trudged up the driveway toward the front door of the property. She clung to his soaking-wet T-shirt, feeling stupid for having fallen off her bike in the first place. She should have been watching the road. If she had, she could have avoided the rut in the road, but she'd been lost in thoughts of Dae. When he'd asked her about the dilapidated barn, her mind had traveled down a naughty path. She'd had thoughts of what it would be like to be stuck in that falling-down building with Dae, with no way to reach anyone outside of the barn walls. Just the two of them relying on each other for warmth and safety. With no outside influences vying for their attention. Oh, the sinful thoughts that sifted through her mind. The idea was ludicrous. They both had cell phones, and there was a farmhouse just across the field, but still, a girl could dream.

Oh no. Am I a self-fulfilled prophecy? Did I cause this?

Now I'm really being stupid.

She wrapped her arms around Dae's neck and felt his grip tighten around her as he mounted the stairs to the porch and carried her out of the rain.

"Did I hurt you? Your whole body just tensed up."

You noticed? "No, it's just the cold."

"I'm sorry, babe. I've got a key. We'll be inside soon." He pulled off his pack and knelt again, cradling Emily against him.

"You have a key?" Even through the shivering cold and shock of falling from her bike, she was excited to be able to see the inside of the House of Wishes. She wondered if it would feel like a magical place that made wishes come true.

"Of course. The assessment is more than just taking in the exterior." He fished around in the backpack for the keys as thunder rumbled overhead. She startled, and he stopped fishing for the keys and wrapped his arms tightly around her.

"I've got you, babe. Sounds like we're in for a worse storm than we'd anticipated."

"Then it's a good thing I fell."

He narrowed his eyes.

"Otherwise we'd still be riding in the rain. We're a good distance from Adelina's, remember?"

He kissed her forehead as he withdrew the keys. "Yes, I remember. How's your ankle?"

She wiggled her foot. It didn't hurt too badly, just a little shock of pain, like when she'd twisted her ankle as a kid. "Twingy."

"Twingy. Even injured you're cute as hell." He rose to his feet and unlocked the door. "Let's get your twingy ankle inside and see how bad off it really is." He had to jiggle the key a few times, but eventually the heavy wooden door creaked open. Dae carried her into a stone foyer that must have been twenty feet deep and only about half as wide. The dampness didn't just follow them in; it greeted them front and center, surrounding them with a moist, cold feeling. Definitely not the magical feel Emily had imagined. A small puddle formed at Dae's feet and trickled along the crevices of intricately laid mosaic tiles beneath his drenched sneakers. Thick stone walls rose to an arched ceiling, and two archways led into other rooms off to the right. A wide staircase curved toward the second floor and took up nearly the entire back wall of the foyer. The door blew further open with a blast of wind as thunder cracked across the sky. Dae tightened his grip on her again and used his shoulder to push the door closed, then tried the light switch.

"Electricity's off. That means the water's off, too."

"At least we're dry. You can put me down. You've carried me a long way, and I'm sure I'm heavy." Emily wasn't overweight, but she didn't want him to feel as though he *had* to take care of her. She had spent her life proving how strong and self-sufficient she was. It took a little getting used to for her to allow herself to be cared for in this way.

His eyes met hers with a look that told her he'd make the decision as to when he'd set her down. And the way he clenched his jaw told her that the decision was not negotiable.

She shifted her eyes away before she barked out that she was fine and could walk by herself. Or hobble, maybe. *Hop?* She had to remind herself that Dae wasn't one of her brothers mollycoddling her, and although she hated feeling like a damsel in distress, she was enjoying being in his strong arms. She allowed herself to lean against him and accept the comfort he offered.

"Look at this place. This type of high-arched stone ceiling isn't very common. It's reminiscent of a thirteenth-century building, and I'd guess this one to be nineteenth century, or maybe even a little later."

He smiled down at her. "You're sexy as hell when you go all architectural girl on me. We're in the twenty-first century now, so let's see if they have someplace comfortable and dry from this era where you can relax and get warm."

She rolled her eyes. "Isn't this the least bit impressive to you?" How could he not be enamored with the design of the house? He didn't have to be an architect to appreciate a beautiful structure. Or did he overlook those things altogether? *No*, she reminded herself. He'd been the one to guide her to the house in the first place. He must have been taken with its beauty.

"You're impressive to me. This place will be more impressive when you're warm and dry and I know your ankle is okay." He walked through the first archway and stopped at the sight of an enormous empty room. Cracks snaked up the stucco walls. The tile floors were laid unevenly and a bit cockeyed. For some reason, that appealed to Emily. Outside, rain thrashed against the large windows that faced the front yard. Thunder boomed, and lightning flashed menacingly in the darkness.

"I don't know why I thought the house might have furniture." His jaw clenched and unclenched.

"Where's the tree?" She'd thought they'd be able to see it from this room. The tree had seemed so large, but maybe she'd misjudged the depth of it. "I want to see the tree from the inside of the house." She heard her voice tremble, and Dae's eyes turned serious. The pelting of rain on the windows sounded like BBs hitting in rapid fire. She tightened her grip on his arm.

"Don't worry, babe. We're safe." He looked around the room. "Huh. Where is that damn tree?" Dae turned with her still in his arms and returned to the foyer.

Now she felt a little silly. She wasn't afraid of thunderstorms. Why was she shaking and clinging to him?

"Dae, really, put me down. I can hobble beside you." Her tone was so soft that she wasn't convinced she meant it.

He ignored the request and went through another arched doorway.

"I like carrying you. And your teeth are chattering."

Are they? Damn, they were.

Dae carried her into a large modern kitchen with dark wooden cabinets, terra-cotta floors, and a substantial marble-topped island. An iron pot rack hung from dark exposed beams in the ceiling. There was a large table with three wooden chairs on the far side of the room. The chairs matched the one she'd seen in the portico off the side of the house.

Her eyes slid around the room. Emily wanted to see the tree, and to see the tree, they had to find the rear wall of the house. The anticipation was killing her. As an architect, she wanted to see the internal structure of the obscurity. As a woman, she wanted to see the tree that gave life to wishes.

"Dae. There." She pointed to a door in the corner of the room. He carried her over and opened the door with ease. Even after carrying her through the rain, his clothing drenched, his shoes sloshing across the tile floors, he didn't seem to be straining under her weight.

The door led to a narrow stucco hallway. There was another door to their right.

"Third time's a charm, right?" He turned the knob and pushed the door open.

"Holy crap," Emily said. "Wow. Go, go, go." She leaned forward, excited by the sight of the massive tree that invaded the back wall of the house. She should have been prepared for how spectacular the image was, but how could anyone be prepared for something that was structurally impossible? She glanced at Dae and realized that she'd also thought he was an impossibility in her life. Not him specifically, but finding a man whom she would never be able to imagine a life without. And yet here he was.

She shifted her eyes back to the tree. Its magnificence rivaled that of the myth it bore. Emily knew she'd never understand the anomaly before her, and maybe she didn't need to. She stole another glance at Dae. Maybe she didn't need to fully understand everything about Dae either.

"This must be the original structure, and then maybe they added the wall separating the original side of the house from later renovations instead of tearing down the tree." She took in the expansive furnished room. It hummed with energy.

"Feel that?" she whispered.

His only answer was a kiss to her trembling lips.

"Red velvet. Now, that's the type of couch I was hoping for." His eyes darted around the room as he knelt beside the couch. "Come on, baby. Let's get you comfy." He balanced Emily on his knee while he brushed dust from the velvet cushions. He eyed two chairs at the far end of the room and a fancy wooden trunk tucked beneath the window.

She watched him silently assessing every inch of the room. She'd never felt safer. Her brothers would look after her in this way, but somehow it felt different with Dae. There was a certain sibling obligation with her brothers that was always present, but with Dae the caring went deeper and was without blood-born obligation.

"You make a great hero, you know that?" She leaned forward and kissed his scruffy cheek.

"Hero?" He laughed, and it vibrated right through him. A deep, alluring sound that Emily wanted to hear every day of her life.

"Yeah. As much as I hate the notion, I'm the damsel in distress and you're the hero."

He laid her on the luxurious couch. "Babe, you could never be a damsel in distress. I have a feeling that left to your own devices, you'd have not only gotten to this villa, but you'd have dragged the bikes right along with you."

She wasn't sure if that was a compliment or if it annoyed him that she was so self-sufficient.

"You've gone quiet on me. Are you okay?" he asked.

He really did notice every breath she took. "Yeah. Do you think I'm not feminine? Am I too—"

"Baby, you're covered in mud, you've got pebbles lodged in your cheek and a twisted ankle, and you're worried about being feminine?" He sealed his lips over hers in a tender kiss. As he drew back, he caressed the side of her face that wasn't scratched. "Not only are you the sexiest, most feminine woman I know, but your strength is part of your appeal. The reason you're not a damsel in distress is that you are the perfect combination of intelligence, femininity, and determination. I wouldn't change a thing."

He kissed her again, and she warmed all over at his loving words. How did he always know just what to say and do? *You wouldn't change a thing*. And there she was having trouble accepting his career.

He pulled his wet shirt over his head and draped it over the edge of the couch. Emily's mouth went dry. Would she ever get used to seeing his incredible body?

He knelt beside her again and ran his hand down her side. "Lean forward, and I'll help you take your shirt off."

"Um..." Despite her injury and the mud soaking her hair and clothing, despite the cold and the unfamiliar surroundings, she was getting turned on.

He laughed. "I'm not a pig, Em. I'm not going to take advantage of you while you're lying here muddy and scratched up with a hurt ankle. I just want to get your wet shirt off so your skin can dry and you can warm up."

She leaned forward, and he gently took off her shirt. He pressed his cheek to hers and whispered, "I'd like to say that I won't look, but I'd be lying." He kissed her neck, then slid his hand down her leg to her ankle. In a flash, the desire in his eyes turned to compassion.

"I'm so sorry that you got hurt." He kissed her shoulder, and the tender touch spiked a dash of pain.

Emily tried not to flinch.

"Hurts?" His eyes were so serious she knew she couldn't lie.

"Just a tiny bit."

"Baby, I wish you hadn't fallen." He kissed the spot below where he'd touched her shoulder.

"It's my own fault. I wasn't looking at the road." She realized that she wasn't embarrassed sitting there in her bra and shorts in front of Dae. She'd never been comfortable naked in front of any of the three men she'd been intimate with. She'd always felt as if she were being compared to other women or looked over altogether like she was a means to an end. She was barely comfortable unclothed in front of women. This was new and unfamiliar territory. Dae looked at her like she was the only thing on his mind, and not in a sexual way, but in an I'm-going-to-make-sure-you're-safe-and-happy-forever kind of way, and she liked that more than anything. He loved her. She knew this deep in her core. She never even knew she was capable of knowing such a thing. Who knew feelings this big existed except in dreams? Then again, everything about being with Dae was new and unfamiliar. The safety and love he lavished on her was more powerful and ran deeper than a family member or friend could ever provide. She trusted him, and as she watched him, she knew she was truly in love with him. Despite her misgivings about their differences.

He unlaced her sneakers and carefully removed them.

"It's not your fault. It just happened. Let's see how badly you're hurt, and then I'll go see if I can rustle up some water to clean you up." His fingers hovered over her ankle. "Can I touch it?"

She nodded and clenched her jaw just in case it hurt.

"I'll be gentle. I promise." He wrapped his fingers around her ankle and applied a little pressure. "Does that hurt?"

She shook her head. "I think it's only when I flex it."

"Okay, let's just be sure." He cupped her heel in one hand and gently squeezed her foot, keeping his eyes trained on hers as he moved up toward her ankle, applying pressure every few centimeters and then above her ankle as well. "You're holding your breath. Does it hurt?"

"No. I just wasn't sure if it would." She held on to his biceps. "Go ahead. You can flex it."

He nodded. She felt his muscles harden beneath her palm and knew he was worried about hurting her. He flexed her foot, and she flinched. The thought of the pain was worse than the twinge she felt, but the concern in Dae's eyes might have helped soften that a little.

"How bad?"

"Not bad."

He turned her foot out a little, and she flinched again and sucked in air between her teeth. *Okay. That smarted.*

He frowned. "It's pretty bad. And don't even try to tell me it's not."

Emily opened her mouth to dispute him, but his piercing stare shut her down, and in truth, it hurt just enough that she knew she shouldn't deny it. Not even to keep him from worrying.

"I think you probably strained a ligament. You need to ice it and take some ibuprofen."

"Ice it? There's no electricity, which means no ice."

"Luckily, your overprepared boyfriend has just the thing." He grabbed the pack and rummaged through it. "Ibuprofen."

"I like it when you say you're my boyfriend. It's been a long time since I've had a real boyfriend."

He caressed her cheek and softened his tone. "I say it a lot so I can hear it, too. I can hardly believe I'm the lucky guy who gets to call himself your boyfriend."

"Dae." He was the lucky one? She'd point out that it was she who felt like she'd fallen from the plane and landed in a four-leaf-clover patch, but he was back in caregiver mode and handing her two pills and a water bottle.

"Swallow 'em down, babe."

"I'll never tease you again." She tossed the tablets in her mouth and took a gulp of water.

"What fun would that be?" He pulled out a light blue bag from the backpack and began kneading it. He folded it and prodded it with his thumbs, then held it out toward Emily. "Ice for my favorite girl."

She touched the cold bag.

"Chemicals are awesome, aren't they?" His lips

spread in a wide smile. "Ready for the cold?"

"I guess." She loved how he kept his eyes on hers while he placed the bag on her ankle.

"Okay?"

"Yeah. It's cold, but fine."

"Here, hold this, and I'll clean you up."

She held it to her ankle as he rummaged through his first-aid kit again and withdrew a roll of gauze. He poured water on the gauze, then tucked her wet hair behind her ears and drew his brows together as he gently cleansed her face. She imagined she looked like a drowned rat, with her hair plastered to her head and her cheeks and nose pink with cold, and she was glad she couldn't see herself.

"I wish I had a dry blanket to wrap you in. Once we get you cleaned up, I'll see about finding something to warm you up."

"I'm okay." She might be wet and cold, but she had never felt more *okay* in all her life.

"You're always okay, but that doesn't mean you're really okay."

She noticed that his eyes narrowed as he moved to her other cheek. "What?"

"You have scratches, and there are two pebbles embedded in your cheek. I can get them out, but I don't want to hurt you, so can you lay your head back and just close your eyes?"

Embedded? She envisioned rocks the size of M&M's stuck in bloody craters in her cheek and reached a shaky hand up to feel them. Dae took her hand in his and eased her onto her back.

"It's not nearly as bad as I said. Maybe stuck is a

better word than embedded. I didn't mean to scare you." He settled the ice pack on her ankle so she didn't need to hold it.

Stuck. Stuck is better than embedded, right? Would she be permanently scarred? Would he care if she was? Would she? Scars weren't the end of the world. *Perspective, Emily. You're fine.* She wasn't fine. She was scared shitless.

He must have noticed the fear she felt creeping through her body, because he stayed there, chest to chest, his hands holding her shoulders, his confident, loving eyes gazing down at her.

"It's okay. They're tiny, and I promise I'll be gentle."

She nodded, breathed deeply, and closed her eyes. She was so scared she wanted to cry, but she felt the press of his lips to hers and felt his hands cup the sides of her head, and it eased that urge away.

"I'm sorry, baby," he whispered. "I wish it were me who fell."

She clung to his arms as he gently wiped her injured cheek, thankful she was in his caring, trusted hands.

"Tell me if I'm using too much pressure."

Every muscle in her body tightened with fear. "Okay." Her voice was shaky.

He touched his forehead to hers. "Open your eyes, Em."

She did.

"I won't hurt you, okay? You don't need to be scared. This is nothing. It will hurt way less than when you landed on the ground. Okay?"

She nodded.

"Okay, I'm going to use my fingernails to get these out since I don't have tweezers." Thunder crashed overhead, and the whole room felt as though it shook. Lightning lit up the room. "I don't want to wait until we get back to Adelina's to clean these out, and I don't want to ask Marcello to come out in this storm to get us. It's too dangerous." He grabbed his wet shirt and bundled it into a ball on the floor. Then he washed his fingertips using water from the bottle and hovered over her again. "Close your eyes again."

He didn't have to ask twice. She slammed them shut.

"Okay, a little pressure."

She felt a little scratch just below her cheekbone.

"There, got one. Not so bad, right?"

She couldn't have answered if she tried. Worry over how much it was going to hurt kept her focused on keeping her eyes shut and clinging to his arms like she was slipping from a raft in a whirlpool.

"Okay, done."

Her eyes flew open. "Done?"

"Yeah. Breathe, baby. Breathe." He dug back into his first-aid kit and withdrew a small vial and a tube of Neosporin.

"Is there anything you *don't* keep in there?"

"Unfortunately, yes. Condoms."

She felt her body flush head to toe. "Oh."

"Not helping," he said with a teasing smile. "Since meeting you, I keep those in my wallet." He held up the bottle. "This is hydrogen peroxide."

He used another piece of gauze to clean out the

cut with the peroxide, and then he cleansed the rest of the scratches, which stung but didn't hurt. He applied Neosporin to the cuts and then sat back on his heels and let out a long breath.

"That's better." He ran his hand through his hair, which was beginning to dry on the fringes. "How's your ankle?"

"Fine. Cold."

"You really need to leave the ice on for another few minutes. It will help keep the swelling down." He glanced behind him at the tree. "How does this myth work, anyway? I think it's time to put it to the test."

"I'm not sure, but I've been putting the pieces together in my mind. I think you're supposed to write down your wish, or pick something that symbolizes it, and put it in the tree."

Without a word he grabbed the notebooks from the backpack and handed one, with a pen, to Emily. "Write your wish, baby."

Before meeting Dae, this would have been her chance to wish for what she'd been telling everyone she wanted for months. This would have been her chance to wish for being swept away in love, cherished and adored. Her chance to ask for love so the green-eyed monster didn't claw at her every time she saw people snuggling together, sharing secrets and touching each other in that way that only lovers could. She'd spent months dreaming of being loved and loving someone so much that everything else came second, and she'd already found that and more with Dae.

She watched him scribbling his wish in the

notebook and the realization that she'd already found love brought a smile to her lips. Her heart was full to the brim, caressed with every glance, every touch. It was just her head that was playing tricks on her.

"Do you think I can make two wishes?"

She laughed. "I have no idea. Maybe?" *Two wishes?* What was he wishing for?

He nodded and scribbled something else on another piece of paper, then tore them free from the pad and folded them into small squares. He ran his hand through his hair and shrugged as he rose to his feet.

"Here goes."

He circled the tree, bare from the waist up but still wearing his wet shorts and shoes. His knees and shins were caked with mud. He'd taken perfect care of Emily and had forgotten to care for himself. It seemed impossible to her that someone would do all those things for her, or that she'd let him. It seemed everything Dae did reinforced how narrow her vision of herself had been before meeting him. She was growing as much as their relationship was.

"This still seems really strange to me," he said. "You know the roots have to snake under the house. How does that work?"

"I've seen houses that have been built around trees, but not with the trees engulfing the actual walls of the house." Emily sat up against the arm of the couch. "And the houses that have a tree growing up the center typically have to be built with a clearance around the tree and above the root system to allow for growth. But I've never seen anything like this."

"Okay, well, here go my wishes." He chose a hole to tuck his wishes into, then pushed them inside. "We'll see what happens."

Thunder roared through the sky. A flash of lightning lit up the room, startling Emily.

"I guess Mother Nature didn't like my wishes." Dae lowered himself beside her and folded her into his arms.

Emily stared at the memo pad. She wasn't sure what to wish for. Should she wish for the ability to find a middle ground with Dae? Or that he wouldn't lose interest in her when he went home and they were thousands of miles apart? Or maybe she should wish that her ankle would get better, or for Serafina's husband's safe return? That was surely more important than anything else. Everything other than Serafina's husband's safe return seemed enormously selfish.

"What am I seeing? Pain or conflict?" Dae asked.

"Conflict." *It's like you're so in tune with me, you can read my mind.*

"Thank goodness. *That* I might be able to help resolve."

"I'm just not sure what to wish for."

"Well, you said matters of the heart, and you already have me if you want me, so what else does your heart want?"

"*If* I want you?"

"I'm confident in my feelings for you, but you, on the other hand, have gone all covert on me."

She loved that he noticed every little thing about her. It was one of the amazing things about him that kept surprising her, but at that moment, with her conflicting thoughts, she kind of wished he hadn't noticed.

"What did you wish for?" she asked in an effort to change the subject.

He smiled and ran his hand down her arm. "Your skin is warming up. That's good."

"You're changing the subject from your wish. Why do you look so...?" His eyes had gone smoky again, but behind those dark, seductive eyes she saw frustration. The space between them heated. His hand slid back up her arm, and every muscle corded tight. She recognized the look in his eyes now as pure sexual need.

He scrubbed his hand down his face. "I'm doing everything I can to distract myself from wanting to make love to you right here on this couch."

"Now, that sounds like a great distraction from my dilemma." She licked her lips.

A deep groan slipped from Dae's lungs as he leaned closer. "Make your damn wish," he whispered.

"I just did."

She took his hand and brought it to her breast. "Love me," she whispered.

"I already do."

He sealed his lips over hers and kissed her until the sound of the driving rain and the whistles of the wind disappeared, and there was only their breathing, the sound of his hand playing across her skin, and the beating of their hearts. Her hands traveled up his back. She loved his back. All those muscles bunching and flexing beneath her fingers. He was always careful with her, careful to ensure she was okay, that he wasn't hurting her, and after the way he'd cared for her and poured his soul out for her, something inside her ripped free of its tether. Her breathing quickened, and the air pulsed with need. She loved his careful touch, his desire to pleasure her, but as the room whirred around her with the energy of their bodies coming together in this magical house that supposedly made heartfelt wishes come true, she didn't want slow and careful. She wanted to disappear into his virility, to burn in the scorching heat she saw in his eyes every time he looked at her. She wanted to stop feeling conflicted over bullshit like his job or hers. She wanted...No. She *needed* to feel their love tear through her, damn it. Despite the cold, despite her injury, despite the torrential storm pounding the rooftop, she wanted to feel his flesh banging against hers, to feel his hot breath in all the places that craved him. She knew the only way to do that was to show him it was okay, because God forbid he would do the wrong thing by her.

With nervous hands and shaky breath, she pressed her hands to his chest and pushed him backward so he was teetering on the edge of the couch.

He cocked his head and gripped her arms tighter to keep from toppling off. His lust-filled eyes narrowed, driving her ache for him deeper.

Oh yeah, that's it. That's what I want. "You need to switch places with me." The words came soft and tentative instead of rough and take charge, as she'd hoped.

"Your ankle."

She forced fierceness into her trembling voice. "I don't give a damn about my ankle. I don't want you to be careful with me, Dae. Take me like you'd take a one-night stand, or I'm going to take you that way."

His eyes darkened to nearly black. "Take you like..."

"Yes. Stop thinking and start touching." She tore at the button on his pants, and he grabbed her wrists. Tears of nerves and sheer need burned in her eyes.

"Hey, slow down." He searched her eyes, and she knew the second he noticed her tears. His grip loosened and his face nearly crumpled. "Baby, what's wrong? Talk to me."

Why are tears running down my cheeks? This was definitely *not* what she had planned. The whole day came crashing around her: Adelina's face when she heard about the demolition. The conflicting feelings she'd felt throughout the day. The overwhelming love for Dae that threatened to strangle her. The pain of the fall and the fear as she'd flown through the air. And then the all-consuming feeling of being safe in Dae's arms. The look of love in his eyes when he cleaned her cuts. And now the way he was trying to figure out why she was sad when all he wanted to do was make love to her.

"I..." She sucked in a jagged breath. "Dae, I have never felt so much so fast, and with everything that's happened, I just want you to let go with me. Love me like you don't have to do the right thing, or hold back, or be super careful."

A smile spread across his lips, but it never reached

his eyes, which were still filled with worry. "Baby. I will love your pain away, but you could never be a one-night stand with me, and what you'll feel in my touch will never be what a one-night stand would feel like." His brows drew together and he inched backward. "Unless you're trying to tell me that you want a one-night stand with me? Because—"

She grabbed his arms and pulled him closer. "No, no, no!" She swallowed her fear and her confusion and let the truth come out. "I want a *forever stand* with you. I love you, Dae. I want you to love me with every bit of the fierce desire I see in your eyes and feel in your body."

DAE TRIED TO temper the mounting desire to take Emily at her word and pound into her, but he had to be sure she knew how he really felt. He was hard, horny, and in love, and that was a dangerous combination.

"Baby, I'll take your body everywhere you want to go. Just know it's out of love."

He made quick work of stripping her of her clothes, but as he drew her shorts and panties over her sore ankle, he couldn't help but notice her flinch, and that was enough of a reminder to reel his lust back a hair. There was more than one way to love a woman he adored and make her forget everything and anything other than them. He positioned himself between Emily's legs, thanking the heavens above that this was an extra-long couch, and kissed her inner thighs. He stretched out on his stomach and lifted her legs over each of his shoulders, careful not to knock her ankle. Her breasts rose and fell with each heavy breath as his tongue touched the moist cleft between her thighs, and she gasped a breath. She was eager and ready, and he knew how to drive her crazy. He reached up with one hand and rolled her nipple between his finger and thumb as his tongue glided over her again. Her sexy, sensual moan filled the air.

He squeezed harder, and at the same time he thrust two fingers inside her, turning that moan into a breathy plea. *Oh, yeah, baby. I'll take you there.*

He lowered his mouth to her as he worked her with both hands. She rocked her hips in to him, and he used his thumb to caress her overly sensitive nerves.

"Dae," she said in one long, heated breath.

He licked and sucked, teased and pinched until the sounds she made were no longer breathy, but forceful cries of pleasure. He loved her until the last pulse shuddered through her body, and before she recovered, he loved her more, taking her quickly up and over the edge again. She was panting, her arms lying spent beside her body, her legs draped over his shoulders, thighs spread wide, and her lips, her beautiful, full lips, formed a gratified smile. She was desire, passion, and sass all wrapped up in a sweet, tender package.

He ran his tongue along her inner thigh. Goose bumps chased the wetness over her skin.

She arched up, urging him on.

"Christ, you're amazing," he whispered. "Promise me tomorrow."

Her eyes fluttered open. "Tomorrow."

He caught a mischievous gleam in her eyes that

sent lust searing through him. He had to have her. *Now*. He pulled her toward him and thrust his tongue in her mouth. She resisted at first. The taste of herself was probably overwhelming. But within seconds she relaxed into the kiss and then met his passion with her own, clawing at his back and thrusting her tongue against his. He deepened the kiss and rose up on his knees. She wrapped her fingers around his hard length.

"Let me taste you as you've tasted me. I want all of you, Dae." She lowered her mouth and took him in.

Fuuuuuck. His head fell back at the feel of her velvety tongue stroking him.

Her hands tightened around the base of his arousal, driving him out of his damn mind. She quickened her efforts, and he gritted his teeth against the urge to come. He fisted his hands in her hair and tugged her mouth free, then kissed her—deep and rough. She pushed at his chest until their lips parted, and she lowered her mouth and swallowed him again.

"I won't last, baby," he groaned through clenched teeth.

She pulled back, releasing his slick eight inches, then licked him base to tip and gazed hungrily into his eyes. "Don't hold back. I want to taste all of you."

Holy. Hell.

"I want to pleasure you like you pleasure me." She licked him again, swirling her tongue over the sensitive tip. "Come for me, Dae," she whispered before taking him in her mouth again.

"If I come, I can't fu...er...love you like you want to be loved."

She narrowed her eyes and spoke in a deep, throaty voice. “You had it right the first time. There are times in a girl’s life when she wants to be fucked. And, Dae, I want that with you.”

Holy Christ.

“But right now I want *this* with you more.” She closed her lips over him again, and within seconds of her sweet mouth wrapping around him, he found his release. Hell if she didn’t swallow every drop he had to give as he grunted through the last eruption that rumbled through him. He took her in his arms and kissed her. Deep, hard, and loving.

Emily might be fighting a mental battle over their beliefs, but he refused to believe that what she’d just done wasn’t her way of showing him that she really was committed to being his *forever stand*.

Chapter Thirteen

DAE WATCHED DAWN spill hazy light into the room. He'd heard voices earlier, and when he'd looked outside, he'd seen a group of women heading into the backyard. Now that he understood more about the property, he knew what those women were there to do. He'd lain beside Emily, listening to the sounds of the women just beyond the wall, and imagined them leaving their wishes for love and babies and other miracles. *Miracles.*

He glanced down at Emily, sleeping soundly with her cheek resting on his chest. *Miracles.* She was his miracle. His eyes slid down to her ankle, which wasn't bruised or swollen, thank goodness. Did the myth apply to wishes for health, too? He'd have to remember to ask Adelina. He could hardly believe that he was contemplating the validity of this place, but he'd wished for Emily's ankle to heal quickly, and he hoped to hell it would. He exhaled and closed his eyes, trying to pull his thoughts back to familiar territory.

Myths and miracles were far from normal thoughts for him.

Emily stirred beside him. He still couldn't get over how strong she'd been when she hurt her ankle, or the look in her eyes when they were making love last night. They'd found a quilt—now draped over Emily's naked body—and towels in the trunk beneath the window. Last night he'd brought in one of the large planters from the side yard. It was full of rainwater, and though it was a bit gritty from residue in the bottom of the planter, they'd used the water to wash up.

He shifted his eyes to the tree burgeoning into the room like a womb full of hopes and dreams. He'd debated making three wishes last night. He'd thought about wishing that Emily would finally realize that they were not that far apart in their beliefs, but something in his heart told him that he didn't need a miracle for that to happen. And his second wish, well, how could he refrain from wishing for Serafina's husband's safe return? After the way Emily had given herself over to him last night, he knew he hadn't needed that third wish after all. A part of him was hoping the House of Wishes did possess some otherworldly power, because he worried that that was exactly what Serafina's husband might need.

Emily had seemed so conflicted about what to wish for. He gazed down at the peaceful look on her beautiful face, her lips slightly parted and curved up at the ends, felt the easy, restful cadence of her breathing, and he knew that she had probably been thinking about what everyone else needed rather than what she wanted. That big heart of hers caused all sorts of emotional conflicts in her beautiful, intelligent mind. He had the urge to caress her face, to kiss the sweet corners of her mouth as he'd done last night, when they'd woken up and he'd taken her again—this time in the manner she'd asked to be taken—rough and reckless. They'd made love until the room vibrated with the sounds of flesh slapping against flesh and moans and gasps thick with raw, unadulterated pleasure. He smiled with the memory. Afterward, she'd let him bathe her. He'd never felt so deeply connected to a person.

She needed her rest more than he needed to touch her cheek.

He slipped from the couch, and she sighed, rolled onto her side, and drifted right back to sleep. Dae moved quietly to their clothing, which he'd draped over the chairs to dry. After dressing, he set two ibuprofen tablets next to the bottle of water for Emily. He hoped she wouldn't be too sore this morning, but he had a feeling she was going to have a difficult few days. He wished he didn't have to leave so soon so he could take care of her, but given how strongly she felt about this property, he needed to have a face-to-face meeting with Frank and decide on his next move.

Outside, shafts of light split the clouds, blazing a path through the dewy grass toward the forgotten bicycles. The scent of rain lingered in the air, damp and refreshing. Droplets of water glistened on the tips of the grass, wetting Dae's still-damp sneakers. His chest tightened and his hands fisted at his sides as he neared the road where Emily's tire had caught. He wished he could have prevented her accident. The urge to protect her was already as much a part of him as the need to breathe.

He picked up their helmets and hooked them on the handlebars before pushing the bikes back toward the house. He parked them on the deep front porch and checked Emily's bike for damage. The tires were still full of air, and the bike was intact, though he couldn't imagine she'd be up to riding back to the resort. Before going inside, he walked around the villa. His mind was ensconced in thoughts of Emily. He envisioned them walking hand in hand across the damp grass, sitting on the patio on the side of the house, having coffee beneath the vine-laced latticework, and as he came to the backyard, he imagined her eyes softening at the sight of the mammoth—*and magical?*—tree. Her eyes had a way of making him forget everything else in the world. He imagined arriving in Denver without her. An empty feeling seeped into him. Emily wasn't someone a person could simply *be* with. She was a woman to be experienced, and he wanted her with him always.

He looked out over the rolling hills and smiled when his eyes caught on a patch of poppies. *Emily, you're everywhere.* He pictured what it would be like to drive into the same driveway at the end of each day. Before Emily, Dae had lived with one foot out the door, never staying in one of his houses for more than a few weeks at a time. How would it feel to know that she was inside waiting for him? *Every night.* The thought of putting down roots was so unfamiliar that it knocked him off balance. On some level, it even scared him. But settling down with Emily was what he wanted. He'd rather be scared with her in his life than empty without her.

EMILY WOKE UP alone on the couch and listened for Dae. The room was quiet. The sound of rain pounding the roof had been replaced with peaceful silence. She noticed the water bottle and pills beside the couch and smiled, feeling happier and more content than she'd ever been. As she swallowed the pills, she thought about the night before and how everything felt as though it had changed. Even the tree felt bigger, more real than it had the night before. She took stock of her emotions and realized that she felt calmer and more settled.

Her muscles smarted as she shifted to a sitting position and carefully flattened her foot on the floor, scrunching her face in anticipation of the pain. She glanced down at her foot, which wasn't bruised or swollen, and pressed her heel harder against the cold floor. She was surprised that it no longer hurt.

She rose to her feet, putting most of her weight on her other foot, and was relieved when she still felt no pain in her ankle as she crossed the floor and retrieved her clothing. She caught sight of Dae through the window. He was filling the planter with fresh water, his back to her. His biceps flexed as he used the hand pump for the well. She wished she'd remembered to tell him about the hand pump last night, but he'd been as resourceful as ever when he'd brought in the planter full of rainwater, then bathed her with so much care she could barely do more than breathe.

She turned back to the tree. The uncertainty of what to wish for had also dissipated during the night. She knew exactly what matter of the heart needed the extra chance. She scribbled her wish and placed the paper in the same hole Dae had placed his; then she opened the door and leaned against the frame, watching her man as he crouched to pick up the full planter. She loved that he was taking such good care of her. She remembered the feel of his hands in her hair as he rinsed out the mud from her fall, the way he'd carefully drawn the washcloth over her skin, removing every streak of dirt, and how he'd frowned at the bluish bruises that were forming on her shoulder and hip. He was all easy movements and striking masculinity as he turned toward her and their eyes caught.

He carried the planter across the grass with a smile that warmed his dark eyes.

"Wow, you're a sight for sore eyes. Aren't girls supposed to need primping in the morning? It's crazy how hot you are."

She felt her cheeks heat up and knew he loved the reaction when he raised his brows in appreciation. He stopped beside her and kissed her. How the heck did he smell so good after all they'd been through? The man made dirt smell appealing.

"You probably shouldn't be standing on your ankle."

"It doesn't hurt this morning, but I took the ibuprofen anyway. Thank you for that." She hooked her finger in the front pocket of his shorts. "Thank you for everything, Dae. You took such good care of me."

"And I always will, if you'll let me."

She followed him inside, knowing he really would always take care of her.

"I thought I'd put this in the bathroom upstairs so you can have some privacy if you want to wash up. I can bring in a few more of these to fill up a tub if you want, although the water's pretty cold."

She followed him upstairs and dipped her finger into the cool water. "I think I'll just use a towel and take a sponge bath."

"That's exactly why I'm spoiling you tonight. When we get back to the resort, I'm giving you a nice warm bubble bath, a bottle of wine, and dinner anywhere you want. All I ask is that you take it easy on that ankle. I won't be here to take care of you if you get hurt again, and that kills me." He lifted her onto the marble sink, parted her legs with his thighs, then moved in close. He lowered her shirt from her shoulder and kissed the spot where the bruise had bloomed. Then he ran his hands down her legs and hugged her to him, holding the back of her head in a way that made her feel like she was one hundred percent *his*.

"I wish I could take the aches away. Are you sure you're not too sore?"

Emily didn't need to be pampered in a fancy tub, or any of those things he mentioned. All she needed was him.

"Yeah, I'm just a little achy, but you've already made me feel so much better. Besides, it's no worse than if I'd been hit by a truck."

He looked down at her with concerned eyes.

"I'm kidding." She laughed.

"You're evil."

"I prefer the word *playful.*" She ran her finger down the center of his chest and thought of her brothers and their fiancées. She was testing herself. Testing her heart. She waited for the embarrassing pang of jealousy that usually accompanied thoughts of them, and when it didn't come, she knew.

"This is real between us," she whispered.

"It sure is, baby."

They held each other for another minute or two, allowing the confirmation to sink in.

"Why don't I get cleaned up and then we can bike back to the resort."

His eyes filled with concern again.

"Don't worry. I promise if my ankle hurts too much, I'll stop and you can ride the rest of the way with me on your handlebars."

"Now you're thinking." He kissed her forehead and left her to wash up.

After she finished, she went in search of Dae and heard him speaking in a heated tone. She saw him just outside the doors of the room where they'd slept. He glanced up and nodded in her direction before taking his disgruntled conversation out of earshot. Emily wondered who he was talking to, but she gave him his privacy and began packing up their belongings. She hesitated when she picked up the two pads where they'd been writing their *preserve or demolish* lists. As badly as she wanted to read what he'd written, she wanted to do it with Dae, and she had a feeling that whatever had him pacing in the yard with his shoulders rounded forward and a pinched look on his face would take precedence over their silly lists. She shoved them into the backpack, along with their other belongings, and a few minutes later she heard Dae's determined steps as he came back into the room. The serious look in his eyes had her concerned.

"Anything I can help with?"

"No, thanks," he said gruffly. "Just work stuff. I'm going to empty the planter and bring it back outside so we can take off."

He took the steps two at a time and was back downstairs in record time. He feigned a smile at Emily as he carried the planter outside. She didn't miss the tension in his jaw or his abrupt movements.

Emily folded the blanket and returned it to the trunk where they'd found it. She bundled up the damp towels and shoved them in the backpack. She'd take them back to Adelina's to wash them and then find a way to return them. Dae came back inside as she was stuffing them into the backpack.

"Why are you taking the towels?"

"To wash them."

"Frank, the owner of this place, won't want or need them." The sharp edge of his voice startled her. "We'll throw them away when we get to Adelina's."

"Are you sure? I don't mind."

"No, Em. The guy doesn't even want this place to remain here. He wants me to demolish it all. The furniture, the tree, everything. He won't give a damn about the stupid towels."

The veins in his forearms bulged as he scrubbed

his hand down his face. "I'm sorry, Em. This whole work thing..." He waved at the tree. "And leaving you..." He kissed the top of her head and folded her into his arms. "It's all got me on edge. I'm sorry. I shouldn't take it out on you."

"It's okay." She was beginning to understand and assumed he'd been talking with the owner of the house. Seeing him upset made her stomach ache, which told her loud and clear how much she loved him.

He came to her side, and his eyes and voice softened. "No, baby. It's not okay. I'm sorry. I just want to make sure you're safe and happy, and I'm leaving soon to deal with this mess. Let's get you home so at least we've got the safe part in place. I know if you need anything while I'm gone, Adelina will take care of you."

"I'm a big girl. I'll be fine." She'd be about as fine as if she'd lost her left leg. Dae had already become not only a part of her life, but a part of her, and even the idea of spending a day without him made her sad, but she was a big girl. She had to be, so she forced a brave face.

"You are a competent, brilliant woman, but that doesn't mean that I won't worry night and day about you when we're apart. And this place, this property that brought me here, and brought us together, I need to deal with it."

Her stomach sank. "To tear it down?"

He gazed into her eyes with an unreadable expression. "I honestly don't know." He slung the backpack over his shoulder. "I want you to see something on the way out."

Emily heard voices when she stepped out onto the porch. "What's going on?"

"I'll show you." He locked the door, then they made their way around back.

There must have been twenty women gathered in the backyard, most speaking in Italian, some fast and heated, others softer, exasperated. She squeezed Dae's hand. This was fantastic! Maybe the community coming together and showing how much they believed in the magic of the House of Wishes would change the owner's mind. Maybe it would help sway Dae, too.

"Adelina must have told everyone she knew that the house might be torn down," Emily said. "Gossip must travel as fast here as it does back home. This is amazing. What a show of faith!" The women were gathered in small groups, talking animatedly and using hand gestures, and there was no shortage of glances being turned in the direction of the tree.

"I bet they're wishing, just like Adelina said she and Serafina would. Isn't it wonderful to see them all coming together like this?"

"Yeah. Great."

His sarcasm wasn't lost on Emily, and that sarcasm served as an unwanted reminder of their fundamental differences.

Chapter Fourteen

DAE AND EMILY pedaled their bikes down the long driveway toward the resort and were surprised to find several cars in the parking lot. They stopped in front of the house and pulled off their bike helmets.

"Wow. I wonder what's going on." Emily watched Dae shake his hair free. He looked like one of those motorcycle guys in a cologne commercial, deeply tanned and glistening with just enough sweat to make her salivate. His unkempt hair partially hid his eyes and amped up his sexy factor by about a million degrees.

"No idea. Maybe there's a reception or something. It is a resort." He hung their helmets on the handlebars. "How's your ankle holding up?"

"A little twingy, but it's fine."

He kissed the tip of her nose. "We'll stay off of it for the rest of the day. I'll bring these down to the shed. Why don't you go inside and get comfortable."

"I can help you." She reached for her bike.

"You're lucky I let you bike home." He snagged the handlebars from her grasp and headed for the barn. "Relax, babe. I've got this."

Relax. She felt like she'd been doing nothing but relaxing for days. It dawned on her that she'd been so consumed with their relationship that she'd actually let go of all thoughts of work. *Damn, it felt good.*

She'd much rather be with Dae than go inside alone and relax. Emily followed him around to the back of the house and watched him descend the hill.

"Emily."

She turned at the sound of Serafina's voice.

"Hi, Serafina."

Serafina's long cotton skirt swished over her legs as she joined Emily. Without Luca perched on her hip, she looked very young. Emily realized that she didn't even know how old Serafina was, but she couldn't have been much older than twenty-five. And she had likely already lost her husband. Emily cleared her throat to try to gain control of the sadness washing through her.

"Hi. My mother was worried about the two of you. Did you have a romantic stay in Chianti after all?" She raised her brows with a hopeful look on her face. Her eyes slid over Emily's face, and the hope quickly changed to worry. "What happened to your cheek?"

"I'm sorry we worried her. We got stuck in the storm, and I fell off the bike. It's nothing, really. It looks worse than it is. We had to get out of the rain for the night." She smiled at Dae as he headed back toward them. "We did enjoy a romantic night. Where's Luca today?"

"I'm glad you're okay." Serafina pointed to the house. "Luca's inside being doted on by more women than I can contend with."

"Hi, Serafina," Dae said as he came to Emily's side. "Hand or arm?" he asked Emily.

"Hand." She reached for his hand. "My shoulder's a little tender."

"Any news on Dante?" he asked.

Serafina shook her head. "I don't expect there to be."

"Don't give up hope," Emily said, even though she was skeptical. "You're praying and wishing at the House of Wishes—"

Serafina's eyes dampened. "Emily, when he was fighting with the other men, every day I prayed for him, and every day felt like a year. I know other women who have lost their husbands and their boyfriends. It was awful, but at least they knew for sure. They watched their husbands' bodies be placed in the ground and knew that when they turned away, they were destined to live without them." Serafina shook her head. "You can't imagine how long a minute feels when the man you love is missing."

"Serafina, I'm sorry. I didn't mean to make it sound easy." Emily felt horrible. Serafina hadn't looked this sad since she'd arrived.

"You didn't. Having hope *should* be easy when it comes to the man you love, but nothing feels easy. Nothing even feels real to me now. I feel like I'm stuck in quicksand. If I don't believe he'll return, I'll drown in it. And if I hold out hope that he'll be found alive, I can't move forward. Isn't that drowning a slower death? Either way I run the risk of taking Luca under with me."

Serafina wiped her eyes and turned back toward the house. "Please don't say anything to my mother about my doubts. She's in there right now with a handful of women who are up in arms over the news of that house being torn down. I swear they've called every woman they know. My mother really believes in these things." She turned her attention back to Emily, and the look of surrender in her eyes made Emily's stomach take a nosedive.

"I swear they're plotting a way to seize the villa." Serafina's voice and eyes filled with determination. "All I want is my husband back. I want Luca to know his father. But all the wishes in the world aren't going to bring him back. It's been too long. We've wished and prayed. I've offered my own life up for Dante's safe return, but...but I know better."

Emily didn't think as she drew Serafina into her arms, her own eyes brimming with tears, and despite her doubts, the next words flowed with sincerity and her own burgeoning hope that Serafina would get lucky and her husband would return. "You have to have faith, Serafina. They haven't found his body, so you can't give up hope." She felt Dae's hand stroke her back.

Serafina pulled away, tears streaming down her cheeks. She inhaled an uneven breath. "It's just too hard. Every morning and every night she drags me to that house. And every time...Every time without fail, I come away hopeful. So damn hopeful that I allow myself to believe that the next day will be different.

That God will hear our prayers and bring my Dante home. And then hours pass, and the terrible days turn into heartbreaking nights, and—" Sobs burst from her chest. "And...then it starts all over again."

Emily opened her arms again, and Serafina fell into them. She felt Dae's arms surrounding them both, and for the first time since she heard about the myth, she saw the harmful effects the myth could have—and she had to wonder if it was a fair thing to hold out hope when Serafina clearly needed closure.

She'd never been more thankful for Dae's strong arms than right at that moment. Serafina needed all of the strength she could muster to get through each day and to take care of little Luca. Dae allowed them both to suck up as much of his strength as they needed as he held them, silently offering his support. He always knew just what she needed, and once again she saw that his thoughtfulness extended beyond the woman he loved, to whomever needed it at the moment.

That realization made her love him even more.

THE AFTERNOON PASSED too fast. Dae wanted to remember every second with Emily. Every passionate kiss, every sweet glance, the way her hand felt in his, and the feel of her body tucked beneath his arm. He stepped from the shower into the steamy bathroom and tied a towel around his waist, thinking of how badly he'd wanted to shower with Emily. It had taken all of his willpower to leave her alone in her room, but after the night she'd had, he didn't want to smother her, and then Daisy had called, and he'd given her privacy with the promise to return after his shower.

As he wiped the steam from the mirror, he wondered briefly why she hadn't invited him to be her date for Daisy and Luke's wedding. Then again, he hadn't attended very many weddings and he had no idea about the proper etiquette for a maid of honor. Maybe she should be solely focused on Daisy and she shouldn't bring a date. Another thought crept in and he didn't like the streak of jealousy that accompanied it. Was she hesitant to introduce him to her family because she was still unsure about him despite what she'd said to him? Despite how she'd given herself to him so wholly last night and the days before? She had talked about staying out of the gossip in her hometown. Maybe that had something to do with it.

The whole thing made him a little uneasy.

A knock at the door pulled him from his thoughts. He answered the door, and his pulse roared at the sight of Emily wearing a skimpy blue halter dress so short it barely covered her panties. Her breasts pressed against the flimsy material, the points of her nipples clearly outlined. Her hair tumbled over her shoulders, and her eyes were seductively heavy. She bit her lower lip as she stepped into his room before he could manage a word. She slid her fingers beneath the edge of the towel and closed the door behind her.

"I missed you." She pressed her lips to his bare chest, and there was no hiding his arousal as her fingers played across his chest.

Her mouth found his nipple. She licked and sucked, driving him out of his mind and making him hard as steel.

"Emily," he whispered.

She pressed her hips to his arousal. "I don't want to think about you leaving, or about the House of Wishes, or the women who are downstairs figuring out how to save it." Her words were breathy as she dropped his towel to the floor. "I want to spend every second drenched in us."

He sealed his lips over hers and lifted her into his arms. Her legs circled his waist as her back met the door, and the tip of his arousal met her hot, wet center.

"Emily," he breathed against her lips. His heart thundered in his chest. *Condom.* He needed one.

"Just the thought of you standing outside my door without any panties on makes me want to come."

He took her in a greedy kiss. Her mouth was like sweet heaven. His muscles strained with the need to be inside her. She was open, ready, willing, and trying her damnedest to slip from his grip and take him inside her.

"Condom," he finally managed.

"I know. I just…" She pushed against his straining biceps and sank onto the tip of his arousal. "A little."

He groaned loudly through his teeth. "You're killing me."

Their lips crashed together in a deep, hard kiss. He fought the urge to plunge into her, barely able to restrain himself from thrusting his hips forward. He held her by the hips against the door, more to restrain himself than her. Her hands traveled down his bare back, then back up, fisting in his hair as she tightened her thighs around his waist and nearly drew the come right out of him. She untied the top of her halter and freed her breasts, pressing them against him, swirling her hips until he was on the verge of release, moving slow and purposeful. Bringing his raging need to the precipice of exploding, until he couldn't take it another second, could barely breathe, as he spun around and lowered her to the bed. He tore open the drawer of the bedside table and it fell from the track and clanked to the floor.

"Fuck." He scrambled off the bed and grabbed a handful of condoms, tossed all but one to the bed.

Emily lay with her dress pushed up to her hips, bare from the waist down, her cheeks flushed, her lips swollen and red from their passionate kisses. The scent of her shower was fresh on her warm skin. He was sure his heart would seep out his pores just to be closer to her. He tore open the packet and rolled on the condom.

"I need to feel you, Em. All of you." He slid her dress from her amazing body and tossed it to the floor. "I can't wait. I need to be inside you."

Her thighs skimmed his hips as he lowered his chest to hers and their bodies joined together. Buried deep inside her, he stilled, overwhelmed by the love consuming him, pulling him under. His head bowed and he closed his eyes, soaking in the feel of her hips pressed to his, the perfect pillows of her breasts against him, and her heart beating in time to his own erratic heartbeat.

"God, I love you." The truth of his words and the depth of his feelings nearly strangled him. Even buried deep inside her, his body strained to be closer.

She grazed her fingers through his hair.

"Open your eyes," she whispered.

He did, half blind with emotions, muscles quivering with desire. The look in her eyes nearly did him in.

"You're no longer possibly mine. You're not even my sure thing," she whispered. "You're my everything."

He lowered his lips to hers and their bodies moved with familiarity. Her words shook him to his core, and coupled with the love he felt for her, his carnal needs took over. They pawed and stroked, fondled and thrust, devouring each other as if this time was all they had. Their bodies glistened with sweat, and the heady scent of their lovemaking hung in the air as hums of pleasure coursed through them. He nearly died at the feel of her lips on his neck and the sharp tear of her teeth grazing his skin. He was lost in the softness of her fingers on his hips. The piercing of her nails as she urged him deeper. His hands slid down her curves, squeezing, wanting, finally clutching her hips, then her lean, supple thighs. He reveled in the shape and feel of her, how perfectly their bodies melded together.

"Yes, Dae," she cried.

He hissed out a breath and couldn't hold back another second. With one final thrust, they both spiraled over the edge.

AFTERNOON ROLLED INTO evening, spilling moonlight across the floor. The comforter lay in a heap on the floor. They'd made love, they'd dozed, they'd laughed, and they'd made love again…and again. Emily lay across Dae's chest, her cheek pressed to his skin as she traced the line of his collarbone with her index finger. He brought her fingers to his lips and kissed them, thinking of how he knew he'd never tire of loving her.

"I can't imagine spending hours on the plane tomorrow without you, or going to bed without holding you in my arms." He shifted her so they were lying side by side. Emily rested her head on her outstretched arm. Her hair spilled over the sheets. He moved closer, so her breaths became his, and slid his thigh over hers. She curled her legs up, and his hand instinctively settled on her hip.

"When I come home Saturday, will you really be at the airport to pick me up? So we'll only be apart for two nights."

"After two long, lonely nights, do you think I'd go a minute longer than I have to without you?" He pressed a kiss to her smiling lips. "When do you go back to work?"

"After you leave, I'm going to work my way through my emails. I was thinking that—"

"Baby, baby, baby. Just because I'm leaving doesn't mean your vacation is over. You work hard all year long. You told me that your life consists of work and your family and then more work. You deserve this break, and your clients can wait a few more days."

"But—"

He silenced her with a kiss. "But wasn't that your goal when you came here? To let yourself enjoy the one place you've wanted to go forever? Don't rob yourself of this chance to explore and enjoy." He felt as though he knew Emily better than she knew herself. He could picture her back in Colorado, moving through her days efficiently from one meeting to the next with to-do lists and sticky-note reminders. He pictured her smiling as she spoke to her family on the phone, meeting them for dinners, teasing and laughing, and he could even envision the adoration in her eyes when she looked at her brothers. He allowed himself to insert his own image into those visions, and it felt good and right.

He listened to Emily sigh over his suggestion of taking time to enjoy herself. He knew in his heart that she was coming to understand that he knew her better than she knew herself.

"But you worked while you were here," she said halfheartedly.

"I, my love, did not come here for a vacation. Remember? Then I found you, and you become my world. I was committed to work while I was here. You aren't." He knew she hated being told what to do, so he tried to soften his suggestion. "All I'm saying is that you deserve more than a fulfilling career, Em. Your heart needs to be fulfilled, too."

"So does my stomach." She grinned.

"Hungry?"

"Starved."

"Let's shower and go in search of food. What time is it, anyway?"

She rolled onto her back and shifted her eyes to the darkness outside his window. "It's way-too-close-to-the-time-you-leave o'clock."

He moved over her, his legs between hers. "We're

not going to count down the minutes. It's too hard."

She lifted her hips and narrowed her eyes. "That's not all that's hard."

"True." He laughed, but he was ready to drive into her and love her until she was no longer hungry. "Food or fun? Your pick."

He watched as contemplation washed over her face. "Food, then fun." She pushed at his chest, but her eyes clearly translated, *Love me. Now. Hard. Fast.*

"Oh, I'll move all right." He rubbed his arousal against her center. "But after that tease, you don't have a chance in hell of leaving this bed."

Chapter Fifteen

AFTER MAKING LOVE again, because it was way-too-close-to-the-time-you-leave o'clock after all, and showering, they went downstairs in search of food. They found Serafina and Adelina sitting at the kitchen table. Serafina's eyes were damp and red rimmed. Adelina held her hand between both of hers and spoke Italian in a hushed tone. Emily's stomach clenched. While she and Dae had been upstairs ravishing each other, getting selfishly lost in their love, Serafina was trying to hold on to her sanity as the shred of hope she'd held on to stretched and frayed. By the looks of the two women, Emily worried that the frail tether Serafina had been holding on to might have snapped.

Emily reached for Dae's hand. "Maybe we should go out to get something to eat."

Adelina said something to Serafina in Italian and Serafina nodded.

Adelina rose to her feet. "Stay. I made dinner for you both, but I didn't want to disturb you."

"You didn't have to do that." Emily felt Dae's hand slip away, and she watched him crouch beside Serafina.

"Cooking is cathartic," Adelina said. "Every woman should know how to cook. We cook with our hearts as much as our hands. Nothing heals the soul like food rich with love and strength from the hands that made it."

Maybe she'd learn to cook for Dae. She wanted to give him back all of the comfort and love he gave her so naturally, and cooking was one more way she could do that. She watched him take Serafina's hand.

"Did you receive news?" Dae asked Serafina.

Emily hadn't even thought of that. She held her breath until Serafina shook her head.

Dae's eyes filled with compassion. "The not knowing is a lot to bear. If he's out there, I'd imagine he's probably more concerned about you and Luca than himself. If he's out there, Serafina, he'd want you to be strong for Luca. I don't know Dante, but I think any man would want his wife to do whatever she needed to do to remain strong."

Oh no! What are you saying?

Serafina's breath hitched. Adelina took a step closer but stopped short when Serafina lifted sad eyes to her.

"Right now," Dae continued, "what matters most is being there for Luca. No matter what happens, I'm sure Dante, like any father, would want you to do what you need to in order to take care of yourself and Luca. Allowing yourself to do that doesn't mean you're giving up hope or forgetting your husband. It means you're raising his son."

Adelina said something in Italian, and Dae raised his eyes to her. "I'm not telling her to give up hope, Adelina. I'm giving her permission to grieve the *absence* of her husband—not the death of him. If she allows herself to grieve for his absence, it might make hoping for his return much easier. I think she's stuck in between. She's afraid to move forward and afraid to remain where she is."

Serafina nodded. "I am, Mama. I'm afraid to cry for his absence. Grieving his absence feels like I've given up on him, but I'm equally afraid not to. It's eating me up inside. Dae said it right. I'm stuck in between."

Adelina's eyes welled with tears. She opened her arms and Serafina walked into them.

"It's hard, all this wishing and praying and not knowing. Maybe Dae is right. If I allow the sadness instead of trying to pretend it doesn't exist, I think..." She drew in a deep breath and took a step back. "Mama, I'm not sure he's coming home. I love him. I want to believe he'll be found more than I want to live, but I can't keep pretending that he hasn't been gone for almost three months, Mama. Three months. Surviving there for this long seems impossible."

Tears slipped down Adelina's cheeks. "You must believe, Serafina. He only has us hoping for his return. If we don't hope, who will?"

"I will hope." Tears came freely now. The tension in Serafina's forehead eased. "I do hope, Mama. But I also have to accept the possibility of him not returning. And I need you to be okay with that. Without your support, I'm not going to make it."

Adelina folded her daughter in her arms, murmuring in Italian. She must have agreed, because Serafina smiled despite her tears.

Dae rose to his feet and came to Emily's side. She couldn't believe he'd said all those things to a person he barely knew. He was stepping into a family matter in a way that she would never have the guts to. And he'd known what she'd needed to hear.

That's it. She was definitely going to learn to cook for him. He had so much to give, and what did she have to offer?

"How did you know what she needed to hear?"

He shrugged.

"Because of your birth mom?" Emily saw a shadow of sadness pass over his eyes. She touched his arm and softened her voice. "You had to allow yourself to mourn her absence in order to move on, because you knew she didn't want to meet you."

"I don't know. Maybe." He met her gaze. "You're the only person on earth who knows that." He laced his fingers with hers, and for a moment they just gazed into each other's eyes, feeling the connection that bound them together.

"Yes, Emily." He paused, and when he spoke again his voice was more distant. "It started as that, but when I saw Serafina sitting there, I started to wonder what would happen if my plane went down."

"Dae! Don't even think that."

"I did, Em. And then I thought about you, and I knew that as the plane soared toward the earth, I'd be thinking that I wanted you to go on with your life. Grieve for me, then move on. You're too special not to light up some lucky man's life."

"I don't want to—"

"I know. Neither does she. But the truth is, she's a single mom with a little boy. She has so many years ahead of her. No matter how much her husband loved her, or wanted to believe that he was her only love, I don't think he, or any man, would want his wife to live her life in limbo. He'd want her to move on, just like I'd hope that one day, maybe when you're a hundred or so, you'd allow yourself to love again."

His smile told her that he was teasing about the *hundred* part, but his eyes told her that he was serious about the rest. She wasn't sure she could ever be that selfless. She was greedy. She wanted him all to herself.

Later that evening, Dae stayed true to his promise. He and Emily shared a bottle of wine, and then he ran a bubble bath and spoiled Emily *oh so good*, in all the right ways. They made love two more times before finally giving in to exhaustion and falling asleep wrapped in each other's arms.

Chapter Sixteen

EMILY WASN'T SURPRISED when she awoke to an empty room. She'd learned that Dae was an early riser, and she knew he was up worrying over leaving her today. He hated leaving her as much as she hated that he had to. She ran her hand over his side of the bed, thinking that this was the last time she'd wake up in this room. They'd stayed in his room last night so he could pack, and just the sight of his bags sitting by the door made her ache with loneliness. She was seeing him in a few days, and they'd agreed to Skype while they were apart, and still his leaving felt tragic.

It won't be that bad.

Only as bad as a root canal.

Or a severed limb.

A few minutes later Dae walked in carrying two steaming mugs. He was showered and dressed in the same low-slung jeans that had stolen Emily's breath the first time she'd seen him. He flipped his wet hair from his eyes and handed her a mug.

"Hey, beautiful. I didn't want to wake you. How's your ankle?"

The coffee smelled delicious. He smelled toe-curling good. So why was her throat thickening? He sat beside her and rested a hand on her thigh.

"It's fine. Nothing really hurts except my heart."

He leaned in close like he was going to kiss her and stopped short. "Aw, that's about the cheesiest thing I've ever heard. And I love it."

She pressed her lips to his. "Cheesy, yes, but true."

"I love you, and my heart hurts, too."

"Good. It would suck to suffer alone."

His eyes narrowed. "Please don't say the word *suck*. I have to leave soon."

She wanted to laugh and cry at the same time. She swallowed past the lump that threatened to silence her and forced the truth to come out.

"I want to crawl into your lap, wrap my arms around your neck, and cling to you like a baby baboon so you can't leave me."

He laughed, and the rush of emotions made her tear up.

"Babe, you'd be the cutest damn baboon there ever was, and I'd give anything not to leave you today, but I need to take care of this business deal."

The business deal. The House of Wishes. Was that all it was to him? A business deal? She shifted on the bed, forcing herself not to try to pick that apart. She didn't want to struggle with anything other than missing Dae right now.

He lifted her chin and flashed that easy smile of his that made her want to melt into him.

"Promise me that while I'm gone you're going to enjoy yourself and not stew over work, the House of Wishes, or anything else. This is your time, Em."

She rolled her eyes. "Fine. I will. But I won't enjoy it as much as if you were with me."

"Well, that's a given."

She swatted his arm. "You're impossible."

He raised his brows and she swatted him again.

"Hey." He rubbed his arm and feigned a pout. "Don't bruise my arm meat."

They both laughed at that. He took the coffee mug from her and pulled her into a hug.

"Think of all the time you'll have to talk to Daisy when I'm gone."

"You'll come to the wedding with me, won't you?"

"You want me to go to your brother's wedding?"

She sensed relief in his tone. "Of course. Didn't I ask you to go with me?"

"That would be a big no." His mouth kicked up into a lopsided smile.

"Oh no. That's rude. I'm sorry. I guess I just assumed you were going with me. See what you do to me? You turn my brain to mush."

"I love your mushy brain." He nuzzled against her neck. "You sure you want me to meet your family? That sounds pretty serious."

She pressed her lips to his. She couldn't get enough of him. "I think the fact that I let you ravage my body and declared my love for you should have clued you in to the idea that we are about as serious as a couple could get."

He kissed her again. "Damn, you're adorable.

Okay, yeah. I'll go. Saturday after next, right?"

"Yup. I'll give you all the details when you pick me up from the airport. That way you're sure to show up."

"Trust me. Nothing will hold me back from picking you up at the airport." He patted her thigh. "You need to shower so you can say goodbye to me outside."

"Dae Bray, are you kicking me out of your bed?" She drew her brows together, trying her damnedest to look offended, and she knew he'd see nothing but how much she'd miss him.

"I'm kicking you out of my bed so I don't miss my plane."

Twenty minutes later they were standing by his car draped in each other's arms.

"You're the best thing that's ever happened to me, Emily Braden." He pulled back and she clung to him. "My sweet monkey, if I don't leave, I'll miss my plane."

She dug her fingers into his back. "You think that's going to help your case?"

"I love you."

She reluctantly let go, and he smiled down at her. The only way she'd make it through this goodbye was by making herself laugh.

"You should go. I hear the next guest is arriving soon, and he's single."

Dae narrowed his eyes and backed her up against the car. "Oh yeah?"

"Mm-hmm." She shouldn't wrap her hands around his waist again, but she had to, just one more time. She promised herself she'd let go this time.

"It's a damn good thing I trust you. You could be in a room with Brad Pitt, Chris Hemsworth, *and* Chris

Pine, and I know these beautiful lips of yours would remain faithful to me." He rubbed his thumb over her lips.

Her knees weakened. How did he do that to her with just a touch, a look, a whisper?

"Promise me Saturday?"

When their lips met in a sensual, loving kiss, she'd have promised him anything.

"Saturday," she whispered.

"And you can be damned sure that I'll be faithful to you." He leaned into his car and withdrew a gift-wrapped package. "Open this after I'm gone, okay?"

"Impossible," she whispered. "When did you have time to get me a gift?"

"When you love someone, nothing is impossible." With one last hug and kiss, he climbed into the car and started the engine. "And you can be damn sure I love you, Em."

"I love you, too."

"I'll call you tomorrow." He slid on a pair of sunglasses, which made him look sexier than hell. "Try to be done with the new guest by then, 'kay?"

She laughed. "I'll be too busy missing you to give anyone else the time of day."

"That's my girl." He blew her a kiss and drove down the driveway.

Emily wrapped her arms around the package and stared after him long after his car was out of sight. She carried the gift to the porch and unwrapped it while sitting on the steps. It took her only a moment to realize it was the beautifully knitted, poppy-red scarf she'd admired in Greve. She picked up the scarf, and beneath it lay a small leather journal with a thin leather strap wound around it. She ran her fingers over the soft leather.

"Dae," she whispered. "Where did you get this?"

She unwound the thin strap and opened the soft leather journal. A photograph of her gazing at the sunflower field slipped out.

"I don't remember you taking this." She ran her finger over the image of herself, scrutinizing it. *I look pretty and happy. I look like I'm in love.* Her lips curved up. *I am in love. So very much in love.* She turned her attention back to the journal. The paper inside was thick and flecked with pieces of parchment; every page was different from the next. She read Dae's handwritten note.

> *Smile, sweet Emily,*
>
> *I'm right there with you—at least my heart is. Hand or arm?*

She laughed. "Arm, you big fool." She read the rest of his message feeling much happier than she'd been only moments before.

> *I hope you find the time to do these things while we're apart.*
>
> > *—Stroll through the vineyard on the way to Chianti. I wrote the address and name in the back of this journal. Ask for Giovanni. He's expecting you. We never had a chance to do that together, and I*

don't want you to miss it.

—Find the exact spot in the picture. You'll know it when you see it. Stop wrinkling those pretty eyebrows of yours and trust me. Just go there.

I miss you already and I haven't even left yet. I'm sitting next to the bed in OUR room, watching you sleep. You're so beautiful that it's hard to concentrate on writing this.

I love you, Dae

He hadn't written a list of tourist attractions or given her the task of seeing all the places she'd had on her initial itinerary. He'd asked her to do only what they had missed out on doing together and to revisit the place where she looked so happy in the photograph. He must have known that all those other touristy places wouldn't mean as much without him there. He must have realized, as she was just beginning to understand, that part of what made the iconic sites such as the musty, dark stairwell of the duomo in Florence so special was that they'd been together. Otherwise, there wouldn't have been a damn thing that was romantic about climbing more than four hundred stairs. It would always be the place she felt his presence the most, the place he first wrapped her in his arms. The place they'd shared their first kiss.

Chapter Seventeen

THE VILLA SMELLED like bread and spices and all things heavenly. Emily followed the scent into the kitchen. Dishes full of sliced salami, ham, and sausage were spread across the kitchen table. A plate of sliced tomatoes and cheese brightened the otherwise dark spread.

"Buongiorno, Emily." Adelina wore an apron tied around her waist and was wrist deep in a large mixing bowl.

"I've made you a special meal, to heal your sad heart from your handsome boyfriend's departure." She moved to another counter and uncovered a bowl. "*Pappa al pomodoro*, a hearty soup. This will help you feel better." She set it on the table and pulled out a chair for Emily.

The dish looked more like a mush of tomatoes and bread than soup, but it smelled incredible.

"Comfort food," Adelina said as she patted Emily's shoulder. "Did you know that every city in Italy has different specialties?"

"Yes, I'd heard that about Italian cuisine."

Adelina nodded as she settled into a chair across from Emily at the wide table. "But no two cities cook *pappa al pomodoro* the same. Ours is the best."

Emily couldn't mask her amusement at Adelina's confidence, but after one taste of the thick, tangy soup, she was convinced.

"Adelina, this is amazing."

"Thank you. Bread symbolizes life, and olive oil symbolizes love. This will bring you strength while you and your Dae are apart."

"I don't know if it's the soup or just being here, but I feel a little better already."

"See?" Adelina patted her heart. "Cooking heals. Did you know that here we bake bread without salt?"

"I didn't know that."

"Yes. Some say it started because of taxation on salt; others say it was because of a rivalry between Pisa and Florence a very long time ago. I say it doesn't matter why we do it. It makes us stronger. We're survivors. Tuscan people are strong and not wasteful." She said this with an emphatic nod of her head. "Today I'm making a feast for friends. You eat; I'll talk."

She listened to Adelina tell her stories of her mother's recipes as she prepared several dishes. Serafina joined her, and when Emily was done eating, she was invited to join their cooking festivities, too. She listened and learned and soaked up as much information about love, life, and cooking as they were willing to share.

Before Emily knew it, daylight was giving way to

dusk. She was surprised to realize that she'd spent the whole day not wallowing in Dae's absence, but reveling in the comfort of these amazing women, who were teaching her things she could share with Dae. And, she realized with a smile, she was beginning to understand and to see the beauty in how a woman could be completely fulfilled by taking care of her family and those she loved instead of building a career outside the home. Emily had always been driven to prove herself to her family, the town where she grew up, heck, even her absentee father on some crazy level. She'd never slowed down enough to learn how to care for others through anything other than giving her time and attention. Cooking, like sewing, and probably a million other handy things, had fallen by the wayside while she strove to prove herself.

After spending the day cooking with Adelina and Serafina, she realized how much more she could offer, how much she'd missed out on, and she now understood why she felt so much comfort when she went to her mother's house for a home-cooked meal. Love came in many different forms. Some were visible: smiles, hugs, kisses. But other forms went largely unnoticed: the effort that went into cooking, the simple act of shopping for just the right ingredients and caring if a person's cup of tea was steeped the way they liked it. How many times had she taken those things for granted?

Too many to count.

As she watched Adelina move around the kitchen with familiarity and appreciation, she realized that Adelina didn't cook for her family or friends because she had to. It wasn't an obligation. It was another way to show how much she cared for them. Emily felt as though she should apologize to her mother for all the times she acted like cooking for her and her siblings was no big deal. It was a very big deal.

Emily watched, listened, and learned, because she wanted to add cooking to her arsenal of skills. She wanted to show Dae she cared in this way, too. Maybe there was something to the old saying that the way to a man's heart was through his stomach.

She was pretty sure there were quicker ways—sexier ways centered around areas below the waist—but this would be fun, too.

Chapter Eighteen

"MARCELLO!" ADELINA CALLED out to the patio where Marcello had been fixing a break in the stone. She ran around the kitchen, her eyes darting from one cooler to the next, as she lifted lids and counted something off on her fingers.

"Come. It's time." Serafina reached for Emily's hand. Serafina and Emily had wrapped all of the dishes they'd made and packed them in coolers.

It was after seven o'clock. Dae wouldn't be landing until midnight Tuscany time. She had nothing but time on her hands, and after cooking all afternoon with Serafina and Adelina, she was excited to bring the delicious meals to their friends.

Marcello made three trips out to the car carrying the coolers. Adelina handed Emily a basket of bread covered with a pretty cloth.

"Time to go to the House of Wishes." Adelina handed a basket of several containers of olive oil to Serafina. "We are meeting women there to make the grandest of wishes together."

Emily had known that they were cooking for Adelina's friends, but she hadn't known that they were meeting at the House of Wishes. Now she was even more excited to see what they had planned.

Marcello came back into the kitchen and settled a hand on his wife's arm. "*Il mio amore,* I have faith in you." He patted his chest over his heart, then kissed each of her cheeks. "Go. Make your wishes. I'll look after my little man."

They arrived at the House of Wishes just as the last hint of daylight melted away. Cars spilled out of the packed driveway onto the side of the road. Bicycles were strewn across the lawn, along with several strollers. The house was dark, but even from the street Emily could see that the backyard was illuminated. They parked across the street, and when they stepped from the car, distant sounds of women's voices brought a smile to Adelina's and Serafina's faces. They exchanged a glance of appreciation. At the sound of voices coming closer, Emily turned back toward the house. A handful of women hurried across the lawn in their skirts and jeans, smiles on their faces, arms waving in greeting.

"They've come to help carry the food," Serafina explained. She brushed Emily's shoulder with her own. "I'm glad you're here. This is what I sometimes forget. When women from all over come together, it's so joyful that you believe they can make any wish come true by sheer will."

One by one Serafina introduced Emily to the women, who each embraced her and air-kissed both of her cheeks. She felt as though she'd fallen into the center of a large family as they laughed and carried on, half the time in English, half in Italian. The women worked in pairs to carry the coolers and bags to the backyard, which hummed with positive energy. It reminded her of her own family gatherings back in Trusty, only there she was surrounded by men and women, but even the air felt alive in the same familiar way.

Tables covered with vibrant cloths were set up in the backyard. Bottles of wine and wineglasses were set along the tables, and chairs lined the perimeter. Candles sparkled in the center of the tables, sending shadows dancing across the place settings. It felt like a festive occasion with voices and laughter rising and falling as the women emptied the coolers and set the tables. Adelina hadn't been pouring strength and love into the dishes for women who were just friends. This was a community of women, extended family even if not related—that much was evident by the familiarity with which they interacted.

Women of all ages gathered around the tables to eat. They filled one another's glasses, bounced babies on their knees, and shared stories that brought laughter and tears. Every once in a while one of the women would leave a table and stand by the tree, her head bowed. Sometimes she'd set a hand on the massive trunk. Emily pictured women doing this for hundreds of years, and she wondered how the myth had begun. What was it about this house, or this tree, that was worthy of being the center of something so momentous?

She listened to the cadence of the group. Even though she couldn't understand everything that was said, she understood enough, and the rest was evident in their eyes. A world of emotions was taking place right before her eyes as they told stories of grandmothers, aunts, mothers, and daughters who had come to the House of Wishes over the years, seeking something. Women spoke of being blessed with babies or finding a lost loved one. Emily couldn't keep up with the stories. Each one was slightly different from the next, but the themes never veered far from the heart.

Emily found herself drawn to the tree, her hands pressed flat against the rough bark. She closed her eyes. She wasn't wishing, and she wasn't thinking about wishing. She was simply being there. Drinking in the beauty and the warm feeling of togetherness these women had draped over the night.

"Missing Dae?" Serafina asked.

"Very much, but I wasn't really thinking of anything. I was just sort of being present." Emily gazed at the others, who were now working side by side, carrying the dirty dishes to the well pump, where another table had been set up beside two trash bins. They worked with practiced efficiency, as if they'd been doing this for years, which they very well might have. Two women rinsed the dishes as four others wiped them dry and stacked them in baskets.

"Do you do this a lot? Get together with all these women?" Emily asked.

Serafina smiled and shook her head. "You'd think it was a weekly affair the way they're so familiar with one another, but the truth is, we barely know them. They barely know each other. When there's a crisis, word spreads fast through neighboring towns and communities, and whoever can make it comes to support the others. When I first came back from the States, Mama took me straight here for this type of gathering." Her eyes filled with sadness. When she continued, her voice was softer. "They make you want to have faith in their energy, don't they? Like if they can create this much energy, they must be able to pull off just about anything."

"They make me want to be around them, and yes, being here and feeling their energy, I believe that the compassion and wills of these women have more power than the house or the tree ever could."

"They do," Serafina said. "This house and this tree, they're just placeholders. They could be anything. A car and a chair. A basket. A shoe. It wouldn't matter. It's the women, and this place, that makes the difference. What they're doing has been done for years and years. Hundreds of years probably. No one knows when it started exactly, only that it's been carried out for generations."

"So, at some point a long time ago, women began gathering and wishing here. It could have been just anyone's house, and it became the House of Wishes?"

Serafina shrugged. "After spending years in the States, I've come to believe that it's probably grown from what you know as a girls' night out. When I try to imagine how it came about, I see a group of friends sharing wine and a meal when their husbands were out working or away at war. I think those women were there for one another through good times and bad, and you know how girls are. We share our hopes and our dreams with one another. I think the myth grew from there."

"I can see something like that happening." Emily thought about her hometown and how fast gossip spread. Word of something so magical would spread quickly. Her thoughts drifted to the bond she had with her brothers' fiancées, making the vision of something magical even more possible. She thought about the place on top of the mountain where her older brother Ross had taken her right before she left for college. He'd said he went there to think, and she'd gone back a number of times since. She realized that she'd even come to believe that if she thought about things there, in that specific location, she'd always figure them out. That was how myths were created. This one was just a little bigger.

"If you ask my mother, she has a whole different idea. She believes it's the energy of the earth and that tree that makes the wishes come true. And see that woman over there?" Serafina pointed to a thin brunette wearing a flowered, knee-length dress. "She believes it was her ancestors who started the whole thing. And that woman there." She pointed to a short-haired woman sitting with a baby on her knee, her head kicked back midlaugh. "She thinks it has nothing to do with any of those things, but everything to do with this exact location and the sun and the moon and the stars."

They crossed the lawn toward the tables. "I don't think it matters how it started or why," Serafina said.

"I think it's just nice to believe, most of the time. Even when it's hard, like the other night when I felt like I couldn't take the hoping anymore, that was a moment of weakness. Right now? My heart is filled with hope for Dante's return. Look around. How could it not be?"

"I'm glad you still have faith that he'll return. I want him to come home to you and Luca. It's what I wished for." She hadn't even admitted that to Dae, but she wanted Serafina to know how much she had come to care for her and Adelina.

Serafina embraced her. "Thank you. That means a lot to me."

"Would it be in bad taste for me to take a few pictures so I can show Dae how much this property means to the women here?"

"Not at all. Go ahead."

Emily took a couple of pictures, and though she knew that Dae wouldn't get them until later, and he wasn't calling her until tomorrow, she sent them off with a brief message that she hoped would make him smile after his long trip home. *Brad and the Chrises didn't show up, but as you can see, I'm in good company. Miss your kisses! Xox.*

Just typing about Dae's kisses made her miss him.

"I guess you don't have to wish for love," Serafina said. "You've found it with Dae."

"Yes, I think I have." Emily glanced over her shoulder at the tree, and she realized that just as she had fallen for Dae, she was also falling in love with the House of Wishes and all that it stood for, the emotions it evoked, and the women whose lives it touched.

Chapter Nineteen

DAE TOOK A long pull of his beer as he listened to his brother Colby tell him about the assignment he'd just completed. Colby had been a Navy SEAL for six years, and although they didn't get to see each other often, they tried to keep in touch with phone calls and emails.

"Anyway, I'm on leave in a few months, and I thought I'd come spend a few days with you. If we can get Wade to drag his ass away from the computer and can convince Leanna and Kurt, then maybe we can all go see one of Bailey's concerts."

"Yeah, that sounds great." Dae walked through his living room to the picture window overlooking the mountains, thinking of Emily. He'd give his left nut to have her with him tonight, the night of the concert, and every night before and after.

"Great. I'll count on it. How was Tuscany? When are you going back to obliterate that villa?"

"That's up in the air right now. I'm meeting with

my client tomorrow. The guy's a real ass."

"You'll seal the deal. You always do."

It's not sealing the deal that I'm worried about. For the first time in his career, he wasn't excited about demolishing a property. He wasn't sure if he wanted to obliterate the House of Wishes.

"So..." Colby lowered his voice. "Did you get some fine Tuscany ass?"

Dae took a swig of his beer and smiled. He was used to Colby's crass remarks. Guy talk, that's all it was. Colby had been that way their whole lives. He wondered why it suddenly rubbed him the wrong way.

"That's your department, not mine."

"Yeah, yeah, Mr. I Don't Want To Hurt Anyone." Colby's deep laugh rumbled through the phone. "Should I take that as a yes but you're not talking?"

"Take it as I met a woman, but she's not a piece of ass, although she is finer than any woman I've ever seen." Dae wasn't sure exactly how his brother would react to his admission, but he knew Colby would give him shit. They pretty much always gave each other shit in a teasing, brotherly way. The problem was, Dae was in no mood for shit tonight. He missed Emily too much, so he hoped his brother would pick up on that and keep his reaction mild.

"Uh-oh. A *woman*. Not a chick. Not a girl. A *woman*. Sounds serious."

Relieved, Dae smiled. "Yeah, it is. She's amazing."

"Serious, like Leanna and Kurt serious, or serious like, yeah, this might last a few weeks, serious?"

"I think we're definitely long-term, Leanna and

Kurt serious."

"Wow, that's some heavy shit. But hey, I'm happy for you. Does she live in Italy?"

"Nope. Colorado. Her name's Emily."

"That's cool, dude. If you're still with her when I'm on leave, I'd love to meet her."

"I will be, and yeah, definitely."

They talked for a few more minutes. After they ended the call, Dae finished his beer, sat on the couch, and kicked his feet up on the coffee table, then dialed Emily's number. It would be seven o'clock Friday morning in Italy. He knew Emily might still be sleeping, but he couldn't stay awake much longer without using toothpicks to keep his eyes open, and he wanted to hear her voice before he went to bed.

He scrolled through the pictures she'd sent of what looked like a party at the property he was supposed to demolish. The House of Wishes. He had a hard time putting the two together. He knew it would just make it harder for him if he ended up tearing it down. The muscles in his neck constricted as he called her.

She answered on the first ring. "Hey!"

"Hey there, beautiful. You sound chipper this morning."

"I am. I've been up cooking with Adelina and Serafina for the past hour. I can't wait to show you what they taught me to make. How was your flight?"

"Long and lonely."

"Aw. I wish I'd been with you. Isn't it like midnight there? I didn't think I'd hear from you until later today. Oh, hold on a sec."

He listened to her telling Serafina and Adelina that she'd be right back.

"Okay, sorry."

"I don't want to interrupt you, babe. I can call later."

"You're not interrupting. I've been dying to talk to you. I kept waking up last night and reaching for you. I miss you so much. Did you get the pictures I sent?"

He conjured up an image of Emily in bed. Of course, in his version she was naked. He cleared his throat in an effort to center his thoughts.

"I miss you, too, more than you can imagine. I did get the pictures. It looked like there was a party going on."

"Not a party, just a gathering, but it was the most amazing thing I've ever been around. Women came from the neighboring towns to…You know, I'm not even really sure how to explain what they were doing. They ate, talked, and wished, but it wasn't like they all wished together at the same time. It was a collective wishing, I guess, but the wishing was sort of done individually, or silently."

"Em, slow down. I haven't slept in twenty-four hours, so my mind is a little foggy. I'm trying to keep up. What were they wishing for?"

"Oh, sorry. They were wishing that the property wouldn't be demolished."

He heard hope in every word. *Shit.* "Em."

"You should have seen them, Dae. It was like being part of this big family. All the women having dinner, taking care of babies, laughing like they'd known one another for years, when in reality many of them had never even met before."

He didn't want to think about the women whom he very well might have to let down. He wanted to have a nice, loving conversation with Emily, but at the same time, he didn't want to lessen the excitement in her voice. He rested his head back on the couch and sighed.

"Hey, babe?"

"Yeah. Sorry. I'm rambling. I miss you."

"Babe, you realize that I can't make any promises about what will happen to that property, right?"

"Yeah." Her voice sounded far away. "I know."

"I'm sorry, but you know this is my job."

"Yeah. I know. I just wish you could have felt the energy these women brought with them. Dae, I know it sounds strange, but I feel so connected to that property now. Being here with Adelina and Serafina and listening to the stories of the women last night, spending the night there and making love with you in that room...It just made the property really come alive."

Dae closed his eyes. He'd felt something when they'd been there, too. And he couldn't help but feel like that room where they'd slept had been left as it was just for them. A ridiculous thought, he knew, but still...

"I know, baby. I know you love that property, and I can't say that I didn't feel something bigger than us when we were there. But I still can't make any promises."

"I know."

He pictured her beautiful brown eyes shadowed

with disappointment and hated knowing that he was the cause of it. He didn't need the income. He could walk away from the job. Tell Frank he wasn't interested in demolishing the building. That would be easy, but wouldn't there just be another building after that? And another? And another? Would this always be a bone of contention between them, or was it just that Emily was overly attached to the people and the myth surrounding this project?

"I'm meeting with him tomorrow. Well, today your time, tomorrow my time. And I'll call you after our meeting. It'll probably be around two my time, so..."

"About ten o'clock my time. I hate the time difference."

"Me too. Why don't we Skype tomorrow night? I really want to see you."

"Okay. Good luck with your decision. I know it's not an easy one, and I hope whatever you decide is what you really want."

She paused, leaving the word *decision* hanging in the silence. How could the decision be what he wanted when he wasn't even sure what that was beyond wanting her?

When she spoke again, the excitement he was used to hearing in her voice had returned.

"You should be really proud of me. I didn't even think about checking email today. Oh!" Her eyes widened. "I loved the gift you gave me. You're so sweet, Dae. Thank you. I'm going to the vineyard and the sunflower patch today."

"I'm so glad. Take pictures and send them to me. And please make sure to take a selfie so I can see *you*."

"Okay. I promise. Guess what?"

"What?"

"Adelina is showing me how to cook a few Italian dishes, and she's explaining the symbolism of the foods. I can't wait to cook for you."

He was glad to hear excitement in her voice again. "I don't care if you never cook a day in your life, as long as you're with me and happy."

"I know, but being here is doing something strange to me. I *want* to cook for you. It's weird. I even want to slow down with my work and, as you said, enjoy the things I like to do. And I want to figure out what all those things are with you, Dae."

He wondered if she'd still want those things if he demolished the building she'd come to love. It had been a hell of a long day, and he was so tired and jet-lagged his eyes were crossing, but he knew he had to ask the nagging question.

"Em, I'm really glad you're having such a good time, and I want all those things with you, too, but are you sure you can handle it if that property comes down?"

His stomach knotted when Emily's silence stretched a beat too long, telling him everything he needed to know.

"Em?"

"Yeah. I…I think so. It's just a house."

Her tone told him that the house had already become anything but *just a house* to her, and the knot in his stomach clenched a little tighter.

Chapter Twenty

LATER THAT AFTERNOON, after spending the morning cooking with Adelina and Serafina again, Emily visited the vineyard in Chianti. The Chianti estate encompassed hundreds of acres atop a hill, with vineyards stretching as far as the eye could see. In the center of the property was a massive, multilevel estate, with heavy wooden doors and multiple terraces, where the winery was housed. Giovanni was expecting Emily. He was a gracious, balding man with a gray goatee, narrow shoulders, and a voice as elegant as the wine he served. He gave Emily a tour of the facilities, which were spectacular for too many reasons to count, but as Giovanni explained how the grapes were cultivated and the wines were made, her mind was tied up in thoughts of Dae. She wished he were there with her, holding her hand, flashing his sexy smile, stealing kisses. She could hardly believe that he'd taken the time to schedule this private tour for her. But then again, Dae had yet to stop surprising her. She missed his voice, his touch, and of course, his kisses, but most of all, she missed the feeling of completeness she had when they were together. She'd been pushing away thoughts about his making a decision on whether or not to demolish the House of Wishes, and as it threatened her good mood again, she closed her eyes and pushed it farther away.

Giovanni led her out the back doors of the winery onto a slate patio overlooking the vineyards. The fresh air brought Emily's mind back to the present. It was too early in the season for the grapes to ripen, but she swore she could smell them in the warm summer air.

The view from the patio was breathtaking. The property rose high above other fields and farms. In the distance, hillsides boasted trees, farmhouses, and roads that snaked through the land. The estate itself was surrounded by rows of abundant grapevines.

"Dae mentioned that you would like to walk through the vineyard without a host. Is that so?"

"Oh." The word came easily, as did the image of Dae's seductive gaze every time she said it. She blinked away the picture in her mind and tried to sound as if she hadn't just experienced a full-body shiver with the memory.

"Sure. Yes, okay, thank you." She wondered why Dae would have wanted her to spend time alone in the vineyard, but he'd surprised her in so many ways already that she didn't hesitate to accept his offer.

"As you wish." Giovanni nodded and his thin lips curved into a smile. "Please take your time. If you need anything, you can ask for me at the front desk."

"Thank you."

After Giovanni went back inside, Emily took a selfie with the stone mansion behind her and texted Dae.

I'm here and Giovanni is lovely. Thank you. The vineyards are beautiful, but I miss holding your hand. Xox.

She tucked her phone into her purse and strolled through the vineyard. The vines held bunches of tiny green grapes. Emily imagined how beautiful the vines would be in a few short months, when plump, juicy grapes would decorate them. When she reached the end of the rows, she paused to take in the view. It really was beautiful here and visually not so different from Colorado. Rolling mountains gave way to bountiful pastures, with telltale horizontal lines of farms outlined by brush and unplowed fields.

But it sure feels different from home.

She pulled the journal Dae had given her from her purse and wrote down what she remembered from the tour so she could share it with him. She'd been too distracted to remember much about what Giovanni said, so she described the wine cellar and the taste of the wines. She smiled as she jotted down the mannerisms that she found quirky about Giovanni, like the way his eyelashes fluttered as he sipped the wine and how he continually flicked nonexistent dust from his slacks.

Her mind traveled back to the evening before, and she described the way the women's voices and faces were filled with so much emotion throughout the evening and how it created a pulse in the air. She wrote about how Serafina's hope was renewed overnight and how Adelina had never looked happier than when they'd arrived back home that evening and she'd fallen into Marcello's open arms as she whispered, *It's done. We did good.*

She set her pen down in the center of the journal and exhaled. She knew it was silly for her to feel so attached to a house that she hadn't even known existed two weeks ago. And it was even more unlike her to let something like that have such a big impact on her life decisions. She adored Dae. He'd waltzed into her life as if he belonged there, and her heart had responded by opening up and embracing everything about him—almost. She was still stumbling over his career, and more specifically, over the darn House of Wishes.

Why had that house become so tethered to her heart?

She pulled out her cell phone and scrolled through the pictures that Dae had sent her. How had her life changed so much? How had she changed so much so fast? She couldn't imagine a life without him by her side. Was she feeling so different and so in love because she was in Tuscany, where every breeze smelled of romance?

She scrolled through the pictures of them together. It wasn't Tuscany.

It was him.

"I do love you, Dae."

She stared at the picture of them in front of the cathedral and touched her lips with the memory of their first kiss.

Emily thought about Adelina and Serafina and the

way Adelina seemed to know just what Serafina needed. Emily was a capable woman, and she thought of herself as having very few issues she couldn't handle on her own, but this one felt a little too big and a little too emotional to try to wade through alone.

She drew her shoulders back and dialed her mother's number.

"Emily? What's wrong? What's happened?"

"Nothing. Why do you sound so frantic? I just wanted to talk to you."

"Emily, honey, do you realize it's only five in the morning here? You scared the daylights out of me. Are you sure you're okay?"

"Oh no! I forgot about the time difference. Mom, I'm sorry. Go back to sleep." How could she have been so wrapped up in her own turmoil that she'd forgotten she was a million miles away?

"Oh, no, you don't. Now that my heart has leaped from my chest and flopped on the floor a half dozen times? No way, honey. Now you have to talk to me. How are you? How's Italy? Daisy tells me that you've been shot by Cupid's arrow."

Catherine Braden had raised six children on her own after her husband had taken off with a woman from a neighboring town. He'd had the nerve to come back to try to squeeze Catherine's inheritance from her, but from what Emily had heard over the years, her uncle Hal, who lived in Weston, Colorado, had gotten wind of her father's underhanded ways and put a stop to them. At six foot six, Uncle Hal was a formidable man, with shoulders as wide as a stairwell and a barrel chest that even in his sixties still roared of virility. Emily didn't want to know what he'd done to her father. Braden loyalty ran deep, and Catherine was every bit as protective of her brood as Uncle Hal was of those he loved.

Emily heard that protectiveness in her mother's voice now, and for some reason it made her feel as though she might cry.

"Italy is amazing, and yes, Daisy's right. That's really why I'm calling."

"Hold on, honey. I need to be up for this."

She heard her mother shifting on her bed and breathing a little harder. She was on the move. Emily imagined her walking through the sprawling house on top of the mountain that Emily had grown up in, making her way down the stairs to the kitchen.

"Okay, coffeemaker is on, sweetie. What's going on?"

Emily sighed, suddenly feeling both a little foolish for having woken her mother up and relieved to be talking with her.

"I don't even know where to start."

"The beginning is rarely best when it comes to matters of the heart. So why don't you start with what's going on right now. I assume if you're calling me at the crack of dawn, then you're having a hard time."

"Kind of, yeah. His name is Dae Bray, and, Mom, he's the most wonderful man I've ever met. We met the first night I was here, and we've spent every day together since." She realized her lips were curved in an effortless smile.

"This is good news. He treats you well, he's a good

man, and all that, I assume? Someone your slightly overprotective brothers won't want to clobber?"

"Oh my goodness, yes. Total alpha, but with a tender side, like they are."

"I'm not an expert on love, Em. You know this. Obviously there's a *but* coming, so lay it on me."

Emily inhaled deeply and blew it out slowly. "He's a demolitionist. He tears down or blows up things. Houses, buildings, whatever."

"Okay. I see. Well...that's not the end of the world. We need demolitionists in our world; you know that."

"Yup."

"You're not a small-minded person, so I can't imagine that you'd feel like you were at odds with this man's career."

Emily closed her eyes.

"Oh, my word. Emily Braden, what has gotten into you?"

"Nothing!" She stood and paced. "I'm not at odds with his career in general. He loves what he does. I'd never try to change that." *Would I? Am I?*

"Then I need coffee more than I thought."

She heard the clank of silverware to cup and imagined her mother in her sleeping shirt, sitting down at her large dining room table, staring out at the mountains and shaking her head at her bullheaded daughter.

"There's this house here that has this myth attached to it. They call it the House of Wishes. Women come from all over to make wishes that supposedly come true. It's an amazing property with an old house that has this massive tree growing right in the wall.

And, Mom, I went last night with the women who run the villa where I'm staying, and there must have been fifty women there. It was as warm as a family reunion, only most of these women didn't even know one another. But they came together to wish for the property to be saved from demolition, and the energy, the sense of community and caring...It was amazing. And that's the house that Dae was here to tear down."

"Ah, now we're getting somewhere. This is the Emily I know and love. You've fallen in love with what that house represents. With the sense of community and the mythical qualities that it brings with it. Em, don't you see? That's how you were raised. We care about family and traditions above all else. It's in your blood. Think about college breaks, when everyone came home, or even now, when Pierce and Jake come into town."

"And we all get together? I love that so much."

"Exactly. It's what has always made you the happiest, being with those you love. I'm the same way. You're so used to our attitude of family and traditions trumping all else that you expect Dae to be the same way. You probably don't even realize it, but a part of you wants him to prove he loves you by not tearing down a house that is attached to something you've come to cherish."

"You don't have to make me sound so selfish." *I seem to be doing that just fine on my own.*

"Oh, Emily. First of all, I know you well enough to realize that you don't actually *need* him to prove his love by not tearing down that house."

"Thank you." She held her chin up a little higher.

"But...I also know you well enough to know that you've been this way your whole life. You see things in black-and-white. Since you were little you judged right and wrong based on what your heart felt, rather than, well, in some cases, what made sense. And you've never had much tolerance for those who didn't see things your way."

Emily hadn't counted on her mother knowing her better than she knew herself, which was stupid, really, because Catherine Braden not only made it her business to know her children well, but she also had no issue pulling them back down to reality when they needed it.

"I think I'm very reasonable." She had to at least try to defend herself.

"Reasonable, yes. But tolerant? Not so much."

"Mom," she huffed.

"Think about it, Em. You're in a field where perfection counts, and you're rarely tolerant of builders straying from your plans. You have always spoken your mind, and when you think you're right, it takes a lot to convince you otherwise. Not that that's bad. I admire your tenacity. I think everyone who knows you does, but, Em, what do you really want from Dae? Do you really want him to make his career decisions based on you?"

"No, of course not." *Maybe a little?*

"You sound certain, but I'm not buying it."

Her mother had always been straightforward, and usually she appreciated that. Today Emily wondered if her mother could try to buy it. Even if just a little?

"Emily, you are a kindhearted, sensitive woman.

You're intelligent, successful, and as strong and stubborn as any of your brothers. And as much as I love you, I'm not going to pretend that those qualities won't sometimes cause you trouble in a relationship. No relationship is easy."

"I know, but Luke, Wes, Pierce, and Ross make it look easy."

"Oh, honey. They adore their girls, but it's never easy. We don't know what goes on behind closed doors. Think about it. Do you think Callie loves Wes coming home with stitches or broken bones from wrestling cattle or mountain climbing or whatever else he does?"

Emily laughed. Callie was very sweet and demure while Wes was a thrill seeker. They'd all seen the way Callie gasped and turned away when he was bull riding or roping steer and how Wes softened when he was around her.

"No. She hates it."

"And yet she knows it's part of who he is and loves him and supports his riskiness. And Rebecca knows Pierce will always try to do everything for her, and when he's able to control that protective nature, it's done with so much restraint that he practically has smoke coming out of his ears."

She smiled at the thought of her eldest brother reining in his protective nature. "So, you're saying that I need to decide if I can love Dae no matter what he decides about this house or any other property?"

"Yes. One day he might implode a building that you feel is an architectural masterpiece. Then what?" Her mother pushed her even further than she'd dare push herself.

Emily pressed her lips into a thin line, fighting against the discomfort of the truth in her mother's words.

"I guess I need to be okay with whatever decision he makes, now or in the future, and I have to trust that his decisions are made with the best intentions." Emily groaned. "I'm being selfish, Mom, and I know that. I mean, I know all of this on some level, but I haven't wanted to see it or think about it."

"I know you do, honey."

"Yeah." Emily laughed a little. "Only you would push me up against a brick wall until I opened my eyes. Thanks, Mom, and I don't mean that as sarcastically as it sounds."

"I know." Her smile was evident in her voice. "It's only fair to you and him if you deal with this now. I'm not going to give you a lecture about the differences between men and women. You've lived through it with your brothers. But you see what the house represents on an esoteric level, and he's a man. Chances are, he sees the tangible structure, the house and the property."

"Yeah, I know that. But honestly, he's so thoughtful that I can't imagine he doesn't see what the house means to the community. He might choose not to think about it, but I'm sure he sees it."

"I guess with you as a girlfriend he has to, because you're not very good at keeping your opinions to yourself."

She heard her mother's smile in her voice. "I wonder where I get that from."

They both laughed, and Emily felt a little better.

"Here's the thing, Mom. I think I know all those things, but it doesn't lessen the hurt I feel every time I think about that house coming down." She thought about their *preserve or demolish* lists and wondered what his said.

"I know, honey. And unfortunately, that's how you're wired. It's in your makeup to be emotional. When you love, you love with your whole heart and your whole being. And whether the focus of your love is tangible or intangible, anything that hinders whatever it is you're focused on feels like a betrayal."

"Like Coco." Coco was the stuffed bear Emily'd had since she was a little girl. When she was young, her brothers would hide Coco in the closet to tease her, and Emily would cry because she believed that since she hated being alone in the dark, Coco would, too. It didn't matter that Coco was a stuffed bear. To six-year-old Emily, Coco was very, very real. Emily still got a pang of sadness every time she thought about Coco being locked in a dark closet. Gosh, could she still be like that?

"Yes, like Coco. It's a house, Em." Her mother laughed, and then her voice became serious. "Myths and traditions survive within us. It's what they mean to us that carries them forward. A house is just a structure, something to focus on while the other stuff is taking place. Honey, the thing you need to figure out is if you love Dae no matter what. If you trust him to make smart decisions that are right for him, even if they're different from the decisions you might want him to make."

Emily sighed. She knew all of this; she really did. It was just piecing it into making a decision that was hard. She couldn't even begin to think she'd walk away from the relationship. She just needed to figure out what was going on in her own head. Talking to her mother helped. It always helped.

"Every time I think of him, I *feel* him, you know? Like he's right here with me. He does this thing where he says, *Hand or arm*. It's stupid, but it's so him. It's like he doesn't have to think about *if* I'll let him hold my hand or put his arm around me; it's just a matter of which one I choose. He knew we were right for each other from the moment we set eyes on each other, and here I am being a doofus."

"A sweet, lovable doofus, at least."

"Thanks." She rolled her eyes.

"Emily, let me ask you something. I heard through the grapevine that Mr. Mangione talked to you about designing the private school he's going to build in Allure. If Dae asked you not to build it as a passive building, would you listen to him and build by conventional standards? Or for that matter, would you turn down the job altogether?"

"This is different."

"Is it?"

She plunked back down beside her purse and journal and exhaled loudly.

"Oh, Em. The heart isn't a rational organ. Nothing ever seems to make sense when you're in love. But I have faith in you. You're a smart woman with a heart bigger than the state of Colorado. You'll figure this out."

"Thanks for believing in me, Mom. Right now I don't feel very smart at all."

"That's what love does to you. It takes you as high as the clouds, and then suddenly you're freefalling toward the ground at breakneck speed. If you're lucky, you figure it all out before you crash and drift comfortably until the next crisis. Or until the next exciting thing happens. Either way, one thing's for sure, and you're not going to want to hear it."

"It can't be worse than half the things I've thought of myself lately, so go ahead; give it to me straight."

"I always do, sweetheart. If it's true love, he won't need to change a thing about himself or what he believes in. And neither will you."

Chapter Twenty-One

ON HER WAY back to the resort, Emily stopped at the sunflower field she and Dae had visited on their way to Chianti. With the photo of herself in hand, she tried to figure out exactly where they'd been when Dae had taken the picture. She looked out over the sea of yellow petals reaching for the sun and sighed. How on earth was she going to do this?

This is impossible.

Dae's voice floated into her mind. *When you love someone, anything is possible.*

She held the photograph out in front of her, scrutinizing the flowers and her profile. She didn't feel like the relaxed, happy person in the picture. She felt like her nerves were pinched, and after her mother's advice, even her stomach felt like it was being squeezed too tight. Was it really true? Did true love mean neither of them should change? At all? What about compromising?

Maybe she should make an offer and buy the

damn house. Take the issue out of the way.

Temporarily.

What about the next house?

Her arms dropped limply to her sides as she wandered along the edge of the sunflower field. She was never going to find the place this picture was taken. She needed clues.

Why would he ask her to do this?

She looked at the picture again. *What was I looking at?*

Memories slid in, soft and welcome. The face she'd made when he first took their picture. His laugh when he said it was a *keeper*.

The tree. Standing sentinel. "That's it."

She looked past the sunflowers to the ridge behind, scanning left, then right, and finally landing on the tallest tree. She inspected the picture again, then sprinted down the edge of the field until she was sure she was close to where she was when he'd taken the picture.

She looked out into the field. What did he want her to see? She walked a little farther, searching the beautiful blooms. Their dark centers were like eyes watching her. Like they were expecting her to see something, too. Her heartbeat quickened.

"Give me a hint, Dae. Is it something about the tree?"

She dropped her eyes to the thick sunflower stems, racking her mind about that afternoon. Had he said something that she'd forgotten? She looked out at the road, then back at the field, and finally scanned the ground in one last frustrating attempt to decipher why he wanted her to go there. Her eyes caught on a flash of red. Anticipation tingled her limbs as a small bouquet of poppies came into focus. It was pushed back between the spiny stems of the sunflowers and tied with a white ribbon. She reached in to retrieve it and realized the bouquet was set on top of the two memo pads they'd used to write down their *preserve or demolish* lists.

Holy crap. What if I hadn't found them?

He had faith she would.

Of course he did.

As she lifted the package from the ground, she noticed the tiny white flowers layering the ground and remembered Dae asking her to look down when they were there the first time.

"You're a tricky creature, Dae Bray."

She walked back toward her car and read what he'd scrawled on the cover of one of the pads.

Read these while you're sitting where we shared our first bottle of wine. I'll be thinking of you. Love, Your sure thing

Emily stopped walking and clutched the memo pads to her chest, fighting the urge to read them right that second. She closed her eyes and thought of Dae, and when she opened her eyes again, she looked back over the sunflower field. This time it wasn't the giant yellow flowers that she noticed. It was the gentle breeze whispering over her arms, the near-silent shiver of the leaves rustling against one another, and the way Dae felt very present, even though he was thousands of miles away.

Chapter Twenty-Two

DAE SPENT FRIDAY morning watching the demolition videos on his YouTube channel. He'd begun posting the videos years ago. He liked to show them to his friends and his brothers and sisters. Hell, he liked to revisit the work he did and relive the thrill of the explosions, the perfection of the tumbling of stone and steel into one beautiful mess.

Around the time he'd decided that flings were no longer an option for him, he'd stopped watching the videos. The thrill of the job had come less from the actual blast and more from the ability to be the best and safest damn demolitionist around. Watching his younger self, arms flung high in the air, eyes wide and excited while a building imploded behind him, he thought about how much he'd changed over the years. He'd never been particularly reckless, but he had never been what he'd consider a candidate for a settled lifestyle, either. He might have nixed having flings and stuck to dating a handful of women for a few months here and there, but he'd never felt one-one-hundredth for any of them as he felt for Emily in the course of a few short days. As if on cue, his phone vibrated and Emily's smiling face appeared on the screen. He opened the message and another picture of her popped up. She was holding one of the memo pads he'd left for her in the sunflower field. The accompanying text read, *Sneaky, sneaky, Mr. Bray. Can't wait to read them. Counting down hours until we Skype. Xox.*

He smiled to himself, glad that she'd found the memo pads. He was prepared for the meeting with Frank as far as data was concerned. It was a pretty straightforward job, and in a few short hours he'd look Frank in the eyes and tell him just that. Emotionally, however, he was nowhere near prepared to make the decision on whether he was going to tear down the House of Wishes or not. He'd forced himself to begin thinking of the property by its name. He could no longer separate the myth, and the community's reliance upon it, from the structure he had been hired to destroy.

Hanging in the balance between his decision and a life with Emily felt like torture. His career was vital to the growth of businesses, areas, even communities, and he was damn good at what he did. He wasn't a hack who tore buildings down for the hell of it or did it haphazardly. He was an expert. A leader in the field, just as Emily was a leader in the passive-house movement. He didn't feel as though his and Emily's ideals were that far apart, but after hearing the hesitation in her voice last night, he had to wonder if she would ever be able to see past the destruction of property to the beauty and the value in what he did.

EMILY STOOD ON the back patio of the resort, holding Luca on her hip while Serafina went inside to get his favorite blanket. She and Marcello were going to take a walk with Luca, and Emily planned on reading through the lists she and Dae had created. She'd stopped at the House of Wishes on the way back to the villa, and she was surprised to see the driveway once again full of cars. There were no tables set up, no meals being shared, but the sense of community and camaraderie remained. Women greeted her warmly. Some she recognized from the other evening; others she hadn't seen before. Women gazed up at the back of the house and the glorious olive tree, and once again, the trail of stories of past wishes ran thick.

The trunk was now decorated with fresh pieces of paper and fabric, spilling out of every crevice in the rough bark. Emily wondered if previous owners had minded women coming from all over, at all hours, and leaving their hopes and dreams in the trunk of the tree.

Before leaving the property, she'd made another wish. A selfish one.

She wished she could understand how to handle the conflicting feelings coursing through her. Now, standing with Luca on her hip, his pudgy little hand in hers, his thick mop of dark hair standing on end, she had another unfamiliar sensation to contend with. A tug at her heart and something else deep inside her. Luca touched her lips, and she instinctively puckered, kissing his little fingers. She sank down into one of the chairs and turned him on her lap, gazing into his dark eyes. It had been ages since she'd held a baby. Her cousin Treat and his wife, Max, had a little girl, Adriana, and she smothered that little cutie with love every time she saw her, but she'd never experienced the desire to have her own children as strongly as she was feeling at that very second. She imagined her babies with Dae's eyes, his silky hair, and his full lips. She even dared to imagine Dae carrying a baby—their baby—in his strong arms, watching everyone who came near, protecting their child.

She gazed down at Luca and wondered how he'd set off her biological clock. She brushed his hair from his face, thinking about Serafina and Dante. She wondered what Dante looked like. Was he still alive, out there somewhere far away, injured or hiding from insurgents? Was he thinking of this adorable little boy and his lovely wife, or was he solely focused on his own survival?

"Thank you, Emily." Serafina joined her on the patio and reached for Luca.

Emily kissed his forehead and inhaled his sweet baby scent one last time. Her arms felt empty without his weight. Her thoughts went to Dae, and she wondered if he wanted children. She'd always known she wanted a large family, but she'd never really contemplated *when* she'd have kids, much less with whom. A fictitious husband was always in the wings somewhere. Nameless. Faceless. Timeless.

Now she pictured Dae's wispy hair and his whisker-peppered chin. It was his eyes gazing back at her from the no-longer-faceless-husband void.

"Are you sure you don't want to take a walk with us?" Serafina asked, pulling Emily's attention back to the present.

"Yes, thank you. I'm sure. I have some things I want to do."

"Okay. Thanks again for watching Luca. Enjoy your evening."

"Thanks, Serafina." Emily gave Luca's foot a little squeeze, then watched them disappear around the side of the house.

She retrieved the memo pads and crossed the yard to the patio where she and Dae had shared their first bottle of wine. It seemed like ages ago and just yesterday at the same time. She'd been so nervous that night, and now she couldn't imagine a life without him. *Love.* Even when she was wishing and hoping to find love, she'd never imagined that it would have this big of an effect on her thoughts and her life. The feelings she had for Dae were bigger than even those she felt for her family. She adored her family, but she didn't crave being with them. Her breathing didn't become shallow and happy tingles didn't fill her chest at the thought of going home and seeing them for dinner or a barbecue. But wow! Thoughts of Dae turned her body into a sizzling, swooning pile of mush.

The breeze had picked up since that afternoon, and the air felt damp, as though it might rain. She folded her arms over her chest, remembering the night they'd met and how she'd lost her ability to think. The feeling had been so unexpected that it had knocked her senseless. She stepped onto the patio, which looked different from the way it had that night. How had she missed the carvings in the wooden table where they'd sat? The deep grooves were crusted over and sloppily etched. She looked up and realized that the wisteria she'd been so taken with had a gaping hole between the vines toward the far corner of the latticework. The floor of the patio was littered with boot prints and leaves. She hadn't noticed much of anything that night beyond the swell of desire when their legs brushed against one another, the smell of his masculinity, and how hard she had to try to remember to breathe.

She set her memo pad on the table and sat down with his. She ran her fingers over the top, thinking about what he might have written. What if he'd written *demolish* for everything they saw?

She flipped open the cover and the first page was blank. She turned the page and then the next and the next. They were all blank. What the hell? She went through every damn page and they were all blank, except the very last page, where Dae had written, *Sometimes the value of something can't be seen with the naked eye. I could no sooner make a judgment call about demolishing these things than I could about tearing down the House of Wishes without proper research.*

That was it.

What the hell?

She picked up her memo pad and scanned the things she'd written. She'd made those judgment calls without hesitation. What was there to research? The dilapidated barn? Why wouldn't you tear down the barn and build a new one? She could see, even from a distance, that the barn was in such bad disrepair it would have been wiser to tear it down. And the sunflower field? How could anyone demolish something so beautiful? Was there even a question?

From the road, the House of Wishes looked like *just a house*, too.

Oh. Shit.

Chapter Twenty-Three

DAE SAT IN his favorite leather chair in his home office, his elbows perched on his knees, palms pressed to his forehead. It had been a long, hot afternoon. He'd had a shitty meeting with Frank, and he didn't have any idea what he was going to tell Emily. He knew what she wanted to hear, and he couldn't make assurances that he wasn't certain he could keep. He glanced at the clock. His gut knotted a little more with every minute that ticked by. Emily had to be up early for her flight tomorrow and it was already after eleven o'clock in Italy. There was no more putting it off. He clicked the Skype video call icon and waited with his heart in his throat as the progress meter circled endlessly. Finally, Emily's deep brown eyes smiled back at him, pushing some of his unease away. He missed her so much. He swallowed against his rising emotions.

'There's my girl. I'm sorry for calling so late."

"That's okay. It's so good to see you. I hate being

apart." She wore a peach negligee that hung loosely from her shoulders. Her hair was tousled, as if she'd been lying down before he called, and her eyes had a very seductive edge to them. Or maybe it was his own desires reflecting back in them. Either way, it was torture not being close enough to touch her.

"Me too, babe. Me too. How's your ankle holding up?"

"Fine. I haven't had any more problems. Gosh, Dae. I knew I missed you, but seeing you...I mean, I *really* miss you. I wish I could crawl through the computer and kiss you."

"If only...I feel the same way. You have a way of steaming up a guy."

Her eyes darkened. "I have a way of steaming you up. That's all that matters."

"Baby, you have no idea." He had half a mind to have a little video sexcapade with Emily, but he was too conflicted about the property to think straight. And he could pleasure himself to thoughts and images of her all he wanted. Neither would ever come close to what he felt when he was buried deep inside her, feeling her heart beating against his, and kissing her luscious lips.

He exhaled loudly and ran his fingers through his hair to try to ground his thoughts. "Tomorrow can't come soon enough."

"Are you sure you don't mind picking me up? I can ask one of my brothers or Daisy to come get me if you're busy."

"I'll be there, and I'm never too busy for you, Em. Ever."

That earned him a smile that warmed him all over.

"I loved the gifts you left for me. And the vineyard was beautiful. I wish you could have been there with me."

"I'm so glad you went, and I was psyched to see that you found the other gift I left in the field."

"Oh, I almost forgot. I have a bone to pick with you, Mr. Bray." She narrowed her eyes, but her smile remained.

"Pick away, baby."

"You didn't write your *preserve or demolish* list. You tricked me."

"No, I didn't. I wrote what I felt to be true. Did you read yours? I didn't think we were that far apart in our beliefs."

She rolled her eyes and pointed at him. He had to laugh. She was trying to be tough, but she was cute as hell.

"How were we not miles apart? I wrote down demolish the barn and preserve the field."

"And I was undecided, so it could go either way. That's not very far apart."

"You are impossible."

"Ha! Totally a sure thing, babe, and when you get back home, I'll prove just how sure of a thing I am." He let his words sink in, loving the instant heat that filled her eyes. "What if the sunflower field was full of venomous snakes? People could get bitten, and you never know who might run into it."

"That's a little far-fetched, but yeah, I see your point. A little research goes a long way, right? I get it. I understand why you wrote what you did. I just...this whole thing is hard for me."

He leaned closer to the screen, wanting to be nearer to her. So much nearer that he, too, wished he could climb through the damn computer and kiss her.

"I know. It's hard for me, too."

Silence stretched between them with longing in their eyes.

"How did your meeting go? Did you make any decisions about the House of Wishes?"

For the first time in years, Dae wanted to tell a bold-faced lie. *Yeah, I'm going to back out of the job.* But when he looked into Emily's trusting eyes, he felt her heart resting in his hands. He could no sooner lie to her than he could lie to himself.

"It didn't go well, Em. He's set on tearing it down, and this is my job, you know?"

"I know. I'm not asking you to give up the job. I realize that you'll probably tear it down. I understand that now. I'm just...I don't know. I've become so attached to the myth and what it means to the women here that I thought it might be easier to deal with the final decision while I'm here, you know?"

He knew damn well. Emily would give her heart to save others sadness. But he also knew that she had in fact become more than just attached to the myth. She'd become enamored with it. He'd seen it in her eyes that night they'd slept in the room with the tree. He heard it in her voice, and he'd felt the energy of something bigger than both of them. He'd tried to deny it all day, but his mind kept circling back to it. He could no sooner deny what he'd felt in that room than he could deny his love for Emily.

"I know. I'm still working things out in my own mind. I've never really had to consider so many people's feelings with respect to my job before. This is all new to me. I mean, how many people become attached to skyscrapers or five-tiered parking garages?" He scrubbed his hand down his face to try to resolve his conflicting emotions. "I'm on the fence about the whole thing, Em, and not just because of you. I'm not a coldhearted person."

"I never said you were. You're just the opposite."

"Yeah. More than you know."

Her voice softened. "I know how thoughtful you are, Dae. It's evident in everything you do. I don't think you're coldhearted at all. But a job is a job, and I realize that there has to be a line between personal feelings and your career. I'm sorry if I've put you in an awkward position. That was unfair of me."

"It wasn't unfair of you, Em. I love that you care so much about the women there and that you believe in something so...so...big?" He'd wanted to say powerful or magical, but both words seemed strange, and *big* seemed too small for the energy he'd felt in that room. "You've become everything to me, Em, and this struggle of right and wrong with regard to this property isn't a bad thing. It's not about what's right or wrong with us. We're separate. Our relationship will always be a separate entity from my work."

"That's what I'm trying to accept." She held his gaze, and he understood exactly what she was trying to tell him. "I know that I need to accept this as if our difference of opinion were something that could happen with every single property, because there will always be something that we don't feel the same about."

"I'm not sure we don't feel the same way about this, Em. I'm struggling with my next step. On the one hand..." He paused, wishing like hell they were in the same room so he could touch her, feel her energy, and know they were going to be okay no matter what. When they were together she wore her emotions as if they were etched in her skin. This video call wasn't all that different, but they were one degree further removed. And he hated that. "And on the other hand, it's my job, and I stand up to my commitments. Always."

Chapter Twenty-Four

EARLY SATURDAY MORNING Emily was wrapped in Adelina's thick, capable arms. By the time Adelina finally released her from her warm embrace, Emily had tears in her eyes.

"You came to Italy in search of something. Did you find it?" Adelina looked just as she had the first time Emily had seen her, wearing a solid gray skirt and top with a pair of leather flats, her gray hair bundled on the top of her head in a loose bun. But where Adelina had greeted her with the excitement of a new guest the first time they'd met, now she regarded her with a thoughtful, serious gaze, similar to the one she'd seen her give Serafina over the past few days.

"Adelina, you are a very wise woman. When I came to Italy, maybe inside I did hope I'd find love, but it wasn't a conscious thought, and I definitely never imagined how much I might learn about myself in the process."

Adelina and Marcello exchanged a warm glance

that spoke of a quiet understanding between them. Something secret and real. Something Emily knew came from years of marriage, and it made her want that with Dae. Inside jokes and the ability to finish each other's sentences without ever uttering a word.

Adelina held out her palm. In the center was a necklace with a silver charm in the shape of an olive tree.

"Marcello and I want you to have this." She placed it in Emily's hand and folded her fingers over the top. "No matter what happens to the Casa Dei Desideri, or the tree we love, you've born witness to the legacy. It will always be in your heart."

"Adelina." Emily's words stuck in her throat. She blinked away fresh tears. "Thank you. I don't know what will happen, but thank you for letting me join that part of your life and your community."

Serafina stepped between Adelina and Emily with Luca on her hip. "Emily, you're going to make me cry so much Luca will need a change of clothes." She laughed as she wrapped her free arm around Emily and hugged her.

"I hope Dante comes home." Emily leaned down and touched Luca's cheek. He smiled and reached for her. Emily hugged him, hoping her doubts about Dante being found were wrong. "I'm going to miss all of you." She handed Luca back to Serafina and embraced Marcello.

"We look forward to you and Dae returning," Marcello said.

He was already giving her and Dae a future, too.

By the time she finally drove away, they were all

in tears.

As the plane descended toward the Denver Airport, it seemed like only an hour ago that they were saying goodbye instead of more than twelve hours. She fingered the charm necklace Adelina had given her and thought about how it had felt like she was leaving part of her family behind. Even the villa she'd stayed in now felt like a home away from home. She could still hardly believe that she and Dae had met in the villa that she'd dreamed of visiting for so many years.

Her mind had spun with a combination of Dae's words—*It's my job, and I stand up to my commitments. Always*—and with her mother's—*If it's true love, he won't need to change a thing about himself or what he believes in. And neither will you*—for the entire flight. Both statements were true. What did it say about her that she had even hoped that he would forgo his commitment because she'd fallen in love with what the property meant to the community and the myth attached to it?

She didn't like the taste of self-loathing as it slid down her throat.

No, she wouldn't beat herself up. She *did* have a big heart, and she shouldn't be ashamed of that. Emily had always believed she was mature beyond her years, but during the last forty-eight hours she realized that she still had growing up to do. She needed to learn to put that big heart of hers into perspective.

As she followed the other passengers off the plane, she wrestled with her uncomfortable thoughts, which were battling her racing heart for her attention.

She was about to see Dae in person for the first time since he'd left Italy. It might have been only a couple of days, but it felt like a lifetime to Emily. Her palms were beginning to sweat, and her stomach felt like she'd swallowed a nest of bees.

She wished the people ahead of her would walk faster. Didn't they know Dae was waiting for her? After days of trying to understand her thoughts, she'd finally realized that her issue wasn't with what Dae did for a living at all. There would always be another house, another property. And if they stayed together forever, as she hoped they would, then there would most likely, at some point, be some other intangible thing attached to a structure that they wouldn't see eye to eye on.

I can't control what anyone else does.

Things aren't black-and-white.

There would always be outcomes she couldn't change, and as she fingered the olive tree charm, she knew that myths didn't become powerful because of what they were attached to. They were powerful because people believed in them.

She didn't really want Dae to change. She just wanted to know that he'd be thoughtful about his decisions and maybe take into consideration how it might affect the community. She needed to know that he'd think things through on every level, not just the physical, but the emotional. And he didn't need to make the same decisions she might make. She just needed to know that he cared enough to make his final decisions, whatever they were, after careful consideration of all aspects. And last night when he'd said he was clearly struggling, too, she'd known that he was doing just that.

She realized that the real question she should have been asking herself wasn't if she could live with a man who might tear down something she'd come to love. The real question was, could she accept—forever and with her whole heart—that Dae was a confident, successful man who had more important and more viable things to base his career decisions on than her hopes and dreams?

The people ahead of her slowed as they entered the terminal and greeted their loved ones. She went up on her toes, scanning the sea of faces in search of Dae. Her heart hammered against her chest as her eyes bounced from one dark-headed male to the next. It was the flip of his chin that caught her attention. Tears sprang to her eyes as their gazes locked, and she drank in his easy smile, which contradicted his purposeful gait as he strode through the crowd, parting people like the Red Sea. She felt her pulse quicken at the sight of his tight black T-shirt and jeans, which clung to his thick thighs as he blazed a path toward her. Her heart was spinning out of control in an effort to reach him. Dae was what her heart desired. He was what she wanted, needed, and craved. Before Dae, she'd only been existing. Once he'd held her, kissed her, and opened himself to her, he'd opened her heart and she'd finally experienced what it was like to love and be loved. She'd finally begun to live.

THE MINUTE HE saw her, nothing else existed. The people who separated them, the noise of the crowd, the announcements of other flights boarding all fell away. There was only Emily, standing at the edge of the terminal, her deep brown eyes sailing over the people between them. His legs moved before he had time to process anything other than *Emily.* He was consumed with her, had been since the moment he first set eyes on her in Italy. Her eyes caught on his as he closed in on her, and for a beat, he felt himself smile, almost forgot to breathe. And then she was folded in his arms. The pillows of her breasts pressed against his chest, her lips on his, her legs—oh, those gloriously supple legs—wrapped around his waist as their bodies and mouths found each other. He didn't need to think; he only needed to be when he was with Emily. Finally, after an interminable two days, she was in his arms again, her hands fisting in his hair and her loving mouth on his. Exactly where she belonged.

"Excuse me?"

The deep male voice brought Dae back to reality. The people behind Emily were trying to move past them. And there they were, making out like teenagers in the middle of the airport terminal. He didn't give a fuck what anyone else thought, but he worried Emily might after she realized they were on display and she was clinging to him like…well, like a woman in love.

"Sorry." Dae smiled against her lips. She was breathing hard, staring into his eyes and smiling like she was never going to stop.

"Don't say anything," she said, and pressed her lips to his again, then replaced her lips with her finger, keeping him mum.

"Not a word until I get this out, okay?"

He opened his mouth, took her finger between his lips and nodded.

She visibly swallowed hard as he twirled his tongue around her slender finger. If she was going to put it that close to his mouth, who was he not to act on what he wanted? Besides, he loved the way her body reacted to him, as it was now, her thighs tightening around his waist, her nipples hardening against his chest. He couldn't have put her down if he wanted to. He didn't care who was watching or what they heard. He needed Emily in his life, and at that moment, he wanted her in his arms.

"I don't want you to change your plans with the house." Her words fell fast and urgent from her lips.

Plans...house...What are you talking about?

His mind was still processing how good she felt in his arms. He blinked through the desires coursing through his body and forced himself to focus. *The house. The House of Wishes. Okay, got it.*

"I don't want you to change one thing about yourself or how you do business or anything. I love you for who you are, and I trust your decisions."

"Emily." Her name rolled off his tongue with familiarity. She'd consumed his thoughts since he'd been home, and now it was all coming together with an overwhelming surge of emotions.

"No, let me finish," she pleaded.

She licked her lips, and he felt himself get hard.

"Em..." He loosened his grip and she clung tighter to him.

"I'm not letting go. You can carry me like this to the luggage area. You can carry me like this to the car.

I'm not getting off of you until you hear what I have to say, and I don't want to talk about it. I just wanted you to know."

She was saying exactly what he'd hoped had been true the whole time. "So you climbed me like a tree and wrapped your little baboon arms around my neck, clinging to me so I can't leave you."

She smiled, looking so damn beautiful and confident that he never wanted to put her down. "Not that I ever would leave you." He touched his forehead to hers. "I know, babe."

"Of course you do. I just told you. That was the point."

"No, baby. I knew you weren't asking me to change before I even left Italy."

She narrowed her eyes. "How could you? I didn't even know."

"I saw the truth of who you were the first day we met, Emily Braden. You're guided by that generous heart of yours, and everything else follows. Sometimes your head tries to take over, but..." He kissed her again. "But it's your heart that drives you. I knew you loved me for who I was and who I am, and I knew that wouldn't change. Now I'm going to put you down so we don't get arrested, because another few seconds of feeling you against me and I'm going to have to take you. Right here. In the middle of the airport. With all the gawking eyes and everything."

She laughed as he set her on her feet.

"Hand or arm?"

"Body." She slid her arm around his waist and tucked herself against him.

He kissed the top of her head as they walked toward the luggage area. "I'm so glad you're home."

"Me too."

He felt like the luckiest man on earth.

"Dae?"

"Yeah?"

She kept her eyes trained on the floor. "Have you decided what you're going to do about the property?"

"Yes."

"So, I guess your meeting went well with your client after all?"

"No. It was shitty. He wouldn't budge." They stood by the luggage pickup area waiting for the luggage to be unloaded. He felt Emily tense against him.

"Oh."

"Yeah. It sucked."

She moved in front of him and wrapped her arms around his waist, pressed her cheek to his chest. "Well, some people don't have the same emotional connections as others. You probably couldn't have changed his mind no matter what you said."

"Yes. You're absolutely right."

"So, when will you go back to...do the job?"

"That depends."

She gazed up at him.

"On when you're free."

She wrinkled her brow in confusion. "I'd love to go back with you. Maybe I can squeeze in a long weekend in a few weeks. It would be nice to see Adelina and the others again and to officially say goodbye to the House of Wishes."

The baggage carousel rumbled to life. When

Emily's bags appeared, Dae lifted them from the rack, tossed one bag over his shoulder, grabbed the handle of her large suitcase, and reached for her hand.

"Do you have a deadline for the project?" she asked. "I'll have to check my calendar."

"Deadline?" He nodded, as if thinking it over. "That guy Frank was a real prick."

"That sucks. Maybe he was having a bad day."

He kept his eyes trained on the exit as he spoke. "Nah. It's who he is. Since I couldn't dissuade him from tearing it down, I bought it."

She stopped cold, nearly tripping him in the process. "You..." She blinked several times, her lips curved into a nervous smile, then formed a worried frown. "You said you always stand up to your commitments. *Always.* Dae, I didn't mean to do this. This is terrible. You've let your client down, and it's my fault."

Her eyes clouded over and her brows knitted together, as if she were caught between anger and gratitude. He pulled her close so they were thigh to thigh, chest to chest. He needed her to understand. As much as he wished this decision had been made only for her, it hadn't.

"Baby, I kept my commitments. *Plural.* My commitment to Frank was to assess the property, not to demolish it. I did that. And I made a commitment to you that I would never do the wrong thing. And I didn't."

"I don't understand. I didn't mean to force you into this."

"You didn't, baby. This was a business decision. I

researched the property, and I researched the myth, which as far as I could uncover, spans at least a hundred years. Don't you see, Em? You opened my eyes to the myth, but you didn't force my hand. I just made the decision that felt right."

"But..."

"No buts. The first time I saw the house, two women rode up on bicycles to visit the tree. I remember thinking that they seemed so at home, they must have lived there, until I saw them hugging that tree. And then you told me about what Adelina had said, and after I got home, I started reaching out to people I know who have relatives in that area. When you sent the pictures of the house with all those women there, that's what really drove the magnitude of what I was contemplating home for me."

A slow smile spread across her lips. "So, you own it?"

"Not yet, but soon. The deal is signed, but there are still legal steps to take. Quite frankly, I think my client was glad to be done with it. He's decided to buy his wife something in the States instead." He took her hand and led her out toward the parking lot. "Now we just have to figure out what to do with it."

Chapter Twenty-Five

EMILY GAZED OUT the window of her hillside home in Trusty, Colorado, wondering how she could have thought that the view from the vineyard in Chianti had appeared so similar to Colorado. Her view from the window overlooked her plush lawn and beautifully landscaped gardens surrounding the patio in her backyard, much like her view from the balcony of the villa in Tuscany. Sure, there were similarities, but the feel of Colorado was different from the feel of Italy. Of course, with Dae by her side, the feel of Colorado was about a million times better than it had been before she left, but the minute Dae had turned down her street she'd felt the familiar rush of panic from having been away. There would be emails to tend to, clients to placate, mail to handle, and every second that passed pushed her further behind. It was those feelings that made Colorado feel so very different from Italy. Real life versus vacation. Could she find a way to recapture that sense of relaxation and happiness without failing in her business?

She felt the warmth of Dae's strong arms circle her waist from behind, his stubbly cheek pressed against hers. She closed her eyes and inhaled his sweet masculine scent. The essence of him seeped into her body, embraced her heart, then burned a path southward. She wanted to find a middle ground. *Desperately*. She didn't want anything to steal what they had.

"Good to be home?" he asked.

Her thoughts shifted to what he'd said at the airport. *Now we just have to figure out what to do with it. We*, not *I*. *We*. *We* was a powerful word. So powerful that even thinking about the future it implied made her knees a little weak.

"Good to be with you." She turned in to his body and pressed her hands to his chest. She loved his body, his strength. His smell. The feel of his arousal against her belly. She tried to push thoughts of work away and allow the desire to be with Dae take over.

I never touched base with my clients.

I need to stop by the office.

The urge to return to the work-obsessed woman she had always been was strong.

"I've wondered what the inside of your home would look like."

She closed her eyes again, willing away those work-related urges. This time, in his arms, it was a little easier. Like when she'd been ensconced in cooking with Adelina and Serafina after he'd left. She wasn't a successful businesswoman because she gave up easily. She could succeed at enjoying their time together and keeping work thoughts at bay. All she had to do was try.

He lifted her chin with his finger and kissed her softly. "It's very *Emily*."

Thoughts of work drifted away. She centered her mind around the cozy and efficient cedar home she'd designed and built using reclaimed wood and massive beams from a horse farm in Allure, Colorado. The exposed beams and the accent walls made from wide-planked barn wood were touches that made her small, comfortable home feel elegant and unique.

"I'm glad you like it. It *is* very me. Some people wouldn't enjoy having such an open floor plan, but simplicity of design and close quarters have always appealed to me."

Wasted space seemed to go along with wasted energy, and using her passive-house expertise, she'd been able to create the perfect setting for tranquility—only it never really felt tranquil. She always seemed to be too hyped up from work to enjoy it. She slid her arms around his neck.

"Having you here appeals to me even more."

"Your body says you want me, but something in your voice tells me you're anxious. Was it the flight? Or is it me?" He slid his hand down her back and squeezed her butt.

Her heart did a little dance in her chest. "It's work. Never you." She felt his heartbeat kick up a notch.

"It's the weekend. There is no work for you today." He slid his hand lower, his fingers grazing the curve where her thigh met her ass, then slid dangerously close to her center as he sealed his lips over hers.

With a pleasure-filled moan, her greedy mouth took over, pushing away all thoughts other than her desire to be closer to Dae. She pressed against him, savoring the sweet taste of him until her body was so full of need she could barely contain it. He gripped her ass with both hands, grabbing, sliding lower, between her legs, coaxing her into dampness. The urgency of her sexual appetite was more than she'd ever experienced. How would she survive it? She tugged at his shirt, needing him naked. Now. One hand left her ass, and she groaned with displeasure. Then suddenly his shirt was off and his hand returned between her thighs, this time from the front, rubbing her through her jeans until she was sure they were soaked right through. She needed him inside her. She fumbled with the button of his jeans, kissing harder, probing deeper. He met her greediness with his own urgency, tearing at her clothes until she was bare chested and her jeans were pushed down to her knees.

"Shoes," she panted out.

But he was already crouched beside her, holding her up with one powerful arm as he tugged her boots from her feet, then rid her of her jeans before stripping himself bare. All those rippled muscles were hers to devour. He scooped her up into his arms, and she crashed her lips to his. In a few determined steps they were in her bedroom, clawing, gasping, kissing, filling her bedroom with sounds of passion. He lowered her to the bed and she refused to let go. They tumbled down together in a tangle of nakedness. Her legs locked around his waist, and his arms slid beneath her and lifted her hips.

"No condom. Please." She needed to feel every inch of him. She didn't want anything between them. This momentarily slowed him. His lips stilled on hers, his eyes opened, and in one heartbeat her feelings were confirmed.

"You're one hundred percent sure? Because I'm sure, Emily. You're the only woman I've ever loved, and I'll love you well past the day we both kiss this life goodbye. But I want you to be sure. You have a career, a life, and there's one percent chance—"

"I've loved you since the moment I set eyes on you. I wasn't searching for love all these months. I was searching for you, Dae. I'm one hundred percent sure of my love for you. You're the only man I want to have a future and a family with. So yes, I'm sure of us."

His lips met hers in a deep, loving kiss that curled her toes. He pushed into her, filling her so completely she never wanted him to leave. Their bodies moved in a familiar rhythm of need and want and a rush of new sensations. An explosion of prickly needles built in her lower belly and shot heat through her limbs, stealing her ability to think. His hips moved powerfully against her, thrusting and grinding with sexual skill that made her whole body quiver. He deepened their kiss, and she had no outlet for the throbbing sensations claiming every inch of her. Her legs fell from his waist to the mattress, the muscles in her thighs flexing. She pried her lips from his, feeling the grip of an orgasm clawing at the periphery of her senses. She gasped breath after breath to keep from dying in his arms from sheer pleasure. He tangled one hand in her hair and tugged. Oh, how she adored that sensation as he angled her and slanted his lips over hers. The feel of being in his control sent her soaring over the edge, and when he buried his tongue in her mouth and lifted her hips with his other hand, she thought she'd split apart from the avalanche erupting deep in her core. He breathed air into her lungs as they rode the waves of their lovemaking. She couldn't think. She was completely and totally under his spell.

BREATHING FOR EMILY, feeling her soft, feminine curves writhing beneath him as her velvety wetness tightened and pulsed, was going to be his undoing. Dae was dizzy with desire and drunk on her love. He'd never felt like he wanted to consume a person before. He wasn't that possessive of a lover, but every time he was with Emily he wanted more. Every muscle in his massive arms ached with need. His thighs were flexed so tight he wasn't sure how long he'd last, but he wanted to pleasure her even more than he wanted to find his own release. She was so beautiful when she came apart, and knowing it was all for him made it that much sweeter.

Her body shuddered through the last of its release. She panted, eyes still closed, and found steadier breathing. He pressed soft kisses to the corners of her mouth, her cheeks, the closed lids of her eyes.

"Promise me forever." He hadn't planned on asking her to marry him. He knew he wanted to create a life with her, but he hadn't thought through the when and how of it. But being with Emily again, he knew exactly what he wanted.

He wanted Emily.

Forever.

Her eyes fluttered open, heavy lidded. They widened in surprise, but she didn't say a word. Her tongue snaked from her mouth and licked her swollen lips. At the same time, she bent her knee, sliding her thigh against his hips. That was all it took for him to lose any sense of control he thought he'd found as his carnal desires surged forward. He plunged in deep, and she matched his efforts, lifting her hips and clawing at his back, sending lightning right to his groin. The room shrank around them, filled with the husky sounds of jagged bursts of air with each powerful thrust. He was drowning in sensual pleasure. Drowning in Emily. She was tight and wet. Her hands claimed his back, his ass, his shoulders, and those glorious legs of hers wrapped around his waist once again. The feel of her destroyed him. Completely, utterly stole his mental abilities until he was powerless to slow his pace, unable to quell the mounting need for release, to fill her completely with him. To claim their love. She gasped tiny gulps of air as she climbed to her own release. He gave in to the landslide of emotions that sucked him under and followed her over the edge as an intense orgasm tore through him, stealing every last ounce of his energy, leaving him spent and so deeply in love he could barely move.

They lay together, limbs tangled, as he slowly regained his senses. Dae rolled onto his back, pulling her in close. Her eyes were still closed, and he realized he hadn't heard her answer.

The air left his lungs.

He felt as if he'd been kicked in the gut. Had he been so lost in her that he hadn't given her a chance to answer? Holy fuck. He was an asshole. He let his own desires take over without regard to what she might have wanted. It wasn't a very romantic proposal either. Maybe it didn't sound like a proposal to her at all.

He closed his eyes and breathed deeply, unable to process his thoughts clearly. She had met his frenzied kisses and thrusts. She had to have been in the same headspace as he was. He couldn't have misread everything.

"Love you." Emily's breath whispered over his skin. Her index finger moved lightly across his chest. She slid her thigh over his hip and pressed her body to his.

Maybe she hadn't heard his proposal. "Em?"

"Yeah?"

"Um...Did you hear what I said when we were making love?"

"Mm-hm."

He drew his brows together. *You did? Well, hell, where's my answer?*

"Okay. Just checking."

She smiled against his chest. "Dae?"

"Yeah?" He didn't mean to sound so gruff, but his ego was taking a kick at the moment.

"Sometimes the beauty of things, even answers, are in the things others don't see."

She was throwing his own words back at him, and her damned finger was driving him crazy, moving over and over on the same spots on his chest.

He exhaled loudly, then stilled her fingers with his hand. *What are you trying to tell me?*

"Am I supposed to read your answer in the way you love me?"

"No. It was much clearer than even that."

He ran his hand through his hair and exhaled. She was fucking with him, and as much as it frustrated him, he loved it. He loved her for having the strength to fuck with him about something so momentous when any other woman would have gushed and probably leaped from the bed to tell the world.

Her finger slid over his skin again. He closed his eyes against the feel of it. The same repetitive pattern over and over. He followed its path with his mind, and—*holy hell. Y. E. S.* She was writing *yes!*

He gathered her in his arms and rolled her beneath him. "You're a sneaky little devil."

"I'm learning from the best."

He pressed a kiss to her lips. "So. Yes? You will promise me forever? You'll marry me?"

She pressed her palms to his cheeks and smiled up at him. Her eyes were warm and loving, and when she whispered, "Yes," the answer clutched him like he'd been waiting his whole life for it.

Chapter Twenty-Six

One week later…

DAISY AND LUKE'S yard had been transformed into a magical world of roses and lilies, with tables draped in white silks and pink satins and chairs decorated with fancy bows. Even Luke's world-renowned gypsy horses' manes had been decorated with ribbons for the occasion. Of course, Luke wouldn't have it any other way. His *girls*, as he called his horses, were as much a part of his and Daisy's life as the love they shared for each other. An enormous gazebo had been brought in for their wedding ceremony, which had everyone in tears as Luke and Daisy exchanged handwritten vows and pledged their love for each other.

The reception was in full swing. Emily watched her cousins Treat and Dane talking with her brother Pierce and his fiancée, Rebecca. Treat kept stealing glances at his wife, Max, who was pregnant with their second child and holding hands with their little girl,

Adriana. She was named for Treat's mother, who had died when he was young. Max and Catherine, Emily's mother, were gazing at Luke, Daisy, Wes, Callie, and Ross, who were laughing about something. Ross lifted his glass toward his fiancée, Elisabeth, and she excused herself from the group she'd been talking with to join him. Emily shifted her attention to Dae, standing with her brother Jake, deep in conversation. Jake was a stuntman who had flown into town for the wedding, as he'd lived in Los Angeles for the past several years. Dae looked striking in his dark suit with his long hair slicked back off his face, sporting a bronze tan, and so handsome that Emily's pulse went a little crazy. One day it would be her and Dae exchanging vows. She smiled at the thought.

"That's a mighty fine man you've got there."

Emily turned at the sound of her uncle Hal's deep Colorado drawl. He and Emily had always been close, and as she wrapped her arms around his burly body, she felt the love and comfort he'd always evoked.

"Thank you, Uncle Hal. It's kind of crazy how quickly we fell in love." It had been a week since Dae had asked her to promise him forever. His proposal was so very *Dae. Promise me tomorrow. Promise me Saturday. Promise me forever.* She couldn't have dreamed up a more romantic proposal. Heck, she couldn't have dreamed up a more romantic man. He'd practically moved into her house, and when they'd met her brothers and mother for dinner last night, he'd stolen away privately with each of them. He'd told her later that he was just making sure they were cool with their relationship. He said they'd been tough on him, but she knew her brothers well, and she knew they were just making sure that his intentions were honorable. Well, that and the fact that she'd received a zillion texts from them last night telling her how much they adored him let her know that her brothers approved of their relationship.

"Oh, I don't know about that. I'm not sure one *falls* in love, anyway." His eyes slid to his second-oldest son, Rex, a brooding cowboy, possessive as ever over his gorgeous fiancée, Jade Johnson. Rex eyed every man who came within ten feet of Jade. Rex and Luke were similar in that way.

"I think love snatches a piece of you from the moment you meet that special person, and the only falling you need to do is into that person's arms." Hal draped a heavy arm over Emily's shoulder. "Not like you have a choice in the matter. The heart takes what it wants."

"Yeah. I think you're right. I couldn't have walked away from Dae without losing a big part of myself in the process."

"Now, that brother of yours, Jake." He nodded toward Jake. "That boy's got something big eating at him. It's gonna take a really strong woman to tame that stallion."

"I'm not sure he wants to be tamed, Uncle Hal. I think he left a piece of himself behind when he and Fiona broke up." Fiona was Jake's first love. They'd dated for two years in high school and had planned to go to college together, but the summer before they left for school, she'd broken up with him out of the blue. He hadn't let any woman get close to him since.

"Love'll do that to a man."

She watched him join his sons, Emily's cousins Josh and Hugh. Hugh's wife, Brianna, was pregnant with their first child together. Brianna had been a single mother to her daughter, Layla, when they'd met, and Hugh had adopted Layla when they'd married. Layla was dancing with Brianna, and Hugh's eyes danced with delight as he watched them.

Emily couldn't wait to start a family with Dae. She hadn't recognized the signs of her biological clock ticking until her trip to Italy. Spending time with Serafina and Luca had cleared the fuzz from her brain, and the closer she and Dae became, the more powerfully she felt the pull of motherhood. Dae wanted a large family, too, and they'd decided to try to start a family right away after they were married.

"Sis."

She turned at the sound of Ross's voice and steeled herself for the brotherly onslaught he was bringing with him. All five of her brothers were heading in her direction. A wall of Braden men, thick bodied and full of confidence, with five sets of serious dark brown eyes locked on her. She searched for Dae and felt his hands circle her waist. She leaned back, letting him take the weight of them closing in on her off her shoulders.

He pressed his clean-shaven cheek to hers. "Hey, baby. Here comes the cavalry." His words whispered across her skin as he laced his fingers with hers across her belly.

Ross's smile was as welcoming as Jake's scowl was serious, but it was Wes's voice that broke the silence.

"I thought I told you not to have too much fun in Italy."

Emily spotted Callie, Elisabeth, Rebecca, and Daisy—in her off-the-shoulder wedding gown—hurrying toward them. *Her cavalry.*

She looked at Jake and drew her shoulders back. "Yeah, well, you also texted me last night after dinner and told me how much you liked Dae." Dae squeezed her hand and moved to her side, draping a protective arm around her shoulder. She didn't need it. She could handle her brothers, but she melted against him, loving his protective nature just the same.

Wes laughed. "My bad. We can't even pretend to give you shit, can we?"

Ross lifted his chin and smiled at Emily. "We're happy for you, sis. It's about time you found your happily ever after."

"Happily ever after," Jake scoffed, and shook his head like they were all fools.

"What? That's exactly what it is, you ass." Ross gave Jake a playful shove.

Jake took a long gulp of his drink. "Yeah, well, you just sound like a sissy saying it."

Elisabeth looped her arm into Ross's. "No, he doesn't. He sounds like a man who knows what it's like to be in love."

Daisy broke into the center of the group and narrowed her eyes at Luke. "What's going on over here? It looks like you guys are ganging up on Emily and Dae."

Luke reached for Daisy's hand and pulled her against him. He smashed his lips to hers with a loud kiss. "We're not ganging up. Just..."

"Staking claim to your sister?" Daisy sighed and gazed at Emily with a dreamy look in her eyes. "Look at her. Have you ever seen Emily so happy? And look at that spark in Dae's eyes. That's love."

"Hey, I have that spark," Wes said.

"Shit, I don't want that spark," Jake said.

Callie touched Jake's arm. "Yeah, you do. You just haven't felt it, so you don't know what you're missing." She sidled up to Wes, and he tucked her beneath his arm.

"I second that." Pierce kissed Rebecca's cheek.

"Jake, I have to say, I agree, man," Dae said. "I never considered myself the settling-down type of guy, but what I realized is that I just hadn't met the right person yet."

Jake crossed his arms, lowered his chin, and glared at them.

"Don't worry about Jake. Being back home brings up memories that turn him into a piss ass," Luke said.

Jake shoved Luke. Luke closed the distance between them, and the challenge in their eyes turned to something more jovial.

"Wanna go?" Luke raised his brows.

"Oh, no. Uh-uh. No way." Daisy squeezed between the two men. "Not at our wedding. You boys are not going to roughhouse and ruin your tuxes."

Jake and Pierce were already handing their jackets to Rebecca. Wes tore his jacket off and handed it to Callie.

"No, Wes. No, no, no." Callie brushed her dark hair from her shoulders and smoothed her dress.

Wes stuck out his lower lip, feigning a pout. "Come on, baby, one little rumble. I promise not to hurt anyone."

"Hold it right there."

They all turned at the sound of Catherine's voice. Her hair hung down her back long and loose, and the smile on her lips wasn't going anywhere, even though her tone was stern.

"Boys, this is a wedding, not a barbecue. We have guests." She pointed to their cousins and friends, talking and drinking and definitely *not* rumbling. "Let's save this for later, shall we?" She turned to Dae. "Besides, you'll scare off Dae before he has a chance to even get to know you guys. Really, Dae, they don't always act like six-year-olds."

"Sometimes they act like teenagers," Daisy said.

"Yeah and you love it." Luke nuzzled her neck and she swatted him.

"There's no chance of scaring me off." Dae took both of Emily's hands in his. "Nothing can keep me from Emily."

Emily felt her cheeks flush.

Jake sighed and held a hand out to Dae. "Sorry for being a dick, man. Just be good to my sister."

Dae shook his hand. "I have sisters, too. No worries, man. I love Emily, and I'll always be good to her."

"Sorry, Em." Jake embraced her.

"You big lug." Emily hugged him back, feeling sorry for him. She wondered if he'd ever get over Fiona.

A cell phone rang, and each of the men reached

into their pockets.

Catherine sighed. "Really? You *all* brought your cells to the wedding?"

Dae held the ringing phone out toward Emily.

"Oh, Emily. You too?"

"Sorry, Mom. I forgot I gave it to him." She took the phone and wrinkled her brow at the international number on the screen as she walked away from the group.

"Hello?"

"Em...Emily?" Serafina was crying.

At the sound of her broken voice, tears sprang to Emily's eyes. *No, no, no. Dante.* She clutched the phone in both hands and frantically turned in search of Dae. She caught his eye, then turned away from the others again.

"Serafina." She could barely push the word from her lungs. "What's wrong?" She hadn't realized she was shaking until Dae's hands on her shoulders steadied her.

"Dante. It's Dante." She sobbed.

"Oh no. Sera..." She turned into Dae's arms, clinging to him in order to remain erect.

"They...they found him...A family was hiding him. He's alive, Emily. He's coming home!"

Emily froze. Sobs wrenched from her lungs. "He's...Oh...Serafina!" She tried to comprehend the rest of what Serafina said, but she was talking fast, and Emily was too overwhelmed to concentrate. Dae held her trembling body against him until she ended the call.

His eyes narrowed. "Baby, is it Dante? Is he...?"

"He's coming home," she said with fresh tears in her eyes. "He's alive, Dae. She said something about a family hiding him until he was well enough that they could sneak him back to one of our military bases. Dae...I know what we need to do with the House of Wishes."

Comprehension washed over him, and his eyes, too, welled with tears. "He's coming home? Really?" He ran his hand through his hair and shook his head. "I'll be damned. That's what I wished for."

"Me too!" Emily searched his eyes. "Wait. You didn't wish for us?"

"No. I knew we'd be together." He pulled her close again. "*You* didn't wish for us?" She pressed her mouth to his, tasting her salty tears as they slid between their lips.

She shook her head. "It seemed selfish. Dae, I think we need to make the House of Wishes into some kind of a women's community center. A place for gatherings, craft sessions, you know, whatever they want. A place where they're always welcome. A place for wishes and dreams to be made and traditions to live on."

"Perfect. Just perfect. Like you." He kissed her deeply, then wiped her tears and kissed her again.

"Hand or arm, Ms. Not-for-Much-Longer Braden?"

"Hand, arm, heart, and soul. Forever and always."

The End

Please enjoy a preview of the next
Love in Bloom novel

Crashing into Love

The Bradens

Love in Bloom Series

Melissa Foster

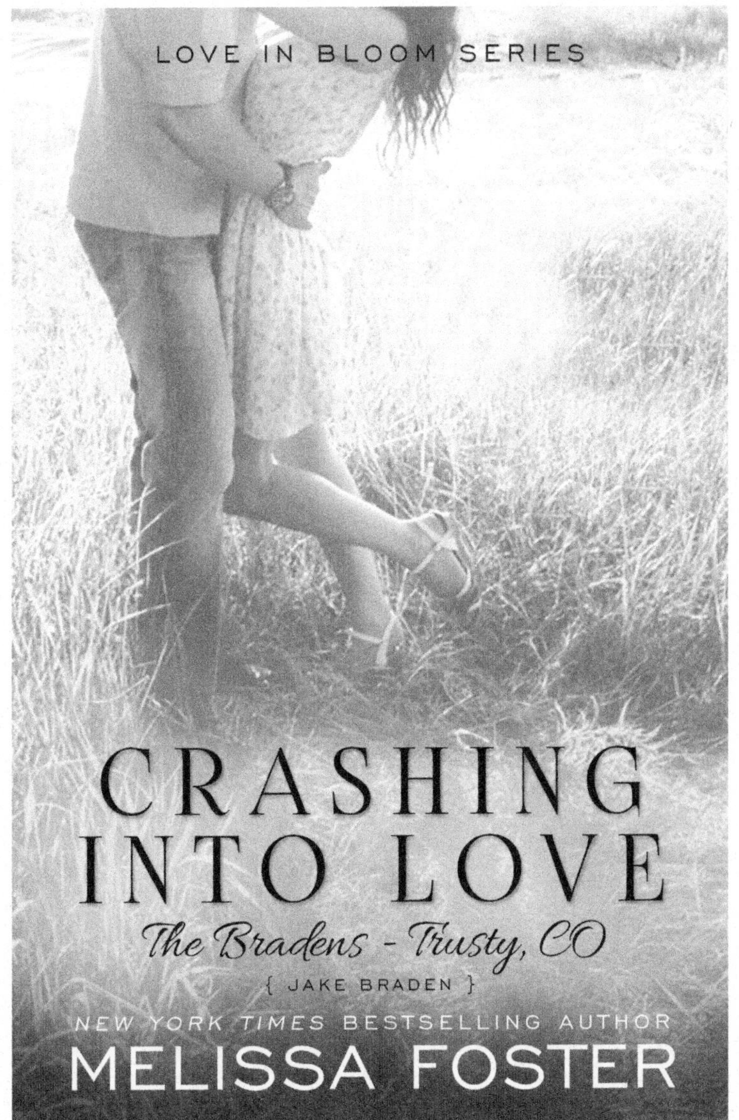
LOVE IN BLOOM SERIES
CRASHING
INTO LOVE
The Bradens - Trusty, CO
{ JAKE BRADEN }
NEW YORK TIMES BESTSELLING AUTHOR
MELISSA FOSTER

Chapter One

IT WAS SUPPOSED to be a quick trip to her hometown of Trusty, Colorado. A few days of hanging out with her parents and catching up with old friends, and then she was off to Los Angeles to meet up with her best friend, Trish Ryder. At least that's what Fiona told anyone who asked—other than Trish, or Fiona's sister, Shea, of course.

Fiona tipped her margarita back and finished it off, thinking about how surreal it had been the night Trish had called her to say that she'd been cast as the lead female in the upcoming action film *Raiders of the Past.* Trish was going to be working with the most famous director in the country, Steven Hileberg. It was one of the biggest events in her acting career to date, aside from the nomination for the Academy Award last year, and she and Fiona had celebrated with a virtual party for two via Skype. That was four months ago, which to Fiona, felt like forever, given how Trish's career opportunity had unlocked a door Fiona had spent years trying to figure out how to open. It had taken Trish exactly ten words to convince Fiona to take a leave of absence from her job as a geologist at the Bureau of Mines and Geology and become her personal assistant during filming.

Jake Braden is cast as the stuntman for Zane Walker.

Done.

"Sis, are you even paying attention to me?" Shea was four years younger than Fiona, and the youngest member of the Steele family. She was as fair as Fiona and her twin brother, Finn, were dark. Shea was also Trish's public-relations rep. Fiona and Trish had met in college, and by the time Trish needed a PR rep for her career, Shea had become well-known in the industry. Fiona had been thrilled with their instant connection.

"Of course." Fiona tossed her chin, sending her long brown locks over her shoulder, and held up her empty glass, indicating to the waiter that she needed a refill.

"Sure you were. Then, what do you think?" Shea blinked her baby blues expectantly.

Fiona winced. She hadn't meant to zone out, but she'd come to the Brewery, a local bar, hoping to see her ex-boyfriend Jake, who she knew was in town visiting his family, and he was nowhere in sight. Her stomach had been tied in knots for the past two hours she'd been watching the door, as if she could will him to walk into the bar. She was sure that when Jake finally came face-to-face with her, he wouldn't be able to resist her. Their connection had been too deep, their love too strong, and their passion had always left them both craving more.

"Just as I thought." Shea leaned across the table, her shiny golden locks curtaining her face. "He's. Not. Coming."

Fiona rolled her eyes. "That would be just my luck, wouldn't it?"

"Finn called me yesterday," Shea said.

"What's my evil twin up to?" Finn was anything but evil, but their family had always joked that one of them had to be more evil than the other. Fiona had dubbed Finn the evil twin. She didn't even know how to be evil—not that he was any better at it.

"Not much. He was visiting Reggie in New York, and when I told them that you were going to finally try to reconnect with Jake, Reggie got all big brotherish and said he was going to check him out. Whatever that means in the world of private investigators," Shea said with a laugh. Reggie was their eldest brother, a private investigator who lived in New York.

Fiona rolled her eyes. "I'll be surprised if Reggie doesn't call Jesse and Brent, just to add a little torture to the next few weeks. As if I'm not nervous enough." Jesse and Brent were younger than Fiona, and they were also twins. Reggie, Jesse, and Brent could be overpoweringly protective. She was glad to have Shea to buffer her with this situation. But Finn had a softer touch, and she wasn't surprised he'd called Shea instead of her.

"Don't worry. I told him to call off the dogs. He knows you don't need hounding right now. I've got your back."

"Thanks, Shea. Do you think there will ever come a time when our brothers aren't looking out for us?" She was just waiting for their younger twin brothers, Jesse and Brent, to get wind of her going to LA. She half expected them to hire a bodyguard for her.

"No way. I think when a brother is born, they come with protective genes, and we sisters are born with big tattoos on our heads that only brothers can see, which read, *Oh my. I'm a girl. Help me. Help me!*" Shea laughed.

The waiter brought Fiona's drink. She thanked him and gulped half of it down. Margaritas served two purposes: They alleviated the ability to focus and provided a false sense of courage. She didn't need alcohol to hinder her ability to focus. The mere thought of Jake took care of that. But she desperately needed the liquid courage.

"The one time I get up the guts to finally try to talk to my ex, he decides not to go out for a beer. Jake always goes out with his brothers when he's home." Fiona had been trying to figure out how to reach out to Jake for the last few years, but Trusty was so small, it was impossible not to realize he avoided her every time he was home. Fear of rejection had kept her at bay, but with the trip to his movie set in hand, she felt like it was now or never. She was finally taking the risk, despite the possibility of being rejected.

"Have you considered that maybe he heard you were going to be here and decided to skip it? This *is* Trusty, Colorado, where gossip spreads faster than chicken pox." Shea finished her drink and sat back, eyeing the men in the bar. "You have a great life, Fiona.

And I know you have your pick of men back in Fresno. Besides..." Shea eyed the guys at the bar. "There are plenty of good-looking guys here."

Fiona glared at her. From an outsider's perspective, her life probably did look pretty damn good, and in some ways it was. Taking a leave of absence to try to reconnect with Jake had been an easy decision when she'd made it, because she'd made it from her heart, completely ignoring her brilliant brain, which was waving red flags and urging her to remember why she worked so hard in her profession and what she was working toward. For a girl who loved geology more than shopping, Fiona's job was exciting as hell. And her social life...Well, her social life probably looked good, too, *from the outside*. Trish was a great best friend, and they got together as often as their schedules allowed. Shea split her time between Colorado, Los Angeles, and New York, so they also saw each other fairly often. And while Fiona was asked out a few times each month, she'd gone out on only the occasional date. And she couldn't really count the invitations, considering that for the last two years she'd turned down all but a few. She guessed that most girls would kill to be asked out by some of the scientists who had tried to woo her. They were well educated, well mannered, and, well, *stable*. *Boring*. Why was it so hard to find a *real* man? The kind who could make her go damp with one hot stare and had hands and a talented mouth that could finish the job. The kind of man who took what he wanted and liked a woman to do the same.

Shea held her hands up in surrender. "I know. I

know. You're done sowing your oats and wasting time. There's only Jake Braden. *Jake, Jake, Jake.*"

Exactly. Jake Braden is the only man I want.

Shea lowered her voice. "Fi, it's been sixteen years since you dated him. Sixteen years. And rumor has it, he's not the guy he used to be. You broke him, and you broke him bad."

Like she didn't know that? Fiona and Jake had dated for two years in high school and had planned to attend the same college, and then they were going to get married. Her life had been planned in a nice, neat package. She'd had every girl's dream at her fingertips. Jake had been attentive and loving, and he wasn't the least bit afraid of commitment. The Bradens were a loyal and kind family, and Fiona knew her life with Jake would have been stable and adoring. Jake would have followed his dream of becoming a stuntman, and Fiona would become a geologist, and they'd have lived happily ever after.

That was the plan.

Reality wasn't quite as pretty.

On her mother's insistent advice, Fiona had ended things with Jake two weeks before they were set to leave for college. She'd taken off for Penn State the morning after breaking up with him, unwilling to stick around for two weeks for fear of giving in to his pleas of staying together—and to see what she was missing. While Jake was hundreds of miles away, she'd buried herself in a new life, which included working her ass off to maintain good grades, sowing her wild oats—which was a ridiculous notion, because she had none—and finally, securing her graduate degree. It wasn't until a few years later, after her career was settled and she slowed down long enough to breathe, that she realized the enormity of her mistake. She hadn't been missing a damn thing. Jake was all she really needed.

And now here she was on a Tuesday evening, back where she'd ended things with him so long ago, wishing she could go back in time.

"Well, Shea. Maybe it's time I put him back together."

ALL JAKE WANTED was a cold beer and to hang with his brothers. They were all in town for the wedding of their youngest brother, Luke. He and his wife, Daisy, had taken off for their honeymoon yesterday. Jake had another week before he was expected on set for his next movie production. He'd given in to family pressure and had agreed to stick around to help his brothers Wes and Ross fix the roof on Wes's shed instead of heading back to LA for what would have been a week of partying. Being back in Trusty made him anxious. He loved his family, but the town was about as big as his thumb, and he'd spent a decade and a half avoiding Fiona Steele. He knew from friends that Fiona was in town, and he didn't need to run into her tonight.

Tonight it was just the guys. Their sister, Emily, had brought her fiancé, Dae Bray, to Luke's wedding. She and their mother, along with their brothers' fiancées, were going to Ross and Elisabeth's house for a girls' night, freeing up Dae and Jake's brothers for a guys' night out. He didn't give a rat's ass where they went as long as they didn't run into *her*.

"Emily said she heard Fiona was going to Fingers in Allure, so we're cool." Wes grabbed Jake's arm and dragged him across the driveway toward their eldest brother Pierce's rental car, where Ross stood by the open door.

"Come on. It's not every day we get to have a beer together." Pierce lived in Reno with his fiancée, Rebecca. Ross, Wes, Emily, and Luke lived in Trusty, and Jake lived in Los Angeles. Nights out with his brothers were indeed a rare occasion.

"Fine, but I'll take my car. Come on, Dae. You can ride with me." Jake climbed into the driver's seat of his rental Lexus SUV. He wanted to hang out with Dae and get to know him a little better anyway, and as long as Fiona wasn't going to be at the bar, then he was cool with it. God knew he needed a drink—or six—after watching his siblings nuzzle up to their significant others all weekend. He loved them all, but he could take only so much of that lovey-dovey shit before he lost his mind. Give him a blonde under each arm and he was a happy dude.

A few minutes later Jake pushed through the front doors of the Brewery with one arm slung around Wes's neck as he ground his knuckle into the top of his brother's head. He pushed Wes away with a loud laugh. Wes smacked him on the back and pointed to the bar.

Music filled the air from the country band playing in the back. As the five men crossed the crowded floor to the bar, Jake spotted at least three hot babes he wouldn't mind taking home for an hour or two. That was, if he were back home on his estate in LA. Picking up women in Trusty posed issues. He'd have to go to their place, which was good for a quick escape, but it was Trusty, which meant he'd leave a buffet for the hungry rumor mill in his wake. And Jake had no interest in feeding that frenzy.

He wouldn't be going home with anyone but his brothers tonight.

Pierce ordered a round of beers and made a toast. "To Luke and Daisy."

They clinked bottles, and Jake sucked down half of his. A hot blonde with hungry eyes standing on the other side of Ross leaned forward and caught Jake's eye. He cracked his most effective panty-dropping smile and checked her out. Even if he had no intention of hooking up with her, a little eye candy was never a bad thing. Not too skinny, nice rack, and...He leaned back and checked out the rear view. Nice ass.

Ross grabbed his arm and turned his back to the blonde. "She's been with half of the single guys in town."

"Do I care?" Jake arched a brow.

"You sure as hell should." Ross was the Trusty town veterinarian. He, like Jake and their other brothers, had never dated women from Trusty. It was easier to date women from neighboring towns and avoid the gossip.

Jake ran his hand through his thick dark hair and sucked down the rest of his beer, set the bottle on the bar with a loud *Ahh*, and motioned for another.

"Emily said you weren't exactly picky," Dae said. All of the Braden men were more than six feet tall, with dark hair and hallmark Braden dark eyes. Dae fit right into the tall, dark, and built-for-a-fight mold, although he wore his hair much longer than the close-cut styles Jake and his brothers sported.

"Life's short, man. Gotta share the love." Jake thanked the bartender for his drink and leaned his hip against the bar, allowing himself a better view of the tables and the dance floor in the back of the bar. "I don't remember there being this many good-looking women in Trusty."

Wes turned around and eyed the dance floor. "Your standards have gone to shit, bro."

"Ouch, man. That hurts." Jake laughed.

"Come on," Pierce said. "Let's get a booth in the back where we can talk." As the oldest, Pierce was used to directing. Their father had left before Jake was born, and Pierce had stepped in and watched over them all. Pierce owned resorts all over the world, and there had been a time when Pierce matched Jake woman for woman—a playboy without any interest in settling down. But meeting Rebecca Rivera had changed all of that. Jake was the last single Braden, and he intended to keep it that way.

"Sounds good to me. I forgot how meat-markety bars are. Haven't been in one for a while," Ross said as he followed Pierce away from the bar.

Jake watched them take a few steps. They were a good-looking bunch, no doubt, but something about the way his brothers carried themselves had changed since they'd each entered couplehood. The sharp edges they'd honed hadn't exactly turned soft—Braden men were alpha to the core—but Jake noticed less of a swagger and more of a confident, my-woman's-waiting-at-home hitch in their gait.

"I'm gonna grab another beer. Meet you there in a sec." Jake waved them off and eyed the blonde again. She was twisting her hair around her finger and eyeing him like he was a big old chocolate bar. *Oh yeah, baby. You can have a piece.*

She smiled and sauntered over. She arched her back and leaned in close, giving Jake a clear view down her sweetly low-cut blouse.

"Jake Braden, right?" she said in a heady voice.

"The one and only." He held her seductive gaze, but hell if in the back of his mind he didn't hear his brother's words. *Your standards have gone to shit, bro.*

Standards. Jake wasn't sure he had many of those left, and he liked his life that way. Uncomplicated. No ties to anyone other than himself and his family. He swigged back his beer and ordered another.

Blondie slipped her index finger into the waist of his low-slung jeans. Her eyes widened as she wiggled that finger against his skin, searching for drawers she wouldn't find. Jake grinned.

"You've got quite a rep around here." She glanced down at her finger, still hooked in the waist of his jeans. "Is it true that stuntmen do it rough?"

Jake leaned down and put his mouth beside her ear, inhaling the scent of her sweet perfume and letting her anticipation build before answering. He knew how to play the game. He was a master at it. Hell, most of the time he felt like he'd invented it. He did a quick sweep of the bar, readying to tell her just how good he could be—*rough and raw or gentle as a field of daisies*—when his eyes caught on Fiona Steele sitting at a booth near the back of the room and staring directly at him. His gut clenched tight.

Fuck.

Blondie tugged on his waistband, bringing him back to the current situation, where he was leaning over a twentysomething blonde who may or may not have slept with half of Trusty. His brain was stuck. He couldn't think clearly. Fiona was there, and she looked so damn good that he felt himself getting hard. If his dick were a guy, he'd knock the hell out of it. He'd done a damn good job of avoiding her for all these years—well, except last year, when in a moment of weakness he'd tried to find her the last time he'd been back in town. He never had found her, but he'd found a brunette from another town more than willing to take the edge off his pent-up frustrations.

He forced his eyes away from Fiona, grabbed his beer from the bar, and stalked toward the back of the bar without a word to Blondie.

"Hey!" Blondie called after him.

He kept his eyes trained on the back wall of the bar with one goal in mind, to find his brothers and drink himself into oblivion.

"Jake."

He hadn't heard her voice in years, and it still sent heat searing through him—and stopped him cold. *Walk. Keep moving.* His body betrayed him and turned to face Fiona Steele. His eyes swept over her flawless skin. Her sharp jawbone and high cheekbones gave her a regal look. Not in a pretentious way, but in the way of a woman so naturally beautiful that it set her apart from all others. His eyes paused on her almond-shaped eyes, as blue as the night sea. God, he'd always loved her eyes. Her face was just as beautiful as it had been when she was a teenager, maybe even more so. He shifted his gaze lower, to her sweet mouth, remembering the first night they'd made out. They were both fifteen, almost sixteen. She'd tasted like Colgate toothpaste and desire. They'd kissed slowly and tenuously. He'd urged her mouth open, and when their tongues touched for the first time, his entire body had electrified in a way he'd never matched with any other woman. Kissing Fiona had made his entire body prickle with need. He'd dreamed of her kisses, longed for them every hour they were apart. They'd made out between classes and after school, staying together late into the night. Her mouth was like kryptonite, stealing any willpower he'd ever possessed.

Until that summer afternoon, when that mouth he'd fallen in love with broke his heart for good.

"Jake," Fiona repeated.

He clenched his jaw and shifted his eyes over her shoulder—not seeing anything in particular as he tried to move past the memory of losing the only person he'd ever loved. He'd spent years forcing himself to forget how much he loved her and grow the hell up, and in doing so, he hadn't allowed himself to even say her name. And now he didn't want to hear it coming from his lungs. Instead he lifted his chin in response.

"You look great. How have you been?"

Maybe no one else would have picked up on the

slight tremor in her voice, or the way she was fidgeting with the edge of her shirt, but Jake remembered every goddamn mannerism and what it meant. Good. She should be nervous.

He knew he was being a prick, but years of repressed anger simmered inside him. The memory of the first time they'd made love slammed into his mind. He remembered the almost paralyzing fear and the thrill of it being her first time, and his. He'd worried that he wouldn't last or he'd do something wrong, but his biggest fear had been that he'd hurt her. He turned away, trying to force the thought away. Little did he know that two years later, it would be her who'd do the hurting.

"Great, thanks," he managed. It was no use. He couldn't resist meeting her gaze again, and the moment he did, he felt himself being sucked into her eyes, stirring up the memories he'd tried to forget. He couldn't look away. Not even when the memory of her dumping him all those years ago came back like hot coals burning him from the inside out. She'd stopped taking his calls, and though she'd returned his texts for the first day or two, after that it was like she'd vanished without caring that she'd ripped his guts out.

She shifted her eyes and he saw them lock on Wes. She smiled in his direction, then quickly looked away.

What the hell was that about? Jake pointed his thumb over his shoulder. "Gotta go meet my brothers."

"Oh." Fiona dropped her eyes, breaking their connection.

Jake's synapses finally fired and he turned away, catching sight of Shea waving from a booth to his left.

She'd been barely a teenager when he'd left for college, as starry-eyed and naive as the day was long. He lifted his chin in greeting and stalked back to his brothers' table.

"I'm outta here." He felt the heat of Fiona's stare on his back.

"What? You haven't even had a beer with us." Pierce smacked the seat beside him. "Sit your ass down, bro."

Jake blew out a frustrated breath. "She's here."

Wes and Ross exchanged a knowing glance that made his blood boil. He got the feeling that they'd known Fiona was going to be there. *What the hell is going on?*

Pierce grabbed Jake's arm and yanked his ass down beside him. "Sit down and have a beer with your family and Dae."

Normally Jake would tell Pierce to kiss off when he was in a mood like this, but something strange was going on inside him. He was too angry and confused to bother. He couldn't get the image of Fiona's beautiful face out of his mind. *Goddamn it.* He picked up Pierce's beer, and when Pierce opened his mouth to complain, Jake shut him up with a fight-me-for-it glare and sucked it down. He should have grabbed the blonde chick and left the bar for a night of no-strings-attached sex. Now he was bound to be up all night, trying to forget the hopeful and pained look in Fiona's eyes—the same damn look she'd had when she'd kicked him to the curb.

"You didn't have to be a dick to her," Wes said. "You look like a rattlesnake coiled to strike."

"That was an asshole move," Ross agreed. "You left her standing there looking stupid when she was just trying to say hello."

Jake looked away from them, breathing harder by the second.

"Jake." Dae's dark eyes turned serious. "Weren't you with her for two years or something? She's probably trying to mend fences or find closure."

"Yeah?" Jake rose to his feet and slammed the beer down on the table. "Well, I'm not that guy anymore, and I have no interest in mending a damn thing." He turned on his heel, stormed over to the bar, grabbed Blondie's hand, and dragged her outside, chased by the forlorn look in Fiona's eyes and the clawing ache of wishing it were her he was helping into his car.

(End of Sneak Peek)

To continue reading, be sure to pick up the next
LOVE IN BLOOM release:
CRASHING INTO LOVE, The Bradens

Please enjoy a preview of the next
Love in Bloom novel

SEASIDE
Secrets

Seaside Summers, Book Four

Love in Bloom Series

Melissa Foster

NEW YORK TIMES BESTSELLING AUTHOR

MELISSA FOSTER

Seaside Secrets

Love in Bloom: Seaside Summers

Contemporary Romance

Chapter One

"I JUST CAN'T believe that Jamie's the first one to get married. I mean, Jamie? He never even wanted to get married." Amy Maples was three sheets to the wind, sitting in a bar at the Ryder Resort in Boston. That was okay, she rationalized, because it was the night before her good friends Jessica Ayers and Jamie Reed's wedding, and she and her friends were celebrating. Besides, now that Jessica and Jamie were getting married and her other three besties had gotten engaged, Amy was the only single woman of the group. Drunk was the only way she was going to make it through the weekend.

"But that was before he met Jessica and she rocked his world." Jenna leaned across the table in the dimly lit bar and grabbed Amy's hand.

Amy saw Jenna's lips curve into a smile as she shifted her eyes to Tony Black, another friend they'd known forever, sitting with his arm around Amy, as per usual. Jenna raised her brows with a smile, implying something Amy knew wasn't true. She rolled her eyes in response. Tony always sat with his arm around her, and it didn't mean a damn thing, no matter how much she wished it did.

Amy and her besties, Jenna Ward, Bella Abbascia, and Leanna Bray, had grown up spending summers together at the Seaside community in Wellfleet, Massachusetts, and to this day they continued to spend their summers there, along with Jamie and Tony. The six of them had spent eight weeks together every summer for as long as Amy could remember. Their parents had owned the Seaside cottages, which they'd passed down to them. Summers were Amy's favorite time of year. Now that Amy's company, Maples Logistical & Conference Consulting, was so successful, she was able to take eight weeks off while her small staff handled the workload. Amy had spent seven years building and nurturing the business, and over the last three years she had turned it into a six-figure venture with clients varying from accounting to full-on logistical consulting. She could hardly believe how her life, and her summers, had changed. Just four years ago she was working part-time during the summers at one of the local restaurants to keep a modicum of income coming in. She loved summers even more now that she didn't have to work. Of course, her love of summers might also have something to do with being in love with the six-foot-two professional surfer and motivational speaker currently sitting beside her.

If only it were reciprocated. She tipped back her glass and took another swig of her get-over-Tony drink.

"Petey, can you please get me another drink?" Jenna batted her lashes at her fiancé, Pete Lacroux. She and Pete had gotten engaged last year. Pete was a boat craftsman and he also handled the pool maintenance at Seaside. Pete nuzzled against her neck, and Amy slid her eyes away. Maybe if Sky, Pete's sister, were there, she'd feel a little better. Sky wasn't currently dating anyone either, but Sky had to work, so Amy was on her own.

Bella and her fiancé, Caden Grant, were whispering nose to nose, Leanna was sitting on Kurt's lap with her forehead touching his, and Jamie and Jessica were looking at each other like they couldn't wait to tear each other's clothes off. Amy stole a glance at Tony, and her heart did a little dance. Delicious and painful memories from the summer before college tried to edge into her mind. As she'd done for the past fourteen years, she pushed them down deep as Tony leaned in close.

God, she loved how he smelled, like citrus and spice with an undertone of masculinity and sophistication. She knew he wore Dolce & Gabbana's The One. She kept a bottle of The One beside her bed at home in Boston, and every once in a while, in the dead of winter or on the cusp of spring, when months stretched like eons before she'd see Tony again, she'd spray the cologne on her pillow so she could smell him as she drifted off to sleep. It never smelled quite as good as Tony himself. Then again, Tony could be covered in sweat after a five-mile run, or laden with sea salt after a day of surfing, and he'd still smell like heaven on legs. Since they were just friends, and it looked like there was no chance of them becoming more, she relied on her fantasies to keep her warm. When she was alone in bed at night, she held on to the image of Tony wearing only his board shorts, his broad shoulders and muscular chest glistening wet, muscles primed from the surf, and those delicious abs blazing a path to his—

Tony pressed his hand to her shoulder and pulled her against him, bringing her mind back to the present.

"Time for ice water?" he asked just above a whisper.

So much for her fantasy. She was always the *good girl* who did the right thing, the only exception being occasionally having an extra drink or two when she was with her Seaside friends. At least that's what she led everyone to believe. Only she and Tony knew that wasn't the only exception—and she made sure that was a taboo subject between them. He wouldn't dare bring it up. She might not survive if he did. She sobered a little with the memory and shifted it back into the it-never-happened place she buried deep inside her. Her secret was lonely in that hollow place, being the only one kept under lock and key.

She met Tony's denim-blue eyes and felt a familiar rush of anticipation in her belly. Maybe tonight she wouldn't be the good girl.

"Um, actually, I think I want another drink."

Tony arched a brow in that sexy way that made his eyes look even more intense. He pressed his cheek to hers and whispered, "Ames, you can't show up for the wedding tomorrow with a hangover."

No, she certainly couldn't. But she'd like him to stay right where he was for a while longer, thank you very much. Since she had a life-changing job offer in hand—a dream job worthy of closing down the business she'd spent seven years building and keeping only a handful of clients—she and her girlfriends had decided it was time for Amy to take a chance and lay her feelings on the line with Tony. She picked up her glass and ran her finger around the rim, hoping she looked sexy doing it. Then she sucked that finger into her mouth, feeling a little silly.

I suck at this whole seduction thing.

"I'm a big girl, Tony. I think I know what I can handle." *And I don't want to handle my liquor tonight. I have plans. Big plans.*

Tony rose to his feet with a perturbed look on his face and rubbed his stubbly jaw. "You sure?"

"Mm-hm." Even as she said it, she considered saying, *Water's good. Just get me water.* She watched him walk up to the bar. At heart, Amy was a good girl. Her courage faltered and she tried to hang on to a shred of it. She needed to know if there was even the slightest chance that she and Tony might end up together. The problem was, she wasn't a seductress. She didn't even know where to begin. That was Jenna's forte, with her hourglass figure and sassy personality. Even Bella, who was as brash as she was loving, had pulled off being seductive with Caden. The sexy-kitten pictures on Amy's pajamas were more seductive than she was.

"Oh my God. I thought he'd never leave the table."

Jenna glanced at Caden, Kurt, and Jamie, still enthralled with their fiancées at the other end of the table. She pulled Amy across the table and whispered, "This is your night. I can feel it!" She sat back and swayed to the music in her tight green spaghetti-strap dress with a neckline cut so low Pete could probably get lost in there.

Amy looked down at the slinky black dress the girls had put her in earlier that evening. They were always trying to sex her up. *One look at you in this dress with these fuck-me heels and Tony's gonna be all over you*, Jenna had said while Jessica and Bella shimmied the dress down Amy's pin-thin body. *Fits like a glove. A sexy, slither-me-out-of-this glove,* Leanna had added. They'd pushed her into a chair, plied her with wine, and sometime later—Amy had no idea how long, because the alcohol had not only made her body go all loose and soft, but it had turned her brain to mush—they were in the bar with the men, and with her friends' confidence, she'd actually begun to believe that she might be able to pull off being übersexy for a night. Her mind might be foggy, but she'd caught a few words while the girls primped her into a hot, racy woman she didn't recognize. Her friends had thrown out words like *sexy, hot, take him* as if they were handing out doses of confidence.

Now she tugged at the hemline of the dress that barely covered the thong they'd also bought for her and insisted she wear. She wiggled in her seat, uncomfortable in the lacy butt floss. She should probably give up even trying and just let the new job change her life. Move to Australia, where she'd be too far for any relationship with Tony, and be done with it, but every time she looked at Tony, her stomach got all fluttery. It had done that since she was six years old, so she was pretty sure it wasn't going to change.

Caden, Pete, Jamie, and Kurt must have taken Jenna's whispers and hot stares as a cue, because they headed up to the bar, and Jessica, Bella, and Leanna scooted closer to Amy and Jenna.

"How about you put those puppies away before the guys over at that table drool into their drinks," Leanna said to Jenna while glaring at the three handsome, leering men sitting at the next table. They finally looked away when Bella shot them a threatening stare.

Jenna wrestled her boobs into submission with an annoyed look on her face. She always acted annoyed about her boobs, but Amy knew it was a love-hate annoyance. Jenna wouldn't be Jenna without her boobs always trying to break free.

"Look at our men up there at the bar." Bella wiggled her fingers at Caden. "Pete has his eyes on the drooling men. Kurt and Jamie are eyeing Leanna and Jessica like they're on the menu, and Tony..."

"*Your* men," Amy corrected her. "Tony's not mine, and he looks mad, doesn't he?"

"Sexually frustrated, maybe. Not mad." Bella took a sip of her drink. "But you'll fix that tonight. I mean, be real, Amy. Who tells a girl to *behave and be careful* whenever she goes out if he's not interested? Why would he care? And not just that—he always adds that you can text him if you need him and he'll come running. Just. Like. Always."

Amy couldn't stop the exasperated sound that left her lips. "You read my texts?" That was the only way she could have known that Tony always offered to be there if she needed him.

"Duh. Of course I did. Consider it a recon mission. I had to know what we were dealing with here from his side." Bella had been pulling for Amy and Tony to get together as long as Amy had been in love with him, which was just about forever. She stood and dragged Amy toward the dance floor. "Come on, sweetie. Time to have some fun."

The other girls jumped up and followed them. Amy sensed Tony's eyes on her before she caught sight of him watching them. It made her nervous and excited at once. The music blared with a fast beat. Amy's head was spinning from the alcohol, and as Bella and Jenna dirty danced up and down her body, gyrating with their hands in the air, Amy tried to ignore the rush of anticipation mixing with nervous energy inside her. Leanna and Jessica danced beside them in a far less evocative fashion that was more Amy's speed, but she could no sooner disengage from being the target of Jenna's and Bella's sexual dancing then she could ignore Tony as he moved to the edge of the dance floor. His eyes raked slowly down her body, making her insides twist in delight. His jaw muscles bunched as he slid his eyes around the bar and leveled the leering men at the table a few feet away with a dark stare.

The sexy dancing, the alcohol, and the way Tony was guarding her like she was a precious treasure—his precious treasure?—boosted her confidence. Amy rocked her hips to the beat. She closed her eyes, lifted her hands above her head, and let the music carry her into what she hoped was a plethora of tempting moves.

"You go, girlfriend," Jenna encouraged her. "He's not going to be able to resist you. You're drunk, sexy, and ready for action. What man could resist that?" She wiggled her butt against Amy's hips.

"Oh, please. He'll probably *never* reciprocate my feelings, which is why I'm seriously considering the job offer from Duke Ryder." *Never again, anyway.* Her chest tightened with the thought.

"No, you are *not*." Bella's eyes widened as she froze and pointed her finger at Amy, right there in the middle of the dance floor. "You are not going to move to Australia for two years. You'll never come back to Seaside in the summers if you're in *Australia*. Can't you tell Duke you'll consider nine months out of the year instead of twelve?"

Duke Ryder was a real estate investor who owned more than a hundred properties throughout the world. He was also Blue and Jake's older brother. Blue Ryder was a specialty carpenter who had renovated Kurt and Leanna's cottage and built an art studio for Jenna and Pete. He'd since become one of the gang and hung out with them often. Jake was an Army Ranger and mountain-rescue specialist. Amy had dated Jake briefly last summer, but he was younger and too wild for her. And...he wasn't Tony.

"No, I can't," Amy answered. "It's a full-time position heading up the creation of the new Ryder Conference Center. The conference center is going to be the focus of international meetings with major corporations. I think I need to be on-site full-time." Amy had worked with Duke on a consulting basis for several years. When Jessica and Jamie had said they were getting married at the Ryder Resort in Boston, Amy had jumped at the chance to help plan the event and work with Duke and his staff again. Amy had known that Duke was negotiating on a property in Australia, but she hadn't realized he'd sealed the deal until she'd arrived at the resort two days ago and he'd offered her a full-time job as director of operations for the Conference Division Center. She'd never been to Australia, and between all of her friends getting engaged and summer after summer of wasted energy spent on a man who treated her more like an adoring brother would than a potential love interest might, she decided it was high time she made some changes in her life.

Amy tucked her straight blond hair behind her ears and moved her shoulders to the slow beat of the music. "I'm not sure being here for the summer is smart anyway. It's like torturing myself." She stopped dancing at the thought of not coming back to Seaside for the summers. Could she really do that? Would she even want to? Could she survive not seeing Tony even if she knew for sure he didn't want her?

This was why she had to figure out her life and make a change. She was becoming pathetic.

She sensed Tony's eyes on her again and forced her hips to find the beat as Bella and Leanna danced closer. "It might be time I move on," she said more confidently than she felt.

"Move on from Tony?" Bella took her hand and dragged her back toward the table with the others on their heels.

Amy saw Tony's eyes narrowing as they hurried past. Why was he so angry all of a sudden?

"He's so into you, he won't let you go." Bella elbowed her as they took their seats. "He texts you almost every day."

"Yeah, with stuff like, *Won another competition* and *Check me out in* Surfer Mag *next month!* He texts me when he's going to miss an event at Seaside. He doesn't text me because he misses me or wants to see me." Tony had started texting her during the summers when they were teenagers, because Amy was the only one who checked her cell phone when they were at the Cape, and at some point, those summer texts had turned into a year-round connection. He'd stopped texting her for a few years when she was in college and he was building his surfing and speaking careers, although she knew the real reason he'd stopped, and it had nothing to do with either. After she'd graduated from college, he'd begun texting again. She hadn't known why he started up again, and after losing that connection for so long, she didn't ask. She was just glad to have him back. Since then, she'd become his habit, but not exactly the type of habit she wanted to be.

"It's not like what each of you have. I want that, what you have. I want a guy who says I'm the only woman for him and that he can't live without me, like your guys say to you." *I want Tony to say that.*

Seeing her girlfriends so much in love was what

really drove home how lonely Amy had become over the past few summers.

"I think he takes care of you like you're *his*. I mean, how many guys text to say they saw a kitty pajama top you'd look adorable in if they aren't gay or interested?" Bella shifted her shoulders in a *Yeah, that's right* way.

"I'm probably the only woman he knows who wears kitty pajamas. He was teasing me, not being flirty or boyfriendish." *Was he?* No, he definitely wasn't. There had been times when Amy had thought Tony was looking at her like he was interested in a more intimate way, but they were fleeting seconds, and they passed as quickly as he'd taken his next breath. She was probably seeing what she wanted to see, not what he really felt, and she'd begun to wonder if she'd really loved him for so long, or if he'd become *her* habit, too.

"You know, he's never brought another woman to Seaside." Leanna's loose dark mane was wavy and tousled. With her golden tan and simple summer dress, she looked like she'd just come from the beach. Her gaze softened in a way that made Amy feel like she wanted to fall into Leanna's arms and disappear. "And look how he treats you. He's always got an arm around you, and when you drink too much at our barbecues, he always carries you home."

Amy wanted to believe them and to see what they apparently saw when he looked at her, but she never had. It was the secret memories of being in Tony's strong arms that long-ago summer, feeling his heart beat against hers, feeling safe and loved, that made her hopeful there would come a day when they'd find themselves there again. But then her mind would travel to the *end* of those recent nights when she'd had too much to drink and he'd carried her home. When he tucked her into bed and went along his merry way back to his own cottage across the road, quickly dousing her hope for more with cold reality. Whatever they'd had that summer, she'd ruined.

"Exactly, Leanna. That's why she's not making a decision about Australia until *after* this weekend," Jenna said. "Right, Ames?"

"Yes. That's my plan. I'm going to talk to Tony, and if he looks me in the eye and says he has no interest in anything more than friendship, then I'm going to take the job. It's pretty stupid, really, because how many times has he had the opportunity to...you know?" She dropped her eyes to her glass and ran her finger along the rim. Amy was as sweet as Bella was brash, and even thinking about trying to seduce Tony and find out where his heart really stood had her stomach tied in knots. When her friends had come up with the idea of seducing Tony, she'd fought it, but they'd insisted that once he kissed her, he'd never look back, and she'd grabbed that shred of hope as if it were a brass ring. Now her fingers were slipping a little.

"Talk? That's not the plan," Jenna said.

Jessica shook her head. "So, seduction? You're going to try?"

"If I can muster the courage." Amy drew in a deep breath, hoping she wouldn't back out. As much as she wanted closure, the idea of actually hearing Tony tell her that he didn't see her as anything other than a friend made her almost chicken out. But she didn't want to chicken out. She had a great job opportunity, and at thirty-two, she was ready to settle down and maybe even start a family. But that thought was even more painful than Tony turning her away.

Tony set a disconcerting stare on Amy as he moved confidently across the floor with the other guys, heading for their table. Her pulse ratcheted up a notch, as his eyes went dark and narrow. She broke the connection, grazing over his low-slung jeans and short-sleeve button-down shirt, afraid to try to decipher if it was an angry or an interested look in his eyes. She'd probably see only what she really wanted to see anyway.

Big mistake. Now she was even more nervous.

Several women in the bar turned and watched the four gorgeous men crossing the floor, but Amy knew they had to be looking at Tony. She was held prisoner by his sun-drenched skin, sandy hair that brushed his devilishly long lashes, and squared-off features that amped up his ruggedness and made her pulse go a little crazy. She reached for a glass of liquid courage, having no idea whose it was, and drained it as Tony slid in beside her. His thighs met hers, and his goddamn scent made her hot all over again. She grabbed another glass and drained it, and another, until the glasses were all empty and the nervous stirrings in her stomach stilled.

"Since when did you become Beyoncé?" Tony grumbled.

Beyoncé? Was that good or bad? Amy couldn't form an answer. All she could think about was that no matter what the outcome, after tonight her life would never be the same.

TONY HAD SPENT the last three hours watching men ogle Amy in that damn skimpy dress of hers. What was she thinking, dressing like that? He worried about her when she drank. She was too small to protect herself against unwanted advances, and she exuded sweetness like she was made of sugar, making her an easy target for a savvy guy. And he knew for a fact that Amy Maples was made of sugar—and spice and all things in between that were delicious and worthy of being savored. But that was a long time ago, and he'd spent years making sure Amy was treated as she deserved to be and putting his own desires on the back burner. Or trying to, anyway. He didn't think anyone else noticed that he could barely hold his shit together when it came to Amy, and he was grateful for that.

She was looking at him in a way that was reminiscent of that summer years ago, and he assumed it was caused by the far-too-many drinks she'd consumed. She never could hold her alcohol. He ran his hand through his hair and ground his teeth together. Maybe he'd take a walk back up to the bar to get away from the assholes watching her. He'd seen Pete stare them down when they were leering at Jenna, but Pete was Jenna's fiancé. She was his to protect.

Well, he wasn't Amy's fiancé, but she needed protecting too.

She's with Bella and the girls. They'll protect her.

He mulled that over for a minute or two. *Bella and the girls*. Yeah, they'd protect Amy. They were about as protective of Amy as he was, but the idea of moving from Amy's side and having some asshole saunter over and hit on her messed with his mind. She was so damn beautiful and way too naive for her own good. One of her gorgeous smiles could stop a man cold, and she was clueless to that fact. *Fuck*. It was so easy not to think about those things when they were in different states during the year, but summers? *Christ*. They were torture. And these last few summers, watching his summer friends fall in love, made this time with Amy even more difficult. But they'd crossed that line years ago, and not only had it not ended well, but Amy seemed to have moved on just fine, while Tony never really had.

He thought about all the summer nights since then that he'd spent checking up on her, making sure she got home safely. The summer she'd turned twenty-two and insisted on going out with that bastard Kevin Palish. What a prick. Tony'd stalked his window that night until she arrived home safely. Normally he tried to ignore the Seaside gossip about who Amy was dating, and she seemed to keep guys away from the complex, as far as he could see, but a few summers ago she'd dated that other guy who came around more than a handful of times. What was his name? Hell, Mr. Tall, Dark, and Annoying. Tony had waited up every night for a week to make sure Amy got home okay—and to make sure the dude left shortly after dropping her off at her cottage. Not that it was any of his business or that he could have done anything about it if they'd spent the night together. That was the problem. It wasn't his business. Luckily, Amy had come to her senses and broken up with the guy before Tony ever woke up to the guy's truck in her driveway.

Amy wiggled in the seat beside him, tugging at that way-too-fucking-short dress. Her thigh pressed against his, and it suddenly got way too hot in there. He unbuttoned another button of his shirt and exhaled loudly, trying to talk himself out of going up to the bar. He should stay right there to ward off looks, like the one the dark-haired guy from the table of oglers was giving her. Amy smiled and fidgeted with the hem of her dress again. *Goddamn it.* Tony's thoughts drifted to last summer when she'd dated bad-boy, mountain-rescuer, handsome-as-Brad-Fucking-Pitt Jake Ryder. Tony had seen all the women at the beach party eyeing Jake, and Amy had acted the same adorably nervous way around him. Jake was younger than Amy, too, which pissed Tony off even more, and he was friends with Jake. He actually liked the guy. But she needed a man, not a boy.

Fuck it. If he couldn't be the man she deserved, he could at least make sure no other jackass treated her badly. He laced his fingers with hers and set their hands on her thigh.

"What?" Amy asked.

Tony nodded at the guy at the next table. "No need to flirt with a guy like that. He'll only hurt you."

"Then maybe you should take me back to my room." She said it with wide, innocent eyes that tore right through him like lightning.

He rose to his feet and pulled Amy up with him.

"We're calling it a night," he said to their friends. He needed to get her to her room before she got herself into trouble—or before he got himself into trouble. "I'm going to walk Amy back to her hotel room. Jamie, Jessica, enjoy your last night of freedom."

"You're kidding, right?" Jamie rubbed noses with Jessica. "Who needs freedom? All I want is to wake up with Jessica in my arms for the rest of my life."

Yeah, and all I want is to wake up with Amy in my arms.

He shifted his eyes to Amy, standing before him pink-cheeked, glassy-eyed, and sexier than hell in that skimpy little black number that looked painted on and high heels that did something amazing to her long, lean legs. He forced his eyes north, over her perfect small breasts to the sleek line of her collarbone, which he wanted to trace with his tongue. Her hair fell over one of her heavy-lidded green eyes, giving her a sultry look that sent heat to his groin. When she trapped her lower lip between her teeth, it took all his effort to force something other than, *Damn, you look hot,* from his lips. Well...how was he supposed to resist her now?

She slid her arm around his waist and leaned her head against his chest.

"Okay, big guy. Take me home."

If she only knew what those words coming from her while dressed in that outfit did to him. As he'd done for too many years to count, he bit back his desires and walked her back to her room. He pulled her room card from his pocket, and it dawned on him that he always carried Amy's stuff. Her keys, her wallet, her phone. At some point, his pockets had become her pocketbook.

Tony held the door open for Amy and kept one hand on her hip as she walked unsteadily past him.

He closed the door and took in her hotel room. Standard upscale fare, it looked like his room, with a king-size bed, a long dresser and mirror, and a decent-size sitting area. Amy's perfume and lotions were lined up neatly on the dresser, along with her birth control pills, which made his gut twist a little. He didn't want to think about Amy having sex with anyone. Well, except maybe him, but—

"Hey." Amy reeled around on him, stepping forward in those sky-high heels. He didn't need to inhale to know that she smelled like warm vanilla, a scent that haunted him at night.

She wobbled a little, and instinct brought his hand to her waist. He'd held Amy in his arms a million times, comforting her when she was sad, carrying her when she was a little too drunk to be steady on her feet. He'd cared for her when she was sick and sat up with her after each of her girlfriends had fallen in love, when she simply couldn't handle being alone. He had a feeling those nights were their little secrets, because he'd never heard Bella, Jenna, or Leanna ever make reference to them, and those girls talked about everything. Now, as she stepped closer and touched his stomach with one finger and looked at him like she had years ago, not like the sweet, too-good-to-be-true Amy that she never strayed from around him unless she was drinking, he found himself struggling to remain detached enough to keep his feelings in check.

He forced himself to act casual. "What's up, Ames?"

She trapped that lower lip of hers again, and his body warmed.

Amy stumbled on her heels and caught herself against his chest. She slid her hands up the front of his shirt, and his body responded like Pavlov's dog. Amy had that effect on him, but he'd always been good about keeping it under wraps. What was happening to him? Was it the romance of the impending wedding? Watching his best buddies whisper and nuzzle their fiancées while he had walls so thick around his heart that he didn't know if he'd ever be able to move forward and love anyone else again?

She gazed up at him with naive curiosity in her eyes, and it was that innocence that threatened his steely resolve. It almost did him in every time they were alone together. Only this time she had the whole hips-swaying, breasts-pushing-against-him thing going on.

Christ. He covered her hands with his and breathed deeply. With those heels, they were much closer in height. A bow of his head and he could finally taste her sweet mouth again.

With that selfish thought, he pressed her hands to his chest to keep them from roaming and to keep himself from becoming any more aroused. She gazed up at him, looking a little confused and so damn sexy it was all he could do to squelch his desire to take her in his arms and devour her.

"What do you need, Ames?"

"I'm pretty sure you know what I need," she said

in a husky voice as she pressed her hips to his.

You don't mean that. You're just drunk. He clenched his jaw against his mounting desire. She was all he ever wanted, and she was the one person he knew he should walk away from.

"Amy."

"Tony." Her voice was thin and shaky.

"You're drunk." He peeled her hands from his chest. She got like this when she was drunk: sultry, sexier, eager. As adults, she'd never taken it this far. She'd made innuendos over the years, but more in jest than anything else. He wasn't an idiot. He knew Amy cared about him, but he also knew she sometimes forgot things. Important things. Life-altering events that were less painful if forgotten. He was certain it was why she drank when they were together and why he'd spent years protecting her. Not that she needed protecting often. Drinking was a summer thing for Amy, and really, she rarely drank too much. She didn't drink when she wasn't at the Cape. He knew this because over recent years, after Amy had graduated from college and settled into her business, he'd begun texting her more often. He'd been unable to ignore his need for a connection to her any longer. He could count on one hand how many times she'd made reference to drinking.

"I might be a little drunk." Her sweet lips curved into a nervous smile. "But I think I know what *you* want."

What I want and what I'll let myself have are two very different things.

He exhaled, took her hand, and turned toward the

bed. "Sit down and let me help you get out of your heels and then I'll go back to my room. I don't want you to break your ankle."

She swayed on her heels and attached herself to his side again. "I don't want you to go to your room."

Tony stepped back. The back of his legs met the dresser. "Amy—"

"Tony," she said huskily, taking him by surprise.

"Ames," he whispered. She was killing him. Any other man would have silenced her with a kiss, carried her to the bed, pushed that damn sexy-ass dress up to her neck, and given her what she wanted. But Tony had made a career out of resisting Amy, protecting her. He respected her too damn much to let her make a mistake she would only regret when she sobered up.

He gripped her forearms and held her at a safe distance.

She narrowed her eyes and reached for his crotch.

For a breath he closed his eyes and let himself enjoy the feel of her stroking him in ways he'd only dreamed of. Every muscle in his body corded tight as he reluctantly gripped her wrist.

"Amy, stop." He'd learned his lesson with her when he was a teenager, and he was never letting either of them go back to that well of hurt. "We're not doing this."

The dark seductiveness that had filled her eyes when she was touching him was gone as quickly as it had appeared. Her shoulders rounded forward, and hurt filled her eyes.

"Why?"

He felt like a heel. A prick. A guy who *should* have

taken her to bed, if only to love her as she deserved to be loved. Even if she might not remember or appreciate it in the morning. He draped an arm over her shoulder and pulled her into a hug.

"Come on, Amy. You're drunk and you won't remember any of this tomorrow. Let me help you get ready for bed."

"Don't you want me?"

Her broken voice nearly did him in, and when her arms went limp, he tightened his grip on her. "Amy," he whispered again.

In the space of a few seconds she pushed away from him, determination written in the tension around her mouth and the fisting of her hands.

"Tell me why you don't want me. What is it? Am I too flat-chested? Too unattractive?"

"No." *Fuck. You're the sexiest woman I know.* Anger felt so wrong coming from her that it momentarily numbed him.

"I know I suck at seduction, but don't these fuck-me heels or this stupid dress turn you on? Even a little?"

"Your fuck-me heels? Boy, you are drunk. You don't realize what you're saying. Come on." He reached for her hand and she shrugged him off again.

"Goddamn it, Amy. Let me help you." *Before I give in to what I really want and lay your vulnerable, gorgeous, sexy body beneath me and devour you.*

"So that's it. I don't turn you on." She paced the room on wobbly ankles, looking like she was playing dress up in her mother's high heels—and it did crazy things to Tony's body. He followed beside her in case she stumbled, fighting the urge to give in and show her just how much she turned him on.

"Maybe if I had bigger boobs, or if I were better at acting sexy, or if I were smarter, you'd want me."

It surprised him that she avoided the secret they'd buried so long ago, but then again, after that summer, she'd never said another word about it. And he'd let her get away with that, believing it was the only way she could survive what had happened. Just like him.

"Amy, it's none of those things." He did *not* want to have this conversation with her. He wanted to fold her in his arms and kiss the worry away.

Tears slipped down her cheeks.

Hell. Tony could handle a lot of things, but Amy's tears melted his heart, and that he'd caused them was further proof he wasn't the right guy for her.

"Then why, Tony? Just tell me once and for all. Why don't you want me? I need to know so I can decide about taking this job in Australia."

Tony opened his mouth to answer, but his thoughts were jumbled as he processed what she'd said. "Australia? I thought you said you weren't taking it."

She crossed her arms, and he hated knowing it was to protect herself from his rejection. Tony felt like an asshole, but he knew that taking Amy up on her seduction would only dredge up bad memories and lead to hurting her. They'd spent a lifetime denying the past between them existed, even to themselves.

"I said I wasn't sure what I was going to do." She dropped her eyes to the floor, and he slid a hand in hers, as he'd done a million times before. It was a natural reaction. Taking care of her. Protecting her. Helping her feel safe. He knew it could send her mixed messages, but he just couldn't help himself. His hand had already claimed its spot with hers.

"You'd give up everything you've built to run Duke's resort? You'd move to Australia?" He had nothing against Duke Ryder. But the idea that Amy would change her life to help him just pissed Tony off.

She sank down onto the bed and buried her face in her hands.

He wrapped an arm around her shoulder, and when she tried to pull away, he tightened his grip and kissed the top of her head.

"Amy, you're sexy, smart, and everything a guy could want."

She cocked her head to the side and narrowed her damp eyes. He felt like the biggest prick on earth, and at the same time, his own heart was fighting tooth and nail against the space he was trying to maintain between them.

"Christ." He scrubbed his hand down his face. "You are all those things, Amy, and so much more, but..."

"But you like me as a friend."

He'd never seen so much hurt concentrated in one person's eyes, and even if he had, it wouldn't have compared to seeing it in Amy's. He touched his forehead to hers, and he did the only thing he knew how to do without doing irreparable damage to their friendship.

His lie came in a whisper. "No. I *love* you as a friend."

He loved Bella, Caden, and the others, goddamn it.

What he felt for Amy was so much bigger than friendship, it threatened to stop his fucking heart.

She didn't say a word, just nodded, and Tony knew in that moment that she wasn't drunk enough to forget what he'd said by the morning—and he almost wished she were.

(End of Sneak Peek)

To continue reading, be sure to pick up the next LOVE IN BLOOM release:

SEASIDE SECRETS, *Seaside Summers*

Complete LOVE IN BLOOM SERIES

SNOW SISTERS
Sisters in Love
Sisters in Bloom
Sisters in White

THE BRADENS
Lovers at Heart
Destined for Love
Friendship on Fire
Sea of Love
Bursting with Love
Hearts at Play
Taken by Love
Fated for Love
Romancing my Love
Flirting with Love
Dreaming of Love
Crashing into Love

THE REMINGTONS
Game of Love
Stroke of Love
Flames of Love
Slope of Love
Read, Write, Love

SEASIDE SUMMERS
Seaside Dreams
Seaside Hearts
Seaside Sunsets
Seaside Secrets
Seaside Nights
Seaside Whispers
Seaside Lovers
Seaside Embrace

HARBORSIDE NIGHTS SERIES

Includes characters from
Love in Bloom series

Catching Cassidy
Discovering Delilah
Chasing Charley
Tempting Tristan
Embracing Evan
Reaching Rusty
Loving Livi

More Books by Melissa

Chasing Amanda (mystery/suspense)
Come Back to Me (mystery/suspense)
Have No Shame (historical fiction/romance)
Love, Lies & Mystery (3-book bundle)
Megan's Way (literary fiction)
Traces of Kara (psychological thriller)
Where Petals Fall (suspense)

SIGN UP for MELISSA'S NEWSLETTER to stay up to date with new releases, giveaways, and events

NEWSLETTER:
http://www.melissafoster.com/newsletter

CONNECT WITH MELISSA

TWITTER:
https://twitter.com/Melissa_Foster

FACEBOOK:
https://www.facebook.com/MelissaFosterAuthor

WEBSITE:
http://www.melissafoster.com

STREET TEAM:
http://www.facebook.com/groups/melissafosterfans

Acknowledgments

As a sister to six amazing brothers, writing The Bradens is one of my greatest joys. Being a sister has its complexities. Finding a middle ground between being strong enough to compete with them (and do I *ever* love to compete!) and allowing myself to be girlie is an ongoing effort. Not just with brothers but in life. I think all women encounter this type of situation on some level, and I hope Emily's story resonates with each of you. I love receiving your emails and messages on social media, so please keep them coming, and let me know how you liked Emily and Dae's story. You inspire me on a daily basis.

If you'd like to find out more about passive houses, Adam Cohen, founder of Passiv Structures and Passiv Science, is an expert in the field. You can find him online at www.PassivScience.com.

I'd like to thank Kristen Weber for "The heart is not a rational organ." That's her line, which she shared with me when we were discussing Emily's transformation. Kristen, I treasure your time and your guidance. Thank you. I'd like to also thank Lynn Mullan, Alessandra Melchionda, and Silvestro Silvestori for sharing information about Italy with me, and Doug Bralsford (Bralsford Ltd.) for reaching out and referring Silvestro.

My editorial team and proofreaders make my work shine with their superb skills. Thank you: Kristen Weber, Penina Lopez, Jenna Bagnini, Juliette Hill, Marlene Engel, and Lynn Mullan. Thank you, Natasha Brown, for the gorgeous cover, and Clare Ayala, for formatting my work.

As always, love to my family for allowing me the joy of writing.